I0619186

Tempest's Embrace

Cavanaugh Sister Trilogy
Book Three

JC Wardon

A *Mystic Waters* Novel

Mystic Waters Books, JC Wardon
Tennessee, U. S. A.

TEMPEST'S EMBRACE
Copyright © 2016, JC Wardon
Trade Paperback ISBN: 978-1-944454-95-1

Cover Art Design by Calliope-Designs.com
Editor, Gilly Wright

Original Digital Release, April 2014
Rerelease March 2016

Trade Paperback Release, March 2016

TEMPEST'S EMBRACE

Three identical sisters…
Three individual mystical gifts…
And Three Thousand Years of warnings to never fall in love….

An out of body experience with a beautiful male soul sends Destiny Cavanaugh running to her sisters in Mystic Waters, West Virginia. But when she finds he's there in the flesh, as well, and is accused of being the serial killer who has plagued the unsuspecting town for years, she has to decide if she can trust her failing instincts, or if she must accept that her ancestors were right all along.

Prologue

Blood froze in Tom Whitehawk's veins when he opened the back door of his small cabin as more than a dozen automatic rifles were quickly raised, pointed at his head and nude body.

"Put your hands in the air!"

"Put your hands up!"

"Get them up high!"

Tom lifted his hands quickly, his gaze darting from one combat-clad FBI agent to another as their hysterical shouts ricocheted and echoed around the mountainous terrain. His ears ringing, Tom stood there fully exposed as his heart pounded painfully against his chest wall. Stunned speechless, he forced himself to remain where he was as two agents advanced on him rapidly though everything inside of him screamed, *Run!*

With a black leather-clad hand, one agent cuffed the back of his neck and roughly pulled him forward so he was standing just outside of the doorway, while the other instantly grabbed his wrists and swung them out and down to secure them together behind his back.

The only things keeping him from shouting in indignation and anger as his shock wore down were the remaining weapons still pointed at him, and the fact that he couldn't seem to breathe. Denying the panic building, Tom closed his eyes to block the sight of those who had trespassed literally and figuratively against him as he sought strength from a lifetime spent in rumination and prayer.

He silently called to the heart of Mother Earth for inner peace and sanctuary, and her response was as it had always been. He inhaled her serenity and let tranquility wash through him as each tension-strung muscle relaxed one by one. The tightness of his lungs loosened as well, allowing him to breathe evenly. Renewed in spirit, calmer, he opened his eyes to look once again at those who had no right to trample what he and his people considered sacred ground.

With his head held high and his shoulders pulled back, Tom studied one agent after another to calculate their strength and touch their minds with his. Relieved to sense none were trigger-happy, he kept his feet planted firmly apart, to give them the show they had apparently come to see. Satisfaction gripped him as a couple of agents broke eye contact and looked away, though their guns remained on him all the same.

For the first time in his life, Tom understood what it felt like to be one of his people faced with an army of aggressive white men, though in this case there were also women present. But he would not cower, nor would he be embarrassed they had come at him before he could relieve himself. Despite the chaos, they had made of his rising, his morning hard-on stood proud and unapologetic.

A shiny black SUV pulled up and a tall man dressed in a black suit and tie, covered with a vest displaying the large white initials of the agency he worked for, emerged to walk by the agents targeting Tom. He looked at Tom, frowned, looked back at the armed agents and began shaking his head. He stopped in front of Tom and removed his sunglasses, uncaring that the weapons were now aimed at his back. "I'm Special Agent Bret Thorne of the Washington, D.C. branch of the Federal Bureau of Investigation. Are you Thomas Whitehawk?"

"Yes. What is this about?"

Agent Thorne pulled an envelope from his vest before opening it and extracting a piece of paper. "This is a search warrant for your home and property. Is there anything you would like to tell me before we commence?"

Completely confused, Tom could only shake his head as Agent Thorne turned to another agent. "Go inside and get this man some clothes."

The barked command told Tom two things and he relaxed slightly; the superior agent had figured out their mistake, and was now going to fall all over himself to fix things, and the man sent to retrieve his clothing was completely intimidated by the more seasoned agent standing before him.

Agent Thorne turned back to Tom, annoyance written in the set of his mouth. "You have been identified as a suspect in crimes committed in Mystic Waters. Do you have anything to say about this accusation?"

Not expecting those words, *ever*, to come out of anyone's mouth regarding him, Tom shook his head, not in denial but in disbelief. He drew in a deep breath as the lead agent's statement had knocked the air from his lungs. Unblinking, he looked the man straight in the eyes. "I say that is ridiculous. Anyone who knows me knows better. I would never hurt another living thing."

"Here you go," the agent said, holding out the clothing to Agent Thorne.

Thorne didn't bother to look anywhere but at Tom's eyes. "Unlock his hands."

The younger agent looked at his superior with brows drawn together. "Sir?"

Agent Thorne finally glanced over at the retriever agent, his mouth set with grim purpose. "Unlock Mr. Whitehawk's hands, *now*," he said quietly, through clenched teeth.

The underling quickly pulled out keys and walked behind Tom. In seconds he felt one, then the other wrist being released. He rubbed his wrists and took the clothing the agent now held out toward him and Tom could feel the younger agent's fear-masked anger. Keeping his eyes on the young man, he bent and pulled on the jeans and then the t-shirt before turning his attention back to the man in charge.

"You could have knocked on the door."

Agent Thorne sighed. "You must have come out before I had a chance to get here." He glanced over to an agent standing apart from the others, his eyes holding retribution. "My orders were to wait until I arrived to engage the suspect."

Tom watched as the man, who held a look of defiance, walked to stand by another agent before he turned back to the man who was obviously in charge. Tom knew that one was itching with nervous energy. It radiated around him in colors of red and black. He turned back to the lead agent yet again. Tom hoped this farce was about over before someone did something stupid—like shoot him.

"I think you will find that you have made a very big mistake. On several levels."

Agent Thorne nodded. "I am aware of the laws governing the lands in this area, and your special rights *here* on this mountain, and as a Native American on these lands. I take full responsibility, and I apologize for the mistakes made here today, by my agents. *However*, we do have a Federal warrant, which supersedes your ability to stop us from searching the premises. Nothing that is not relevant to our investigation will be disturbed. And your land will be treated with respect, and to the best of our ability without harm."

Though his heart was pounding again, Tom didn't allow himself to react as he took the paper and looked it over. Once he was done reading, he handed it back. "I would have been more than happy to cooperate with you, assuming that you are also searching every home in Mystic Waters.

"Unless that *is* your plan, I will have no choice but to look at this as a direct and prejudicial attack against my people as well as myself, and I'm sure charges will be filed on our behalf against the United States Government for yet another broken promise."

Agent Thorne nodded once. "I understand. I've had the opportunity to read the documentation, and as such, I am trying to make sure that you and your ancestral lands are treated with the proper respect. Again, I apologize for the inappropriate way in which you were…handled."

He remained facing Tom, his gaze assessing and unwavering, as he addressed the others. "Put the damned weapons down!

"Henson, Parks, get inside and look around and make it quick!"

Tom stood there trying to come to grips with what was happening while he opened his mind to rescan those around him, starting with the one directly before him. The senior agent gave off an even vibe. Though his irritation at his agent's was obvious, Thorne's sense of authority and perhaps even his personality didn't lend itself to spikes of heated aura or even an increased heart rate that would normally be apparent in someone given the volatility of the situation.

Thorne's calm demeanor wasn't common at all, which piqued Tom's curiosity. He put what was happening around him aside as he focused, delving deeper into the agent's psyche. What Tom found fascinated him: absolute calm. Purity of purpose. A hard line dividing the agent's sense of right and wrong.

Because Tom could read such things in people, it calmed him further to know the agent wasn't faking his ability to handle the situation completely and that he was a man of integrity. But what the agent may or may not have known was Tom's threat hadn't been idle. The council would be up in arms and be ready to spend whatever it took to handle this insult to their spiritual leader.

Tom hoped it wouldn't come to that. If he were ever needed to fight physically for his people and their rights, he would be there in a heartbeat, but until that time came, he planned to continue living the life that had chosen him. That meant peace and solitude. The last thing he wanted was to become a public spectacle.

"It won't take them long. I live a minimalist lifestyle."

Agent Thorne said nothing as they waited, and Tom

realized while he'd been assessing the agent, the agent had been assessing him. Neither broke eye contact, until a minute later when one of the agents who went to inspect Tom's cabin returned to stand next to his superior. He had a pistol dangling from a gloved finger on his left hand, and a plastic wrapped brick of what was obviously a dried green plant in the other.

Tom looked at both items and then at the agent as real anger gripped him. "We both know that isn't mine." He turned back to Agent Thorne. "*You* know that isn't mine!"

Thorne looked at him a few seconds more then turned and walked around Tom to go into the cabin. He was gone only a few minutes before returning to address the agent still holding the contraband. "Bag those and get a detailed report to me within the hour." He turned to the others who stood waiting for instruction. "Search the area. You have one hour. Leave everything as you find it unless it is relevant to the investigation. And I want a report on what you find, if anything.

"And I had better not hear that one word of any of this has been leaked privately, or to the press."

Finally he turned back to Tom. "I'm going to have an agent re-cuff you. It will go a lot better for you if you cooperate."

Tom shook his head, unable to believe what was happening. "It isn't mine," he reiterated from behind clenched teeth. Agent Thorne nodded so slightly Tom was sure he was the only one who saw it.

"Just cooperate. You will ride with me."

Tom put his arms behind his back although it went against every fiber of his being. Something about the senior agent's demeanor made him want to trust the man, but he wasn't sure that he trusted his own judgment at the moment. Physical violence was foreign to his spirit yet everything inside of him screamed for retribution. He called once again to his Mountain Mother, and was relieved when the alien feelings seeped away. Tom remained silent while being re-cuffed, and while being led to Agent Throne's

SUV.

The agent directed to lead him to the vehicle touched the top of his head as he was seated inside, then a seatbelt was placed around him and locked into place. The sound of the lock went through him and he wondered when, if ever, he would ever be free again.

Within minutes Bret Thorne was buckling his own seatbelt, telling another agent that he could ride with someone else. The look on the underlings face said it all, and Tom was getting more concerned by the minute.

After they pulled away from his home, Tom couldn't hold back the question. "What's really going on here? Do you really think I've done something involving that gun?"

Thorne shook his head as he looked in this mirror. "No. I'm going against every protocol there is by doing this, but I'm going to ask you to work with me."

Tom locked onto Thorne's gaze reflected in the mirror, although the agent continued to look between him and the road. "What are you talking about?"

"There isn't an FBI agent worth his salt that couldn't see what we just found is a set up. My guys laughed at how easy it was to find the gun and the drugs. Unfortunately for the person who put them there, they forgot to take the evidence sticker off.

"I'll have to have you piss in a cup so I hope you don't have anything in your system, but I would stake my badge on your fingerprints being nowhere on that gun."

Tom hung his head as the air left his lungs. "Thank God! I was sure your guys were setting me up. I just didn't know why.

"I can guarantee you there isn't anything in my piss. As for the gun, I've never touched it. Where was it?"

"It was under the mattress, at the foot of the bed closest to the wall. It was obvious that it had been shoved there quickly, with no concern to hide it. In fact the butt of the grip was visible, and I'm thinking that was on purpose."

"So, in spite of finding a gun and drugs at my place, you believe me?"

"I'm pretty good at what I do, Mr. Whitehawk, which is why I'm leading rather than following this task force. And my gut is telling me several things. One is that leaving a weapon where it can be found quickly isn't something a man as smart as you would do. Not to mention you have thousands of protected acres—that would take us *years* to search—at your disposal to hide things that could incriminate you should you ever decide to become the criminal I doubt you are.

"I had an agent pull your life history as soon as we got the report there was something to investigate at your address; an address, by the way, that has no actual physical address on a Federal level. So the caller who blocked the number they were calling from knows something the average person wouldn't have known, and will turn out to be the one who is trying to turn the attention away from them, and toward you.

"And even if I didn't know all that, there was the fact that although you were angry about what was going down, you were calm, which I have to give you credit for. No way could I have stood there naked and been more intimidating than the taskforce of agents holding their automatic rifles at me."

Tom couldn't help the smile that crinkled the corners of his eyes. He'd never thought of himself as intimidating on any level. He wasn't about to admit he'd been shaking on the inside like a little girl. He held his thoughts without sharing them as the agent seemed willing to talk. The more he talked the better Tom felt.

"Knowing how easy it was for us to find condemning evidence would have had a guilty man sweating, at the very least, and talking his head off to try to divert our attention. There are other things I can't disclose at the moment, but put your mind at ease. This all smelled worse than two-day-old fish lying in the sun."

The agent's eyes crinkled as he looked back. "I just bet you were calculating how much you were going to sue the government for when my agent walked out with the contraband."

Tom almost smiled at that, too, but this time didn't. "What can a report on me tell you? I live too simple a life for anyone to know anything about me unless they know me personally. I don't use the Internet. I don't get involved in politics. I am a spiritual man who seeks a higher power to help those who ask it of me, but I don't advertise myself in any way."

Agent Thorne made a sweeping turn before bringing the SUV to a standstill at one of the mountain's lookout rest stops. He undid his seatbelt and turned in his seat. "Unfortunately for us all, the government knows a lot more than they should about pretty much everyone. But I don't have time or the authority to go into that.

"This is the thing; I'm taking a big risk here not only with my superiors, but with you as well if by some chance you aren't who I think you are, by telling you what I already have. But I'm going with my gut on this, and it tells me you are innocent. But more importantly, it tells me you can help us catch those who are responsible for the deaths of those young men, and possibly the White kidnapping if you're willing.

"But for now, publicly, I'm going to have to treat you like a serious suspect. The only people who know any differently at this point are the two agents who went inside your cabin expecting to find something because I told them to, and you and me. Those men are worthy of my job and can be trusted. If you are willing to help us, we may be able to save Gavin White's life. I believe that kid is still alive and the sooner we get to him the better his chances are of staying that way. I just hope he holds on.

"I know I'm asking a lot of you. Your reputation will suffer for a while. Your family will be hurt and angry. But I promise you in the end everyone will know of your innocence. You'll never be convicted of this."

Tom didn't know if he had any choice but he needed time to process what was happening. "Can you give me a few minutes?"

Agent Thorne nodded as he put his seatbelt back on. "That's all I can give you. If I take too long getting you to the Mystic Waters police station to be booked, questions will be asked that I don't want to answer yet."

He started the vehicle and pulled forward, then turned as he backed up, before dropping it back into drive and pulling out onto the road in the direction they'd originally traveled. Tom knew he couldn't pass up an opportunity to help the White family, though very distant, they were a part of his own, but he didn't know how he could stand the hurt to his parents or those who trusted him with their spiritual cares. His parents would be devastated for him over his arrest, although they would know he wasn't capable of what he was about to be charged with. It would be the same with all those who knew him, and it would be a black eye to his people when they were all committed to fighting old prejudices by the ways in which they lived their lives.

"Will I have to remain in jail for long?"

Thorne glanced in the mirror. "That will be up to the judge. As soon as I can get clearance for all this, I'll let him know you are actively cooperating with us and are not a flight risk. We'll get you bonded out as quickly as possible, but you may be safer locked up. People can get pretty daring when a child is involved."

"So everyone will think I've committed these crimes."

"Unless they know you well, and maybe even some of those folks will be unsure for a while, but if you can get the man that's currently being held to talk to you, I think there is a pretty good chance we can wrap some of this up fairly quickly.

"I'm going to keep Captain Grammar in the loop because I can tell he's a good man, but no one else on the force because, at this point, I believe there are two different people committing these crimes, and I believe one is a dirty cop. He's the man being held now, but we can't charge him for any of this yet. I'm hoping Captain Grammar has charged him with domestic assault. It will buy us some time."

Tom took several deep breaths as he processed Agent Thorne's information. "I don't really have a choice. The Whites are good people and have been family friends for generations." He didn't mention the several generations-back relationship. There wasn't any point.

"I hate that they will think I had anything to do with any of this. And it will kill my father and mother. They're pretty old. If I do this, can you at least let them know the truth? It will save both of us a lot of trouble; me worrying about my parents' health and you not having my very powerful father fighting what you are planning."

Thorne looked in the mirror as they approached the town. "I don't know...but not yet. I'm usually a by the book man, but there are always shades of gray in these cases and my immediate superior had my position before her promotion. I expect her full cooperation and support on this.

"Until I get clearance from the director, I'm powerless to do anything more, so from here on out I have to follow protocol. I believe it would go a long way with her superiors if your father is willing to stand up against any tribal or racial fallout that may result. This case is complicated enough with what I believe are at least two, and possibly three, different criminals committing these crimes. The last thing we'll need is an uprising.

"If I can get approval to carry this forward my way, your father would have to be willing to do it without letting anyone else know, and that could cause him problems."

Tom nodded. "I understand that more than you do. Can you get us alone with him where no one else can hear or record us? I think I can take care of all of that."

Thorne drove for a minute before nodding. "Once I have the go ahead, I'll make it happen."

Chapter One

Destiny rubbed her eyes hoping to alleviate the blurriness of her vision. She knew she needed to take a break as she'd been reading every waking moment for days in an attempt to find out if the out of body flight she took across the country she'd experienced was real, or not.

While using the extensive notes from her sister Rayne's years of study, Destiny delved into the diaries containing the Cavanaughs' long history. They were huge and heavy and filled with handwritten entries that were in a variety of languages. She eventually had to start reading in the later tomes that were only a few hundred years old to garner her own knowledge. But when she began her quest for understanding, she had gathered Rayne's stack of notebooks and looked through the older diaries whose pages Rayne had painstakingly preserved.

The very oldest were more than three-thousand-year-old mats of papyrus. Rayne preserved them by placing each between two sheets of quarter-inch ultraviolet-filtering Plexiglas she'd lined with Swiss silk bonding-cloth and then sealing the Plexiglas sheets together. These sealed pages were then stacked and divided by more silk before being placed in the large, hinged, wooden lockbox Rayne had commissioned to have built and sculpted by a local artist.

The elaborate carvings covering most of the lid were of a raised oblong circle encasing raised hieroglyphic symbols. Outside of the distorted circle were the sharp tipped blooms of the Egyptian water lily. But the most interesting thing, Destiny decided, was the large uncut jewel placed dead in the center. At times she was certain it glowed, but when she'd look closer, she wondered if it wasn't just a reflection of light from either a lamp or the sun coming in through the glass walls.

Though only a few of the sheets made from the processed pith of the papyrus plant were still completely intact, Rayne had pieced together others as best she could, even preserving the broken bits and pieces of the ancient diary pages forever lost.

Destiny was amazed by how dark the ancient Egyptian glyph script still was. And even more astonished that Rayne's translations indicated the most well-preserved ones were from the Nineteenth Egyptian Dynasty where she believed their royal lineage may have began, and the hereditary magic began to triplicate.

Destiny became mesmerized with Rayne's neat handwritten notes and forgot about everything else as she read about the auburn-haired Egyptian Pharaoh Ramesses the Second. Their esteemed ancestor, who had ruled Egypt from 1279 BC to 1213 BC, had married and fathered eleven children with the woman who became his most beloved and favorite wife, Queen Nefertari.

Though they married before his ascension to the throne, when she was thirteen and he fifteen, what was believed to have been a politically inspired union grew into an amorous relationship that left the Pharaoh bewitched. Nefertari was a goddess in his eyes. She was said to have had such mighty powers over the heart of the Pharaoh that he built elaborate monuments and statues in her likeness well beyond what was expected or acceptable at the time.

Though the names of all of their sons and the other two royal daughters were well documented, as well as the other ninety or so children he'd had with his other wives, Rayne noted, without surprise, that she had never been able to find the names of the three auburn-haired identical triplet princesses in any Egyptian history books.

Rayne surmised the papyrus' had probably been written by the queen's personal scribe shortly after the girls' births. It was probably hidden away along with the endangered triplets after the Pharaoh was told by his most trusted seer these children were the foretold precursor to the ultimate demise of Egyptian rule.

The scribe recorded Queen Nefertari's fury when she was informed the only way to preserve the Egyptian Dynasty was for the newborns to be sacrificed, and for their hearts to be cut out and burned upon a tray placed before the statue of the solar deity, Ra.

As the Pharaoh had always called his beloved *The One for Whom the Sun Shines,* Rayne noted it must have added insult to injury for the queen to be told the sun god required the sacrifice of her children to gain Divine protection.

A footnote at the bottom of this ancient document, stating their lineage as well as the triple births, also told of the mighty storm Queen Nefertari unleashed in a fit of anger as her begging for their lives was denied, and the king turned on her with an anger never before displayed. The scribe further detailed and recorded what Rayne believed was the curse she shouted.

Lightning and thunder fill the sky
Cleanse now my heart
Love is a lie
Protect my descendants from males who come
Perpetuate my line through only one
Should unqualified love ever-be
This curse be then ended
by The Three

This was followed by the detailed secret killing of three piglets whose hearts were cut out and delivered to the High Priestess and the Pharaoh as proof of the children's deaths and for the sacrifice.

Though Rayne noted she could find no record where the babies were sent, or who took them in, the next decipherable entries were flattened scrolls of parchment made from calf and goatskins and were written in Aramaic. These too were preserved and placed in a second smaller box, which visually matched the first, minus a jewel.

The written language used to record their lives before

and after the time of Jesus of Nazareth spanned several generations, and it was at this point the name Kavanaugh first appeared. The detailed entries spoke of periods of Kavanaugh triplets procreating while amassing great wealth and high societal position, until they once again reigned over a kingdom. Though the names of each set of female triplets were well documented, there was never any indication of who had sired them. Rayne noted this omission was probably a direct result of the Pharaoh's misguided actions.

Rayne's written interpretation held several question marks at that point, but she noted she was certain many years were lost in the broken bits and pieces of papyrus she had preserved. She also considered the possibility of a span of years where none were added for some reason.

Destiny figured her sister must had mulled over the missing years for quite a while as Rayne added many more question marks on her notepad before adding a doodle of the deity Ra.

Following the drawing of the falcon headed Egyptian with the sun-disk sitting on his head, Rayne wrote their ancestor's next recordings were in the Old Norse language using the Runic Alphabet also known as *futhark,* which modern scholars surmised were created by the Vikings around 800 AD. The Runic alphabet was completely new and did not include letters from any other language being used at that time, she'd added, and then she'd drawn a smiley face that made Destiny smile in response.

Destiny glanced at Rayne's notes often while looking at the older diaries. She now knew, in Old Norse, the word *rune* meant text or inscription. But more importantly to her ancestors, likely the Vikings who created the independent language to protect their private history, the word also meant mystery and secret, which translated into *Magick.*

Though the written language was eventually shared with their subjects and became so popular it spread throughout Europe, as far as Rayne had determined, only members of the Kavanaugh Royal Family knew the mystical meanings. Those *special* meanings were never recorded in the diaries until the Runic Alphabet was taken from southern Europe and was carried north when her ancestors fled their castle to join up with nomadic Germanic tribes.

In an effort to escape the sudden persecution that had forced them from their lavish home, the identical Kavanaugh princesses changed the spelling of their last name by dropping the K and replacing it with a C, as well as dropping their royal titles. By the next generation the recordings began to be written in a slightly different way as the alphabet evolved and eventually became known as Old German.

It seemed, Rayne wrote, for the first time in their recorded history the family had to practice magic in secrecy, only displaying their gifts publicly with individual or multiple runic letters being used for important rituals and magic, as well as for their own protection. Sometimes those public displays were chiseled into the side of a cliff as they travelled; more often into the stone walls of each home they moved into or on large rocks strategically placed in their gardens.

Now very careful, as the Age of Magic had passed and Christianity had finally taken hold, the Cavanaugh women only used their magic to survive and prosper. They could no longer help the masses, as had been their charge since the original three where saved. Many who claimed to be followers of The Christ used what was meant only for good for their own evil purposes.

But nature would eventually override caution, and the need to help others, being as natural to the Cavanaugh women as breathing, would eventually capture the attention of those who sought their elimination. Thus generation after generation of Cavanaugh's were targeted and persecuted as pagans.

Subsequent diaries written in Ogham and Picts, which were primitive Irish and Scottish languages, revealed a period of peace for the sisters, as the peoples of these islands still believed in magic. But even later diaries written in Old East Slavic, followed by the Italian romance language of Piedmontese proved a safe haven never lasted long before one or more of the Cavanaugh women were once again persecuted, and all would be forced to flee.

On and on the stories of her ancestor's lives went. Good trying to survive in a world filled with evil; only one sister of each set of triplets procreating and perpetuating their bloodline; finally, inevitably, the men who had once loved them would turn on them in fear and with contempt before attempting, and sometimes succeeding, in killing them.

Destiny couldn't help but wonder if her ancestors had made the same mistake she had made by not learning of their own history. It would have helped her so much to know they had always been doers of good. It would have made such a difference to know they were special for a greater purpose. And maybe, at least she hoped, it would have helped her better deal with the death of her mother.

She knew now it was time to let go of the anger and resentment she had carried toward Celestia Cavanaugh since she was fifteen years old. Had her mother known what Rayne had so painstakingly uncovered, maybe she would have been wiser in her choices and her three children wouldn't have had to grow into womanhood without her guidance.

She fought tears but lost, so Destiny gave herself a moment to mourn the beautiful creature who had given her life and to silently ask her mother for forgiveness. But she owed others an apology also, as she had harbored anger at her sisters for being able to move on when she had so stubbornly stayed behind.

Even knowing nothing about their lives had been going right she had stayed; determined to get her gift back on her own, determined to show them she didn't need them or anybody else. Just determined to be determined because she was hardheaded that way.

First she owed Rayne an apology; she hadn't valued

her youngest sister enough and hadn't given her sufficient credit when they had all lived together. Destiny had mistakenly thought Rayne lazy and something of a spoiled brat, and that her need to take seemingly endless years of college courses that allowed her to interpret and preserve the diaries had been a waste of energy and time.

Destiny knew now she had been so very wrong.

If not for Rayne's notes, she wouldn't have been able to make heads nor tails from the Royal Books of Kavanaugh or the later books written in anything but English.

And she owed Haven an apology as well. She had allowed fear to turn her into such a nutcase that Haven had fled without a word, and rightly so. It made Destiny sick now to think she had considered having Haven committed to a mental institution when her sister lost her ability to heal and subsequently fell to pieces. All Haven had needed was support and understanding.

And I failed.

Shamed, Destiny left the kitchen table where she had Rayne's notebooks and the large boxed and leather-bound diaries stacked or laying open, and walked to the glass wall facing Los Angeles and the Pacific beyond. She watched as large and small waves broke on the glistening surface of the sea and wondered if she would ever figure out whether the out-of-body experience had been real or only a daydream so detailed she doubted she could ever replicate it.

She thought of the man with the beautiful face and body, with the soul that had reached for her own. She wanted him to be real, if not for herself, then for the universe, as she had never known such an exquisite essence walked the earth.

Which meant he wasn't real, of course, as no man was so pure of spirit.

In a way it was a relief. She knew now that to join with a man, *any* man, would end in disaster. But that didn't take away the longing that had driven her to the diaries to begin with. The reality that she shouldn't want to find him almost brought more tears to her eyes, but she chose to call to him instead.

Just to see.

Just to know.

Just so she could let him go.

He had filled every dream she'd had over the last few nights, every fantasy while she was awake. The only thing able to distract her was the history of those who came before. But even her studies were *because* of him. She wanted some evidence, some proof, she could return to him again.

Destiny hadn't found anything helpful. But even knowing what she now knew, she still needed to see if she could travel without her body going with her. And honesty required she acknowledge she *needed* to see him again, even if it was for the last time.

No, the diaries hadn't really helped yet, but there were centuries and centuries to study. The Cavanaugh women before her generation had chronicled nearly every day of their lives. From the mundane to the magical, from the highest joys to the most devastating losses, they were all in there waiting to be read and acknowledged and learned from.

Destiny considered going back to the table to study some more, but she was tired of reading and her eyes were still blurry. More than anything she just wanted to let go and fly away as she had in her vision, or dream, or whatever it had been.

She started as she had before, allowing every part of her body that bent or moved to bend and move as extremely as possible. Slowly at first, and then more smoothly, like liquid silk…. Destiny began humming, and then transformed her movements into a sensual dance as the humming fell into the song Celestia once sang to her children. At the end of the simple song, she glided to the floor to sit with her legs bent at the knees and her feet tucked onto her thighs, as she faced the city of angels.

With arms outstretched, Destiny closed her eyes and

began to hum again as she envisioned herself a mist rising from the floor. She held the image then pushed it a little further… Only nothing happened. She opened her eyes and shook her head and arms hard to loosen herself up before returning to the pose.

Determined not to give in to defeat, she held tight to the images and resumed humming, but the longer she went with no results the angrier she got. Still she kept trying, and kept trying, but nothing would change the fact that gravity was holding her firmly to the floor. Furious, exhausted, and completely defeated, she cried out her anguish, and gave in to reality.

As soon as her body relaxed, Destiny's spirit soared.

Surprised and delighted, she laughed and squealed with joy. There was no fear as she flew through ceiling and roof of their elaborate home, and on up until the clouds tickled her essence.

Destiny studied the landmarks below following the same ones she'd seen before, like a goose returning to its birthplace after a long winter abroad. She embraced the spirit of freedom and envisioned herself turning and diving before once again soaring toward the clouds.

She felt the joy of her laughter as it coated the clouds while she played her way across the country. It wasn't until what felt like hours later that she settled down enough to focus on the ground below and the sight of the pine-covered mountains flooded her heart with happiness. She was close now, so very close, and all she wanted was to find him once again.

Destiny crested the mountain's peak and began her descent, excited and nervous at the same time. She wondered if he had thought of her, if he had missed her, if he still believed she was his.

He had called her by name, *my Destiny*, he'd said, though that was the moment she had been so abruptly pulled away from him to be dragged back across the country, back to the west coast, back into her home, and finally back inside her body.

The loss had nearly destroyed her. For the first time in her life, she had faced a crisis with no one there to care. Her sisters were gone, as were her aunts, and she'd been too embarrassed to show them her weakness and seek them out. Desperation and loneliness finally won, and she had turned to her ancestors' diaries for help.

In their own way they had.

If nothing else she now knew the Cavanaugh women were never defeated if they stuck together and had the courage to persevere. And persevere she would by using whatever magic she still held, while honing this new skill she never knew she possessed.

Destiny located his cabin and the animal skin tent he used as a meditation sweat lodge, but even before she flew into it, she knew he wasn't anywhere close. Disappointment tugged at her. She feared it would pull her all the way back home, but she wouldn't let that happen again. This flight had been by *her will* and would remain so, and she wouldn't leave until she was good and ready. And that wouldn't be until she found him, and touched him, and let him know she was real, just as her heart now knew he was.

His land was quiet, as was the sweat lodge when she flowed through the opening at its top. She allowed herself a moment there, to envision him as he had been, sitting with his legs bent at the knees, his bare feet tucked into thick muscular thighs. She recalled his manhood as she had first seen it, lifeless yet long and thick and nestled below the flat stomach that lead upward to the rippling ribcage nestled below his broad muscular chest.

Then she pictured his face when he'd lifted his head and his long, silver-streaked hair no longer shielded it from her view. He was a beautifully tanned work of art that bespoke a heritage whose lineage was surely as deep as hers, though his was clearly native to this land and the lands to the north. Yet his eyes, *those purest of blue eyes*, had been a startling surprise; not only because of their beauty, not only because of his heritage, but because she knew now that they saw what others did not, could not. His eyes beheld *magick*.

Now that she was back in his place of enchantment, she knew his lips, so wide and full and filled with truth, had called to her spirit that first time. And though she hadn't known the language, her soul understood purity and had answered his call.

It was humbling to realize her magic had only been set free because of the power of his.

Though overwhelmed to realize he was a sorcerer, she was still dizzy with want, just remembering him as she had first seen him. Shaking with desire, she recalled his shaft filling and rising when he had felt her presence, and though she had been torn between amusement and embarrassment at the time, she knew even then they were meant to be.

After seeing him so intimately, Destiny had no idea how she would look him in the eyes should she ever get to meet him face-to-face, but she wanted to, more than she wanted to take another breath.

After one last look around she made her essence leave the sweat tent, its rocks now as cold as the torture of his absence.

As nothing more than a dry mist she floated to the roof of his cabin where she entered through a circulating air vent. Once inside she hung back as the feel and scent of others permeated the structure, sending chills through her essence.

Though there was a taint of evil in the single room structure, those who had last been there had been of a more natural spirit. But that did not comfort Destiny. She sensed they came with an unsettling purpose she could not identify, yet knew bode ill for her beautiful man. Confused and feeling suddenly suffocated, she took only seconds to see how plainly he lived before returning outdoors.

Breathing easier now that she was away from the dark psyche that polluted his cabin, Destiny floated a short distance into a stand of trees. She found a hidden structure, and though it was newer than the one she'd just left, its external siding held the feel of age.

Once inside she looked in awe at the wooden shower

house with its modern toilet. It was built for comfort, but other than the commode, it too was made to look as old as the original structure he called home.

Though no evil taint was present, Destiny departed the shower house quickly. Those others had invaded that space also. Darkness was falling now, and she no longer wished to float around. Picking up speed, she flew through acres and acres of forested land that had known him intimately; his clean scent and love for the land and its animals lingered in the air.

But all around her essence was dark and still and held a silence as deafening in its own way as thunder would have been in the center of a cyclone. Neither cricket nor frog sang their night songs. The air was so stagnant not one leaf trembled. Deer, raccoon, possum nor mouse stirred. It seemed the nocturnal creatures sat as if frozen in place, their presence only discernible if the moon's reflected light touched upon their shiny black eyes.

The overwhelming feeling of sorrow caused tears to choke her essence, but Destiny refused to give up easily. She continued to search franticly for hours for any sign of him or an indication of the direction he might have been forced to go, only stopping when the mountain suddenly groaned and shook, and the animals frantically howled in mourning over his loss.

Knowing now he was truly parted from the land that called him family, Destiny took to the sky and headed west. There was nothing for her here anymore, and though she knew it was for the best, she couldn't shake the feeling he was *meant* to be her lover, her mate, and the other half of her whole.

Tears mingled with the mist she had become. He had truly vanished, and the evil she had acknowledged within the walls of his home gave her little hope she would ever see him again.

****

The earth shook and moaned for nearly three minutes, and Tom blew out a breath and acknowledged *Her* anguish when it stilled.

He was exhausted and disgruntled and felt dirty even though he'd been made to shower in the large room upon his arrival. The confines and rough cotton of the orange jumpsuit they gave him to wear scratched his skin and bound his broad shoulders. It wasn't nearly large enough.

The day had started out horrible, and had only gotten worse once he'd had to face the throng of people waiting outside the police station. Agent Bret Thorne's attempts to delay news of his arrest obviously hadn't worked, and a lynch mob had descended on the city's jail.

The humiliation and terror had only increased when he'd been taken to the courthouse, shackled at the wrist and ankles, and had to shuffle before the judge as the real lawbreakers of Mystic Waters sat back and watched. The arraignment took only moments, but he'd had to turn back to face the crowd filling the court's pews in order to be led back to the side door where he would once again be walked to the jail.

In that few minutes of facing the citizens of Mystic Waters he caught a glimpse of his parents, and the suffering he had so wanted to keep from them was written in the deep lines of their faces and in the sadness and moisture in their eyes.

He looked around for the agent who had promised him all this would go differently, but the man was nowhere in sight, and he'd been returned to the jail to be caged in a cell across from the only other man being held.

If he'd understood Agent Thorne correctly, that was the man they were really gunning for, and was also the man responsible for Tom's current situation. Although he'd never been one to lash out in anger, it took all he had now to look at the obese little man and not want to choke him to death.

Being a man of the earth and one whose freedom had long ago been procured, Tom couldn't stand the idea of being caged. He missed his home, he missed his land, and he wanted his life back.

Hoping he hadn't misplaced his trust, Tom turned from the amused stare of the dishonored police officer and went to sit on the bed where he could stare at the far wall. As the cell was only eight foot by ten he didn't have far to look, so he laid his head back on the cold concrete wall and closed his eyes, forcing himself to take slow even breaths.

The only escape he had for now was his mind, so he allowed it to open as he sought the image of his home. The mountain was his mother as much as the lovely woman who had nurtured him inside her womb, and he sought Mother Mountain's comfort now.

Instantly he was home, walking her paths, smelling her bounty. He touched soft leaves and inhaled the scent of pine. He ate her berries and communed with her pets. His bare feet felt the chill when he stepped into her spring as the pure waters sped toward the magic lake below. Overwhelmed with thanksgiving for all that she was, he sat on the large bolder she provided for his rest. There, he wept.

She soothed him with the gentle fingers of the wind and enveloped him with the warmth of the sun. She whispered to him through the trees, and spoke of the one who had come. He dried the tears as he listened to the story of his Destiny's long search, his heart breaking anew when he learned she had left brokenhearted when he was nowhere to be found.

"You asleep over there, Injun?"

Abruptly Tom was back and he sighed in sorrow and irritation. He looked through the cell bars at the hate-filled man, ready to tell Burt Thompson exactly what he thought and felt, but Tom held back the words. If he was going to clear his own name, he had to get that man talking. Telling him to eat the fruit of the White Baneberry, and die, probably wasn't the best way to go.

But being too friendly wouldn't work either, Tom knew, as the man's spirit held the stench of evil, and evil was always suspect where there was goodness. "What do you want?"

"Name's, Thompson. Burt.

"So you're the guy they've been looking for."

Thinking it odd the man didn't know Tom knew who he was, since it was apparently something pretty much everyone in town already knew according to the FBI agent, Tom kept his knowledge to himself. He decided it was time to start the game of wits. Still, he was unable to believe the gall of the man; if he was the one guilty of setting Tom up, he knew good and well he wasn't who the police and FBI were looking for.

"Didn't do anything."

Burt nodded. "That's what they all say."

Tom kept himself from saying more in the hopes that keeping his mouth shut would open the other guy up.

"Don't talk much, do you?"

Tom shrugged, trying not to grin. "Nothing to say."

"They are going to nail your ass to the wall."

Tom just looked at Burt, though it was becoming a struggle to keep quiet.

"You're a pretty thing. Bet you get some nice meaty boyfriend when they send you to prison."

Tom turned away; he was choking on anger. That the man would go to such a disgusting place with a perfect stranger was beyond his understanding, but he'd never been in such close confines with someone whose spirit of evil was so prevalent, either. Knowing he'd have to be careful with such a good liar, since the honestly in him didn't allow for such, Tom hesitated in answering.

"Got nothing to say, pretty boy? Mulling around what it will feel like to have some big old guy's diseased dick sticking in your tight little ass? Probably hold on to all that girly hair while he rides ya!"

Burt burst out laughing, the amusement in his voice when he spoke again confident. "Looky here, pretty boy. I'll show you mine! That way you'll know not everyone's is all that hard to take!"

Tom kept his lips pressed together and his eyes averted. He wasn't going to allow the monster to provoke him into such a discussion, and the last thing he ever wanted to see was that man's body. But he couldn't help sending a jab of his own. "Hope you aren't planning on going anywhere soon."

The laughter instantly died. "Bet I am now that they have you."

Tom slid a glance in the direction of the other inmate, relieved to see his jumpsuit was intact. He allowed himself a grin of his own as he shook his head slowly. "Don't think so. They are investigating two to three different murder types. They are only targeting me for one. And like I said, I'm innocent. I never touched the things they found in my home. Bet the FBI is dusting them for fingerprints now."

An evil gleam entered Burt's eyes. "They'll just say you wore gloves."

"Don't own gloves."

Now Burt's face reddened. "Look you cocky son of a bitch, don't play stupid. They will say you dumped them!"

Tom took a deep breath and allowed a hum to leak out with it. "But I don't have access to the evidence locked up here."

Burt frowned at him. "What are you talking about?"

Tom smiled and turned away to go lay on his cot. "I'm tired. I'm going to sleep."

"Like hell! What did you mean about that last comment?"

Tom lifted his head, his features relaxed. "Just something one of the FBI guys said." He closed his eyes to lie back again, nearly laughing when Burt threw something in his cell.

"Don't be so smug, pretty boy. I have connections in this town."

Tom shook his head and wished someone would turn off the lights, but he had a feeling they stayed on all night. Which was just great. He was tired, exhausted actually, which just went to prove he shouldn't be where he was. He was never tired during the day. Ever.

"I'll be out of here by tomorrow night. They can't hold

me if they can't charge me."

"Hmmm…."

"Everybody knows you're a sissy girl. Probably took those kids so you could do 'em. Like them *boys*, do ya, sissy girl?

"Maybe I was wrong… I bet you've already had a man take you, unless you like to do the taking. Bet they charge you with raping *all* them boys and chopping them to pieces. They will fry you like a piece of bacon!"

Tom refused to let the maggot get to him, so he just kept his eyes and mouth shut, which apparently was the right thing to do.

"I like girls. Got me a helluva woman. She likes it dirty and rough, and once I get out of here I'm going to finish tearing her up.

"Damned cops interrupted my little lovefest with the wife when they came to get me. But I'll fix them for that."

Sickened, Tom rolled over to face the wall.

"What? You don't like hearing about it? Too damn bad. Wake your ass up! I'm not tired and I got things to say."

Having had enough, Tom sat up. "I have no interest in hearing about your depravities." He laid his head back down on the hard pillow, only to hear laughter.

"Got'cher goat that time! Well, if you don't want to hear about mine, why don't you tell me about yours?

"Talk, dammit!"

"Didn't do anything," Tom said, between clenched teeth.

"Sure you didn't.

"What was it like getting those boys and making them bend over for you? Pretty good, huh? Well, I like it from behind too, if you know what I mean. Wife is more than accommodating! Likes to scream and cry, but she likes it just fine."

Burt laughed uproariously, and Tom felt the goodness of spirit leave him. "Shut up! I don't want to hear it."

The steel door separating the jail from the operation

rooms of the police station opened, and the female officer he'd given the report to about someone breaking into his cabin just a couple of days before walked in. She didn't even look at Burt as she approached Tom's cell.

"You all right in here? We had a little earthquake, but no damage as far as I know." When neither man responded, she shrugged.

"Mr. Whitehawk, you have a visitor. Please come to the door and give me your hands," she said, pulling handcuffs from her belt.

Tom rose, glad to be able to escape, hoping he was going to get a chance to talk to the FBI agent. He needed to know his father and mother would be okay. He placed his hands in the opening and waited while she cuffed him before stepping back. She opened the door of his cell and he walked out, and then waited until she unlocked and opened the steel door.

The squad room was not as bright or as cold as the jail had been, and it helped soothe his burning eyes and chilled body. He allowed the woman to take his arm and lead him into another room, but the man standing waiting for him wasn't the agent, or even his father. It was the uncle of the missing child, Gavin White.

Tom kept his gaze on Garrison White as he was led to a hard metal seat and made to sit. His handcuffs were attached to two U-bolts attached upside down on the table. The officer looked at both men before she turned to leave. Tom glanced at her retreating back and then looked up to where Garrison White stood.

Garrison walked to the other side of the table and sat before placing his elbows on the table and putting his hands together. "Tom."

"Garrison."

His friend looked as tired as Tom felt and he seemed at a loss for words. But Tom didn't know what to say either. He had no idea how to keep his undercover mission a secret. He'd never been deceptive before. But at the least he could tell some of the truth. "I haven't done anything."

Garrison nodded, his features grim. "I figured that."

Surprise lifted Tom's brows. "Thanks."

Garrison stared at him a moment, then shook his head. "I've known you all my life. What I don't understand is why they found a gun and drugs in your home."

Tom didn't know what to say. If he said he was being set up, he would break the agreement with the FBI agent; so again, all he could say was the truth. "They aren't mine. Until they were found I had no idea they were there.

"How come they've let you come in here?"

Garrison sighed. "Captain Grammar is allowing it because he knows I need to understand what's happening. I can't stay long though. I just needed to ask you myself… Do you know anything about Gavin? *Anything at all?*"

Tom held the tear filled gaze of the man who had suffered for months over first the murders of his brother and sister-in-law, and then the loss of their son when he went missing. "I swear to you on all that is Holy, I have had nothing to do with his disappearance and have no knowledge of his whereabouts."

Garrison nodded and rose. "What can I do to help you?"

The unexpected and most generous offer hit Tom hard, making his eyes water. "Check on my parents, please. Make sure they're okay."

Garrison nodded and glanced at the small, wire-woven glass window of the door. Immediately the officer entered and walked to Tom's side. She unlocked the padlock attaching Tom's handcuffs to the chain and took his arm. He stood, and he and Garrison looked at each other for long moments before the officer nudged his arm.

Tom stopped just before they reached the door to look back. "Thank you," he said, before being led away.

Chapter Two

Garrison took his time going home though he was so tired he knew he shouldn't even be driving. He rode around the silent dark streets of Mystic Waters, thinking over the events of a day that had spanned too long.

The news there had been two arrests, regarding the murders of his brother and sister-in-law, the multiple remains found, and his missing nephew, had given him mixed feelings. Of course, he was relieved something was finally happening after so many months of nothing, but the holding of suspects, one of which made no sense, didn't bring his nephew back.

Though he had spent the better part of the day denying the possibility of Tom Whitehawk being involved in the murders, as he knew the man didn't have a mean bone in his body, he couldn't help the niggle of doubt that still remained. After all, Tom was the last person anyone would suspect of anything, so who better to commit a crime, or several?

Tom kept to himself for the most part, only known to leave the vast area of mountains his tribal family owned to deal with his rental properties both on the mountains and in the valley below. To Garrison's knowledge, he never dated or attended social event unless they were with others members of his tribe. And given the fact that Garrison had really gotten the chance to know Tom over the last few years, he doubted the man socialized much at all, even with his own.

Tom was a good guy. He had been extremely generous in helping when Garrison first wanted to purchase the land where he'd built his cabin and workshop, even though they were only very distant cousins on his father's side. The council had balked at first, because Garrison's Native

American blood was thinned with generations of Anglo-Saxon, one of whom removed the Hawk from the end of their name, shortening it to White.

Tom had argued with the council on his behalf for over two years, even helping Garrison trace his ancestors back to the same great chief who had first made a treaty with the United States Government, allowing their people to keep the much smaller plot of mountainous lands than they had originally hunted and lived on since before the white man's toes ever touched the continent.

Though he had known Tom casually before their joint venture, the time they had spent together working to procure the land had cemented a friendship Garrison wanted to trust. He just couldn't reconcile the man he knew with the one who was being targeted for one or more of the crimes that had plagued Mystic Waters.

His heart heavy and his head reeling with fatigue, he finally turned and headed back toward the mountain he called home and the woman he loved.

Twenty minutes later he pulled into the space he'd carved out to park his truck and as tired as he was he couldn't help but smile. His fiancée stood on the long porch of the cabin he'd built, awaiting his return.

Garrison made his way up the huge upside down split logs he'd shellacked and made into steps, and felt instantly better when he had her in his arms. "Hey beautiful."

"Hey, yourself." Rayne pulled back and smiled at him, her gaze filled with questions.

Garrison sighed, tired and confused. "I talked to him. I just don't believe he has anything to do with anything. I don't think John Grammar thinks so either, or he wouldn't have let me in there to speak to him."

"What did Captain Grammar have to say about the arrest then?"

Turning to walk them into the house, he shrugged. "Not much. Just that they had to hold him because of evidence found in his cabin. But the more I've thought about it, the more I believe he's been set up.

"I told you about his help in my buying this place, but I didn't tell you about all the time we spent together when I was designing and building it. He had some great ideas that I incorporated into my design, the porch and steps being one, and the bathroom shower being another.

"I guess you could say outside of immediate family and Logan, he's about the closest friend I have here. Or anywhere, for that matter. Even the men and women I fought with, who became brothers and sisters over the years, don't come close to the feeling of kinship I have with Tom.

"His being arrested doesn't make sense, unless someone is using him as a scapegoat. And what is sad about that, other than the obvious, is he isn't the kind of guy who will do well locked up in there. Tom is an outdoorsman. Not in the typical sense, but in the sense that he lives his life on the mountain because he is a part of it somehow... I don't even know if I'm making sense. It's just he has this spiritual connection to it. I wouldn't have even understood what I'm saying if I hadn't spent so much time with him.

"He knows things. Things others don't about nature. He took me on several hikes when I was working on the cabin, so I could look for the right woods to use and to show me how to make my home blend with the land.

"It was fascinating to listen to the reverence in his voice when he talked of the Mountain, the gentleness with which he touched the plants, and the trees, and even the rocks. But his actions weren't effeminate, if you know what I mean, it was like he was listening to them and knew them like a man knows a woman he loves, like family...like I love you...."

Garrison shook his head. "I know that sounds crazy, but I swear, I was so at peace when I was with him... I don't know how to explain it."

"You have explained it very well." Rayne studied him, her eyes filled with appreciation and adoration. "You are a good man, yourself, and you recognize goodness in others. I think you can trust your instincts on this. If you feel Tom is innocent of all wrongdoing, then I'm certain he is.

"But you look about to drop."

Rayne led him to the bathroom and began unbuttoning his shirt. "When Tom is cleared and released from jail, I'll have to remember to thank him. I love this shower."

Garrison grinned as he started unbuttoning hers. "Yeah, me too. Especially now that you are always in there with me."

Rayne laughed, her airy giggles lifting his spirits as well as his manhood. They continued undressing each other until they were nude, then Garrison took a step back just to look at her. He shook his head, always in awe such beauty was his. He moved back to stand right in front of her. His hands shook with the passion he felt for her as he placed them on both sides of her jaw. He held her there, just looking into her amazing emerald eyes, before pulling her to him to take her lips.

The magic and taste of Rayne's mouth had become home to him, the warmth of her spirit and toned body his refuge. Everything about her had saved him from the drowning despair of loss and worry. He pulled back and sought words, but there were none that expressed how thankful he was to have her in his life.

Rayne placed a soft hand on his cheek, her eyes filled with unshed tears. "What?" she asked, her voice breaking.

It was only then he realized that the overwhelming emotions she brought out in him were now trailing down his cheek. He swallowed and cleared his throat. "I am so blessed."

She smiled then. "No more than I."

Garrison took her mouth again, this time pouring all of his heart into it, wanting her to know, to never doubt, his eternal devotion and love. They made their way into the large walk-in shower and he managed to turn the water on, but he couldn't let her go.

Hungry kisses transformed into body worship, hands and lips, pioneers. Words of love and adoration were shouted and screamed as male and female conjoined with a need for speed that scratched and bruised in the fight to reach pleasure's threshold. Heightened ecstasy detonated into rapturous fireworks that shattered souls and shook limbs. Spent, humbled, and so in love he could barely breathe, Garrison held her in his arms as long as he could before allowing her long legs to slide down the outside of his.

Weakly they clung each to the other as they endured the ritual of cleansing. Rinsed and wrapped in towels they stumbled their way from the bathroom through the living room before crawling up the open-backed stairs to cross the small span of wood flooring leading to the bed.

Garrison took their wet towels and hung them over a rack before falling with her onto cool sheets. He pulled her close and inhaled the scent of her hair while whispering words of forever love. As she snuggled back into him, he released one big sigh before sliding into sleep.

****

Rayne awoke to the sound of soft knocking. She glanced back at Garrison and was relieved to see he still slept. Careful not to wake him, she slid off the bed before grabbing a robe. Hurrying, as the knocking was getting louder, she made her way down the stairs and to the front door. She peeked through the magnified glass peephole Garrison had installed only days before and sighed. Her sister Haven was on the other side, and it looked like she was gearing up to start banging.

Rayne unlocked and opened the door with an index finger to her lips, which was a good thing because Haven's mouth was already going. Haven closed her mouth and nodded as Rayne pointed to the loft. She stepped outside onto the porch as Haven moved back and couldn't help but smile.

Of the three sisters, Haven was always the funniest: quick with a joke or prank. Her happy nature was a relief to Rayne's own studious personality and Destiny's *way too serious* demeanor and often-dour attitude.

Somewhat flighty normally, since her engagement to

Garrison's best friend, Dr. Logan Hansen, Haven had become a bouncing ball of happiness. Her joy of life radiated like she was her own solar system. Her large smile now was no stranger to her face, and there was no way not to respond.

"You are not going to believe this!"

As badly as she needed a cup of coffee, which a habit Garrison had introduced her to, she knew it would have to wait. "Well, tell me!"

"Destiny called! She actually got through, which is a miracle in itself, but the bigger one is she has packed up and closed the house, and she's coming here, and she's bringing the diaries with her!"

Rayne was stunned. To put it mildly.

Destiny was the oldest, and so adverse to change, her leaving Los Angeles was major news.

"And even better, she apologized to me. For not being there when I needed her. And she wants to make amends and apologize to you, too."

Rayne knew she needed that coffee now. Destiny apologetic? As far as Rayne could remember, Destiny had never apologized to anyone for anything. But she couldn't help but wonder... "What does she have to apologize to me for?"

Haven shrugged. "I don't know. I was so shocked by what she had already said I didn't think to ask. But isn't this exciting?"

"Astounding is more like it. I wonder what made her change her mind...."

Again Haven shrugged. "Does it matter? Now we can tell her everything. I think it will make a difference for her. She's been so lost and unhappy since Mom died.

"Not that it ever mattered to me, but I think she and mom were closer than mom and us; like Destiny needed her more than we did. Of course I was always more interested in spending time with Aunt Lune Brille, and you were always stuck up Aunt Soleli's butt."

Rayne frowned. "That isn't a very nice way to put it."

Haven laughed. "You know what I mean. You badgered that poor woman all the time wanting to pick her brain apart so you could study it."

There wasn't really anything Rayne could say to that. Haven was right. "You know I need to understand things."

Haven nodded. "Thank God, *I* could care less. It about killed me just having to study to get my nursing degree. It was like pulling every tooth I have, but it was the only thing I could think to do that would allow me to use my gift, though I figured out soon enough *that* was a bad idea."

Rayne smiled, as a frown of deep thought rarely touched her sister's face. "Well, we've all been there. If I had known helping others, by responding to the requests of their deceased relatives, would eventually cause me all the problems it did, I may have ignored them altogether."

"Yeah, I know what you mean. But did we ever really have a choice?"

"No," Rayne acknowledged. "We didn't." She smiled suddenly, as excitement blossomed. "This is great news. I can't wait until the guys get a load of the three of us. It will freak them out!"

Rayne and Haven laughed together, their matching eyes shining with devilment, which was what Garrison saw when he opened the door. He looked from one to the other as they burst out laughing again.

"Oh Lord, what are you two up to now?"

Chapter Three

Destiny's plane landed after an exhausting day of travel, and she was still at least a couple of hours away from seeing her sisters again.

She knew they would have met her at the airport, but she wanted to surprise them. Although she told Haven on the phone the night before she was coming, she hadn't told her when. Haven, flighty bird that she was, never thought to ask questions.

Which was the biggest reason Destiny had reached out to her first, instead of Rayne.

Rayne would have picked her brain apart. She would have needed to know every detail about how Destiny closed up the house, how secure were all the family treasures, if she moving for good—and if not—how long she would be staying, and on and on until they would have been on the phone forever. And with the ridiculously early flight-schedule, she would have lost valuable sleeping time.

As exhausted as she already was, that would have been a disaster.

Less than a half hour later Destiny was in the rental car, a late model white convertible she'd badgered the rental attendant to upgrade to, her loads of luggage stored in the trunk. Except for the suitcases filled with the diaries. Those, which the airline had charged an arm and a leg extra for because most were way beyond the weight limit, were in the back seat, covered with a solar-shielding blanket to keep them cool and protected.

The drive was incredibly peaceful, the country scenery and majestic mountainous terrain amazingly beautiful, and Destiny settled in for the drive, only looking at the map once she was underway.

A peace she hadn't felt in years enveloped her forty-five minutes into the drive. She wound her way up the Blue Ridge Mountains on the Tennessee side, and the feeling only increased as she crested the mountain and began the decent on the West Virginia side.

She had to hold back the sudden need to cry when she realized this land looked exactly like the land she had visited when her essence found the man she still mourned. She knew it was unrealistic to think she would ever see him. The mountains covered thousands and thousands of miles, but it was a fantasy she couldn't shake.

Though it took considerable effort, she finally forced her thoughts away from him and toward the sisters who she hadn't seen for months. Though they had always been identical in looks and size, she wondered if the brief separation—which had felt like years—had changed them physically. From the few brief conversations they'd had over the last months, she knew Rayne now drank coffee and ate foods none of them ever touched, and she knew Haven was starting to eat differently too.

Destiny grinned to herself, wondering if they were getting fat.

Since a niggle of guilt followed the amusing thought, Destiny tried not to enjoy the vision of plump sisters for too long. She figured if any of the three of them were to put on weight, Rayne would be the last. Her need to study the world and how it worked was only matched by her need to exercise. If she wasn't studying, she was running or walking or moving around.

Haven on the other hand was a ball of energy even when she was sitting still. If scientists could find a way to bottle her zest for life, no one would ever need to diet. *L'essence de Haven* would make billions, and the world would be a happier and thinner place, and aromatic to boot!

It was funny, Destiny realized, that she was suddenly seeing her sisters in a different light. For all these years she had only thought of their personalities in negative terms, and she now saw them as they had always been. The problem hadn't been them at all. It was she, and the depressed outlook on life that had weighed on her since her mother's death.

Determined not to get bogged down while she was so at peace, Destiny didn't let the tragedy that had orphaned her and her sisters linger in her mind. She was still coming to terms with what had happened, though now she understood why.

She turned her thoughts again to the landscape and was rewarded with an amazing sight. An adult male eagle flew just overhead, so close she could see the strange blue of its eyes. It called out so loudly she jumped, swerved slightly, and then had to exhale through a shaky laugh.

Keeping her eyes on the road got harder and harder as she felt compelled to follow its magnificent movements. The large wings flapped laboriously but with strength and purpose. Its large body with the legs tucked back looked to weigh as much as she did. It flew overhead, then ahead, and then would circle around to come back. Destiny was certain it was watching her as closely as she was watching it.

She finally found a spot designed for travelers to pull over so she took it. As quickly as possible she was out of the car, mesmerized as it flew closer and closer, certain now it was interested in her for some reason.

Amazingly, it landed smoothly on the jut of mountainside less than fifteen feet above her head. She stared at it as it stared back and something inside of her melted. Not knowing why she cried, but unable to prevent the salty liquid from spilling down her cheeks and into her mouth, Destiny wiped one tear after another from her face.

She continued to watch it, transfixed, enraptured, and then jumped slightly when it let out a loud cry. After what was only seconds yet seemed an eternity, it flapped its wings and jumped. Her heart skipped a beat as it nearly reached the top of her head before heavy wings flapped and it was once again heading for the sky.

She had no idea how long she stood there blindly staring into the distance where she last saw it disappear into the clouds. Her eyes finally blurred over, and she remembered to blink and then to breathe. Stunned by the experience, she made her way to the car, her steps uneven and disjointed. She was glad there were no policemen around to witness her movements. She would have had to argue she hadn't been drinking.

Once she was finally seated in the car she took a moment to relive the experience, knowing no one would ever believe the connection she had felt with the large bird. It wasn't until it had flown away that she'd recognized that connection, because she'd suddenly missed it. And was even now mourning it.

She was Intuit by birthright and was once able to know and understand the true souls and motivations of others, but her abilities, when they had still worked, had only applied to humans. There was something about that beautiful bird that had called to her spirit, and she could only wish she had the ability to understand why.

It was almost like losing *him* all over again.

Destiny threw the car into gear and pulled out, knowing she was close to her destination. With the eagle still flying in her mind, she maneuvered the winding road until she reached the mailbox with the address that told her she had finally arrived.

Chapter Four

Tom inhaled sharply as he returned to his own body, awakening it from the dormant shell it had been while his spirit sought, requested, then entered Friend Eagle. The bird had been generous, willing to let its mind be put to sleep so Tom could have complete control of its body.

He had been in the cell for a full forty-eight hours with no word on what was happening on the outside regarding his case. The only people he saw were the officers who came in to feed him and walk him to the shower and back, and the fat little man whose smart mouth had finally been closed after he returned from being slapped with the domestic assault charge.

Boredom had driven him crazy so Tom pretended to sleep while he'd escaped the confines of the jail. He hadn't had any particular destination in mind, only the desire to smell fresh air and to stretch his mind. The exercises he did in the cell helped a little in keeping his body fit.

As soon as his essence was free, he'd headed for his home, willing to let Mother Earth embrace and soothe him. But something had pulled at him, and he'd passed over his cabin without looking down. The spirit that called to him was familiar, and when he processed what it meant, his energy level spiked, reminding him of the reaction he'd had to her when she first came to him.

He had never been with a woman, had even questioned his sexuality because of the lack of desire women inspired in him. Until *her*. Since then all Tom had to do was think of that moment when he'd sensed her, then felt her wrapping herself around him as he'd inhaled her intoxicating scent, and he was instantly hard and throbbing.

Now he woke every morning ready to burst, his engorged penis so hot and heavy he wondered how he held it up. He'd dream of her, and to his shame he would always picture her as Garrison White's woman.

He hated that part. It shamed him. He had never taken what belonged to another, but even to imagine it, to covet her, was a sin in his eyes.

He had prayed about it, had asked for the desire he felt to leave him, but nothing would shake the hunger she inspired in him. He had exercised vigorously before being incarcerated, and afterwards to the best of his ability in the confined space, hoping to wear his body out so his mind wouldn't dream.

But to no avail.

His dreams were vivid, and erotic, and mystical. She was a witch, a sorceress, and a genie in one.

She wove spells that drew him to her no matter how hard he tried to fight the diamond-encrusted silver chains she ensnared him with. She spun the earth so fast the gravitational pull melded them together, making them as one. She fulfilled his every sexual fantasy, making him believe it was her wish as well, until the delightful torture overrode any objections he wanted to voice. It shamed him a little more each morning upon waking because each night his objections grew weaker. He was beginning to not care that she belonged to his friend.

Even as the mist his essence had been sexually charged, and he knew he had to find her before she left the area again. The eagle came when he'd called out, ready and willing to be possessed, as he had allowed Tom the privilege many times in their years together. He sang of his gratitude as they flew side by side before wrapping his essence around Friend Eagle and soaking into his large strong body.

The sudden weight of the large bird threw him off for a second as it always had, but almost immediately he was raising and lowering the long span of wings then holding them out to soar as he'd searched the earth below. A hawk thought to distract him, and Tom had to send a sharp warning before the other reached him and they collided. It turned immediately and headed back toward the earth. As he watched it pass over a white convertible, he saw her shining red hair glittering with sunbeams and, when she looked up, her amazing face.

The difference in her stunned him, threw him off, and he'd had to get a closer look. He'd met Garrison's woman only once, and though she had looked identical to the woman in the car, her soul had been completely different. He hadn't known that then, but with a bird's eye view, he'd been blessed with understanding. With understanding came a relief so great, he'd had to bow his head in thanksgiving.

To find that this woman was not the love of his friend's life had filled him with endless joy. He *hadn't* been coveting another man's woman; he'd been coveting her twin. Unable to help himself he had flown over her again and again, thrilled each time she looked up at him with those incredible sparkling green eyes. His heart had nearly busted through the bird's chest when she suddenly pulled over, got out of the car and instantly sought him. He had landed as close as it was safe for his friend. He was not willing to endanger the bird, even though he wanted to land at her feet and pay homage to her as she deserved.

She was his queen, his sovereign, and she had come for him. She had come to save him. She was his destiny.

He called to her with the eagle's voice, wanting her to know it was him, and he watched as tears filled then ran from her eyes as if he'd broken her heart. His own heart swelled even more as he inhaled the exotic scent he'd dreamed of night after night but had never really expected to experience again.

His heightened emotions had awakened his friend, and Tom had no choice but to extricate himself from the borrowed body. He thanked the bird again then hovered in invisible mist as his friend jumped from the small mountain ledge. His heart nearly stopped beating when Friend Eagle nearly landed on top of her head before he flapped those impossibly long wings and took flight.

Tom watched her as she watched the eagle fly away

until he was finally out of sight. He felt her confusion and her sorrow and wondered if she somehow sensed the connection. As she walked back to her car, Tom figuratively held his breath, fearing for her safety. She swayed, zigzagging slightly, but made it without falling. She took a moment before starting the car, and he would have given anything to know her thoughts.

When she drove away he thought to follow, but he knew he needed to get back. He had to get word to the FBI agent and get himself released as soon as he could because he had no idea how long she would stay this time.

If she had indeed come for him, if she was in fact his destiny, then he couldn't let her go.

****

Rayne opened the door and squealed, and Destiny laughed as Haven ran up behind Rayne and squealed, too. The three hugged and laughed and cried, and Destiny knew she should have come sooner. They pulled her into the amazing cabin, shooting question after question at her, and she was overcome with the joy of being in the bosom of her family once again. It took a good twenty minutes for them to calm down enough to let Destiny head to the bathroom, and that was only because she had threatened to pee on the pretty hardwood floor.

When she returned Rayne was making fancy drinks and Haven was slicing the most decadent-looking chocolate cake Destiny had ever laid eyes on. Her gaze instantly went to her sister's waistlines but, no, neither had added a pound as far as she could tell. She laughed at herself and both Rayne and Haven looked at her with smiles.

"I'm so happy to see you looking so…well, happy," Rayne finished, as she slid a glass to Haven and carried one to Destiny.

"Me too! You are absolutely glowing!" Haven's smile faltered and her brows drew closer together. "Are you pregnant?"

Rayne's smile slipped a little too and Destiny knew why. "No, you guys! I'm just so happy to see you!"

The relief in their eyes spoke volumes, and though she had never given a thought to which one of them would be *the one*, she knew it would be hard for either of her sisters if it were someone else. She, of course, had absolutely no interest in bearing children, so they could worry over that all by themselves.

"So, catch me up." She looked at the three large slices of cake and then at Haven. "If you expect me to eat more than a bite or two, you're mistaken."

Haven simply smiled at her and handed her the saucer and a fork. "Suit yourself. But my fiancé made it, and I can guarantee you'll have an orgasm before the first slice slides down your throat."

Rayne laughed and nodded before taking a big bite of hers. She moaned as soon as the fork hit her tongue, and Destiny shook her head, unable to believe her sisters had become chocolate addicts in the short time they had been parted. She took her fork and cut off a more reasonable-sized bite before putting it in her mouth.

As soon as her taste buds got over the shock she looked at Haven, then Rayne, with eyes open so wide they hurt. She chewed slowly then swallowed. *"Oh. My. God!"*

Peals of laughter followed her reaction and she had to join in. "This is horrible!"

Both Rayne's and Haven's laugher dried up instantly, and they looked at her like she'd lost her mind. Destiny enjoyed the moment before making her confession. "I mean it's horrible because I'm not only going to eat this piece, I'm hiding the rest from you both."

Identical expressions of shock slid into identical knowing smiles. Destiny knew she was in trouble. She loved these women more than life, and she already knew this move was permanent. "I guess I should have put everything in storage just in case, because I think we need to sell the house."

Haven and Rayne's identical expressions of shock returned, nearly made her laugh. Her heart was so full of love for both of them she felt more like crying.

"Are you serious? You're staying? Just like that?"

Destiny nodded at Rayne, so at peace with the decision she questioned it. "I don't know why, but as soon as I was on the mountain I felt this... I don't know how to describe it."

"Freedom?" Rayne shot at her.

"Peace?" Haven added.

Knowing she must have the same shocked expression as her sisters now, Destiny nodded. "Yes. So you felt it too? When you first came?"

Both sisters nodded enthusiastically. "It was like coming home," Rayne said, before she stuffed another forkful of chocolate sin into her mouth.

"Like the mountain had just been waiting for me," Haven added, before she took her first bite.

Her throaty moan was long and low, and Destiny decided Haven was enjoying the cake just a little too much. Until she took *her* next bite. The cake was truly an orgasmic confection.

"So let's see..." Rayne said, setting her plate down. She looked at it longingly for a few seconds then turned away abruptly. "Okay, we need to get you settled in somewhere. I would ask you to stay here, but we are in crisis mode at the moment, which I will tell you all about later."

"And I would let you stay with me and Logan, but I'm afraid we would embarrass you to death. We only have the one bed and its up in an open loft. And we have sex... well, every possible minute."

Rayne rolled her eyes at that. "She isn't kidding either."

Destiny was glad her mouth was full of cake; it gave her time to ponder rather than react. After their enthusiastic greeting it hadn't occurred to her she'd need to find herself another place to stay, at least not *immediately*. But maybe it was for the best.

Unlike the Cavanaugh ancestors she'd read about, she and her sisters had stumbled into living without each other for a period of time, and though she had certainly been lonely and had missed them, she'd enjoyed not having someone else always around with their noses stuck in her business. And as she still had a lot of thinking…and research to do, it was best she have alone time to concentrate on both.

"Do you think there is rental property available I could get into quickly? I hate hotels. Bed bugs terrify me."

Rayne's lips puckered and her brows pulled together. "Well, the guy I rented the cabin from, that Logan and Destiny are now occupying, is in jail. Which is part of the crisis I need to tell you about. So he isn't an option. Unless…. Oh wait! I had forgotten, but I actually talked to his dad when I first called about renting it. I think the father handles getting renters, and the son just takes care of things when there's a problem. Since I didn't have any, problems that is, I didn't even meet him until much later." She grinned. "And when I did he stopped me in my tracks.

"If I hadn't already been head over hills about Garrison I would have made a fool of myself." She grinned again and shook her head. "But I digress.

"There is a cabin a little further up the mountain that hasn't ever had a For Rent sign in front of it, but from what I have observed when Garrison and I went walking in that direction, I don't think anyone lives in it either. If it's one of the Whitehawk cabins and really is unoccupied, it may be a quick option. I bet the same guy owns it. He owns everything around here. I have no idea what it looks like inside. And like the place I rented when I first got here, you can't see the cabin from the road."

She frowned at Destiny, her eyes filled with worry. "We could go look at it, though, if you want to."

After a full day of travel, the last thing Destiny wanted to do was get back into a vehicle, but it didn't look like she had a choice. "Do you have a number?"

Rayne grinned again, her relief evident. "Have you ever known me not to keep records?"

Destiny smiled through a sigh. Exhaustion was settling in now the rush of adrenalin, caused by reuniting with her sisters, waned. "What was I thinking to even ask?"

In less than forty-five minutes, they had taken the short drive, looked into the isolated cabin by peeking through the large windows, and called Mr. Whitehawk. He not only told them where the hidden key was kept but also said he'd been keeping it readied for the third—which they all thought a rather strange statement since no one knew there were three of them. Destiny had a place of her own to move into immediately.

The speed with which everything had happened reactivated Destiny's energy long enough to get her back to Rayne's cabin, to get her own rental car and belongings, and to get her back to the cabin she would call her own. Since it was nearly dark by the time all this had been accomplished she carried in only one small suitcase, changed into her pajamas, brushed her teeth, and climbed the loft to the queen-sized bed.

After eating the rich cake, she hadn't cared about the meal Rayne had tried to talk her into staying for or meeting the men they both had fallen in love with, which was an issue she needed to address with them both, eventually. Even a shower would have to wait. She was dead on her feet. Tomorrow was another day. For her, this one was spent.

****

Destiny awoke to complete darkness, and for a moment she was afraid to move. She stayed still, listening to the silence, before reaching over to fumble around until she could turn on the small lamp at her side. The instant light eased her, but the isolation was bit overwhelming.

She forced herself to get up and turn on the other bedside lamp. Feeling a little better, she made her way down to the main level, turning on every lamp she passed as she headed to the small kitchen. She stopped at the small island separating the kitchen from the sitting area, remembering she didn't have anything in the cabin to eat or drink.

She glanced over to the sink and debated drinking the

unpurified water. Since her throat was so dry even swallowing from anxiety was nearly impossible, she knew she had no choice. Even a lifetime of germ phobias couldn't trump extreme thirst.

Destiny opened a couple of cabinets before finding the one with the dishware. The quality of the fine china as well as its delicacy surprised her. If anything, she'd been expecting to find something cheaply made since the cabin was a rental. The glasses were special, too. She knew Fostoria when she saw it, and she had to give the Whitehawks credit for making her feel right at home.

Though sparkling clean, old habits, and phobias, couldn't be broken easily, so Destiny searched and was relieved to find dish soap beneath the sink, and dishcloths neatly folded and placed in a drawer. It took only a minute after opening the tap to remember she'd been told the hot water heater had to be turned back on.

Groaning, giving up, and knowing she was acting ridiculous, she turned off the hot and turned on the cold tap before filling the glass. She held it up to the little florescent light over the sink and studied it. It looked pure, but her eyes didn't have microscopic lenses. She knew she was taking a chance.

Destiny took a tiny sip and allowed it to roll over her tongue and around her mouth before she swallowed. The liquid was ice cold and surprisingly refreshing, so she took another larger drink, amazed at how really good it was. Before she knew it she had emptied the glass and was refilling it to carry it with her back into the sitting area.

Though she expected it, Destiny was disappointed the small flat-screen television had no reception. Mr. Whitehawk had told her on the phone she would have to contact the cable company to have the cable turned on, if she wanted it, and that the electricity would have to be transferred to her name if she planned on renting the cabin long-term. He hadn't said anything about the water, but maybe that was included in the rent.

She took another sip and decided she was getting a big

bonus if she was actually getting the water for free. It tasted even better than the air-infused water she had always paid big bucks for. It was crisp and energizing, which made little sense, but that was how it made her feel: like she was suddenly just bursting with energy.

Destiny stood and walked to a row of light switches. She flipped the first one closest to the front door and was happy to see soft yellowish lighting when she stepped back and looked out onto the porch through the large front window. She turned it off and flipped the next switch and had to blink when she looked out the front window this time. Bright white lighting bathed a large area surrounding the house and made the uncurtained interior very light as well.

Liking the security aspect, she turned them off and hit the next switch. The light above her head lit up and then the next one turned on the large ceiling fan that hung from beneath the point of the high ceiling. She kept that switch on, liking the slight stir of a breeze in the room.

Destiny looked around, amazed and amused that she had landed such a wonderful home. She examined and touched the finely made furniture that was in too good a shape to be old, but looked antique all the same. She ran a finger over several surfaces, but there was not a speck of dust to be found, and then squatted down to feel the texture of the braided rugs on the floor, amazed anyone would have enough patience to make one so large. But it wasn't until she reached what looked to be a hand carved oak mantle gracing the huge stone fireplace that her interest was really captured.

It was exquisite and must have taken the artist years to sculpt. The workmanship of the carvings was simply breathtaking, and she couldn't imagine what a museum piece was doing in a little rental cabin in the mountains of West Virginia.

Every wooden hair was visible as was the fear in the eyes of the buck and doe as they jumped from tall individually carved blades of grass, while a pack of hungry wolves chased them. The movement sculpted within the work made her heartbeat pick up, as if she too were running for her life. There were pine trees and oaks, maples and sycamores, and each one so perfectly chiseled and carved that their identifying leaves and trunks couldn't be questioned.

A rushing stream ran a third of the length of the mantel in a snakelike pattern that was so masterfully crafted Destiny expected to feel the spray as it flowed over a ledge of boulders where the wooden water rolled and foamed before sending echoing waves outward into a small lagoon, which finally veined out into smaller streams. Cattails and tall grasses grew around the lagoon; the blades and leaves touched the water as they swayed, as if windblown, in the direction of the waves.

A large bear stood on its hind legs in the foaming water with a fish in its mouth as it looked and leaned toward the shore where her twin cubs sat on the sidelines. One cub was looking up at a fish about to jump from its paws. The other was completely focused on the momma bear as if waiting for its turn for a meal.

It was all so lifelike she almost expected them to start moving. When she could finally tear her gaze away, she looked on, toward the more heavily forested area that started just past the lagoon.

At first Destiny thought the artist must have gotten tired of working on the piece and was taking an easy way out, but upon closer inspection she saw just the opposite was true. Within the dense carving of tree trunks, beneath the heavy canopy of leaves, were rabbits and raccoons and even a fox with her pups. Tiny yet amazingly detailed birds in various poses sat on limbs or in nests. Destiny could only wonder if the artist used a giant magnifying glass, because she could actually see the individually woven, minute sticks used to build their homes. Squirrels frolicked in tree branches and on the ground, and an owl watched with interest from above.

As Destiny continued to study the workmanship and

the story it told, she sidestepped her way down the mantel until she reached the remaining third where the trees opened enough for her to see the little cabin nestled within their protection. Her breath caught, and held, as she realized she knew the cabin, and looking back down the mantel, the entire area.

It was the home of her man. That magical wizard had to have created the mantel. Excitement collided with joy and Destiny's eyes filled and spilled over as she returned to the beginning of the scene to make certain. She reached out, afraid but feeling she had no choice, and touched the tip of the buck's antler.

Instantly she was drawn into the scene with the animals as they ran and jumped in fear. The wolves where close on their heels, and her heart beat like a piston ready to explode. The yellow-brown color of the narrow oak mantle changed to an endless open landscape of vibrant colors. She laughed as she ran to keep up with the deer, somehow knowing, even if she stopped, she would not be harmed.

Destiny had no idea if she was awake or asleep, but it didn't matter as she embraced the experience. As the proportions of the carving had been dead-on, she knew she had a long way to go, but she wouldn't stop running until she cleared the stream and passed the lagoon, with the hopes of finding her wizard in the little cabin.

It felt like forever, yet only a moment passed as she entered the clearing to the cabin. Unlike her trips to his home in the past, there were no other buildings. Gone was the temporary one he used to sweat and meditate in, as well as the one he'd built to bathe in. But it made sense. This scene, this work of art no mortal man could have created, was the mountainous land as it had been before he was even born.

She approached the front where a weathered old door hung and didn't bother to knock. She opened it out toward her and stepped in, and there, filling her heart with joy, was he.

Chapter Five

Gavin White flexed his biceps in the bathroom mirror and smiled. He had been working really hard to build his strength and his muscles in the little room where he had lived for the last two weeks. It was nice to know the shows on the television allowed him a sense of time. That was something he had missed all those months he'd been forced to live in the darkness of the cave Ma'am had taken him to, following his abduction.

He was still a little confused about how long ago everything had happened. He felt it had to be nearly a year. At least he thought so. It seemed like forever. And that scared him.

It was aggravating not to be able to remember simple things. Like what he and his parents had been celebrating right before bullets flew into their dining room window, and the chaos that followed. His dad had died instantly. His mom, minutes later. He'd been hiding then had come out just in time to see that monster try to rape his mother's dead body.

Everything from that point on was really fuzzy, so he knew he must have gone into shock. But he needed to remember. Needed to fight through the curtain of fog that had cloaked him through the days and weeks that followed. It wasn't until he'd awakened to find someone dragging him into the darkness that he'd really been clear-headed. By then it was too late. Not only had the person, who he now knew was *Ma'am*, hit him with her car when he'd been riding his motorbike, she'd nearly beaten him to death when he had struggled to get away from her.

The days that followed were all too clear: the pain, the cold, the solitude, the hunger, and more than anything, the fear.

The fear was the worse. Not knowing where he was or why he was there. Not knowing if the person who killed his parents would come back with more food, and fearing they'd come back and kill him. Not knowing if he'd ever see the light of day again.

He'd all but given up on that one.

That he didn't want to remember. That made him relive the fear and he didn't ever want to go back to that place because it made him feel weaker; like the little boy he'd been back then. Gavin shook his head, realizing what a brat he must have been.

He'd had everything. Parents who had loved him above all; friends who thought he was the bomb. He'd been so popular at school for both his athletic ability, as well as his looks. His parents made sure he'd had the best of everything; clothes, sports equipment, transportation to anywhere he wanted to go. At the time he'd taken it for granted. Now he knew he'd been spoiled rotten with their love.

Tears threatened but Gavin held them in. He wasn't that little boy anymore. He was a man who had survived unimaginable treatment, and he had survived, and was still surviving, being a prisoner of war.

Because this was war.

Ma'am thought she had him right where she wanted him. He was going to continue to let her believe that while he built an arsenal, even if that arsenal was only made up of his brain and body. His body was coming along. His brain was still questionable. That's why he had to let the darkness go, and clear his mind and remember. It was the only possible way for him to get back into the light.

He had to remember *the before*, that time between his parents' death and his capture. Maybe if he could remember everything that had happened while he'd been in the hospital and while he'd been living with his uncle, he could figure out who Ma'am really was, and then maybe know why she wanted him. Most importantly, why she would go to such lengths to take him, try to break him, and be so determined to turn him into somebody else.

He was trying really hard to piece everything together. Not because it changed anything in the short term, but because he was afraid Ma'am was winning. She called him Jimmy all the time now, and he responded to that name because he had to. But that wasn't who he was, and it wasn't who he wanted to be.

I'm Gavin White. Son of Grey and Joy White. Grandson of Garrison and Mary White. Nephew of Garrison White, Kaye White-Miller, and Gary White. Cousins to Johnny, Jillian, and Caleb White.

Although he couldn't say the words out loud, in case Ma'am's video had audio as well as video, Gavin felt better.

That's who he was. And no matter what Ma'am did or said, that's who he would remain.

So he went through his immediate family again, the grandparents, aunt, and uncles no longer just extended family. They were his immediate family now that his mom and dad were gone. Ma'am couldn't take that away from him as long as he kept it to himself. If she had any idea he even gave them a thought, Gavin had no doubt she'd destroy him.

She'd made it perfectly clear she was all he had, and she was all he would ever have…as long as he lived.

Though the threat hadn't been voiced, he knew she'd meant as long as he accepted her as his one and only, he got to live.

That's why he never allowed himself to think too far beyond the next moment, at the most the next day, because he had come to accept that he had to live in the moment and try not to think about escaping unless the opportunity presented itself.

After so many months of being held in the dark, dank, cave that had nearly cost him his life, he was thankful for the clean bright bedroom with its private bath. The last thing he wanted to do was make her mad so she started shackling him again, or worse, put him back in that dark hole of despair. Death would be preferable.

Ma'am had relaxed quite a bit with him, and though he was still required to stay on the opposite side of the bed when she entered the room, she no longer carried the stun gun in her hand when she brought him his food and clean clothing. She talked to him more often now too, telling him of plans she had for them. That concerned him greatly, but at the same time gave him moments of hope. He had to believe the day would come when he'd be able to escape her, as long as he acted like he never wanted to, in the meantime.

He still had no idea who she was, or why she had kidnapped him in the first place, although he knew she knew who he was.

At times he forgot and believed it too. And that was the problem.

Gavin mentally repeated his family names again and felt better for doing it.

He was glad each day his head got clearer, at least mostly, and his body was not only firmer, it was starting to bulge in all the right places. Gavin was even pretty sure he'd grown a couple or maybe even a few inches in height since he'd first been taken.

He looked in the bathroom mirror at his face and shook his head at the changes that had taken place on it since he last saw his family. He face was longer, his jaw more squared, and he was starting to grow a beard and mustache to go with the long hair Ma'am never allowed him to cut.

She had noticed the changes too, commenting on his becoming the man she wanted him to grow into. She seemed *so* pleased by the changes in *her* Jimmy. It made him nervous at times, but it also gave him security. He rarely ever felt like she was going to kill him anymore. And that helped to get through the endless days. *A lot.*

Gavin heard the sounds of her footsteps approaching his door, which had become more common over the last few days. It had taken him a while, after he'd first been moved to the house, to figure out she had probably lived somewhere else, since the house was always silent until she approached his door. But that seemed to have changed. Now he heard sounds early in the morning, and even in the evening. She ran a washing machine. He could hear when it was spinning. And he heard when she showered. Knowing now that she had been gone most every night, he had to keep from beating himself up for not trying to escape sooner.

But he hadn't known.

He had just believed that his room was well insulated, or soundproofed, and sounds didn't carry to him. Now that he knew differently, it was too late. It seemed she was around a lot more often, even during the daytime.

Still, he never knew when she was in or out since she'd gotten in the habit of leaving a television on in the other room, and he never knew when she was watching the monitor that kept a constant feed of his activities throughout the day and night.

In the last couple of weeks Gavin believed she left only to go to work or shopping and he'd been certain, at least at first, that she had rigged the door so harm would come to him if he touched the doorknob. Now he wondered if he had just been overly paranoid, but fear of harm or being put back in that horrible place had kept him in line.

Which she no doubt banked on.

He still hadn't found that camera she kept on him, but Gavin knew that at least was real. She would comment on something he had done while she wasn't in the room to see it, just to let him know she really was watching his every move, he was sure. And knowing she watched, he never had a chance to search for the device without it being obvious.

The sound of several locks being sprung preceded her opening the door, and Gavin wondered why he hadn't noticed before. Next time he heard her approach he had to remember to count them. It could be important....

As always Ma'am had her head covered with a hat that was covered in thick black netting. Though it hid her features, he had learned to gauge her moods by the flash of teeth he'd sometimes see behind the black, or by her overall demeanor. Today there was no flash of teeth, and she held something in both hands that instantly put him on guard and had his stomach churning.

"Hello, Jimmy."

Gavin stayed where he was, determined not to tremble. "Good morning, Ma'am."

The hand with the stun gun stayed at her side, but she lifted the other. The syringe was between her index and middle fingers, and her thumb was over the plunger. "I need to give you a vaccination."

It shamed him, but Gavin couldn't keep the panic from his voice. "For what?"

She shook her head making the netting swing from side to side. "You don't ask questions without permission."

Swallowing, trying to get his trembling under control, Gavin nodded. "I'm sorry, Ma'am. May I ask for what?"

He saw the flash of teeth then.

"It's a tetanus shot. To make sure you don't get lockjaw if I cut you while shaving the scraggly stuff. My Jimmy always has a neat appearance."

Remembering she had promised to trim his beard and mustache, since she wouldn't allow him to have a razor of his own, he nodded. Not because he trusted her, but because he really had no choice. If he refused, Gavin had no doubt she would finally use that stun gun on him, and then he'd have to take the shot anyway.

"I want you to attach yourself to the restraint, Jimmy."

Getting sick to his stomach, Gavin walked to the side of the bed where there were still shackles attached to the metal railing. It had been so long since she'd used them, he had almost forgotten about them, and that he had slept in a hospital bed since first being brought to the house. He lifted the metal railing and locked it into place then closed the open cuff on his wrist.

"Good boy. Now lie down."

Gavin sat then lay back and swung his legs up. He

knew there was no way to protest what he feared was something other than what she said was in the syringe, or she wouldn't continue to believe he was going along with whatever she dictated. He held his tongue as she cautiously walked around the bed, and his stomach lurched when she told him to hold out his other arm so she could lift the railing and strap him immobile.

Once he was secure he saw the flash of teeth. But for the first time since he was too sick to notice, she was close enough to him that he also saw she wore sunglasses to further shield her eyes. He forced himself to relax before she pushed the needle into his arm. In a heartbeat she was pulling it back out and other than a little sting, it wasn't so bad.

"Now you just relax while I go get shaving supplies."

Gavin waited for her, relieved he'd been wrong as he felt nothing, until a moment more when he realized he was getting woozy. He fought it, but nothing would change the fact his brain was floating on a cloud that made him even more nauseated. When she appeared again, she held her cloaked head close to him as if she was looking into his eyes. He saw the flash of teeth again.

"As you've probably figured out by now, that was a sedative. I gave you just enough to make it safe for me to shave you. It won't hurt you, so relax and enjoy the high."

Gavin couldn't help the tears that leaked from the outer edges of his eyes. He had always been a good kid and had taken care of his body. He'd had friends who had experimented with various drugs, but he'd respected his father too much to even consider trying any.

"Can I ask you a question?"

Ma'am lathered his face in the areas she meant to shave. "Okay."

Gavin took a shaky breath as the small disposable razor got closer and his body suddenly felt heavier. "Why? I'm shackled. I didn't fight you."

Ma'am shrugged. "Be still. It's just to make it easier on us both. I see that look in your eyes sometimes like you want to try something, and I've seen you when you didn't know I was watching. You eventually remember to mask it, but I see.

"It's a good thing you haven't tried to come at me or tried to escape, because I would hate to have to hurt you, too. This way I don't have to worry about replacing you.

"It's a win-win situation for us both."

Gavin stayed very still only opening his mouth when told and closing it when told again. Ma'am took her time as if she was creating a masterpiece. All he could think about was her words. There had been others? He wasn't the first? How many? Who were they? Was it anyone he knew? And where were they now?

That question scared him to death.

She finished and looked at him for a good minute before the netting bobbed up and down. "Good. You look very nice, Jimmy. Very nice indeed.

"And you are growing so nicely too."

She took her time letting her covered head indicate she was looking up and down the length of him. Gavin was horrified to feel his penis grow and fill as she continued to look at him there. He shook his head as anger at them both tore into him. She turned back to him again and though the teeth weren't visible, he was certain she grinned.

"Don't be upset with yourself Jimmy. You're a healthy young man, and that is a natural reaction to a woman looking at you. But don't be afraid. We have another year of training before I make you mine.

"I want a man. Not a boy."

Ma'am stepped back and pulled out the cap for the needle then covered it before pulling out the keys to unlock his restraints. Gavin's first reaction was to try to grab her with his freed hand, but he couldn't lift his arm. He realized then that was the real reason she drugged him; not so he would behave while being shaved, but so he wouldn't fight her when she was done doing whatever she wanted to do to him. He watched as she released his other wrist then stood back and looked him over again.

"Be a good boy Jimmy and let me have my way. Other's didn't, and their families have had to throw them going away parties. I've even attended some of the funerals and got to hug the distraught parents. But you don't have a family anymore, do you? It would be a shame to go without anyone to throw you a party.

"The drug will wear off soon and you won't be any worse for it. So the next time I tell you to connect yourself to the shackle you had better do exactly what you did this time. Do you understand me?"

Gavin nodded, knowing there was no other answer he could give, but he knew now that the time for being timid had ended. He had to get away or die trying. And she was wrong. He did have a family; a *great big family* that would tear her limb from limb if they ever caught her.

Chapter Six

He was just as Destiny remembered him; at least six inches taller than her five-foot nine-inch frame, very broad of shoulder, a muscular chest, rippling abs, and every other inch of him long sinewy muscle. He was naked this time, as well, making her think it was his way when he was alone. Since she'd grown up in a family of women who believed it healthy to feel the air on their skin, she had no problem with his nudity. Not that she would have anyway, Destiny decided, thinking him as incredible a work of art as the mantel she now dwelled within.

Though the cabin was empty save the two of them, she felt warm, almost hot even, but then that could have been because of the heat he radiated, or perhaps the heat he caused to ignite within her.

Surprise and delight lit his incredibly blue eyes as a nearly blinding smile lifted his lips showing perfectly straight teeth. He was before her instantly though she never saw him move, his eyes taking her in, his heart pounding visibly against his broad chest. She trembled, needy and desperate, wanting more than anything to feel the strength of his strong, heavily muscled arms wrapped around her form.

"I found you," she said softly, inhaling the scent of him. He smelled of the wind and the rain, of the earth and the trees. He was everything and he was solidly before her, and Destiny was lost in the wondering of it all.

Find me, he mouthed, but no words left his lips as he continued to absorb her with sky blue eyes that caressed, yet still held an edge of urgency.

He reached for her then, wrapping her in even more warmth as she was pulled against his body. The security of his arms was everything she'd dreamed of, but there was desperation in his grip as well. Though she didn't understand the cause for his distress, she hugged him tighter. He said nothing more but she felt his body tremble so she pulled back to look into his eyes. "But I did! Don't you see me? Feel me? I'm here!"

He said nothing as he continued to look at her.

"Don't you see me?" she repeated. Apprehension filled her, making her tremble as well.

His eyes took on a look of terror as he glanced at the door. Destiny turned to see what he saw but there was nothing there. She took his hand and pulled him with her as she headed toward it, determined to find the reason for his distress.

When she stepped out of the cabin, nothing was there except the trees and the grass. She turned back to question him as her hand fell empty. Disbelief nearly took her to her knees…he was gone.

Destiny shook her head in denial, unable to believe he had left her. She took off at a run and ran all the way around the cabin but he wasn't *anywhere*. She ran into the forest circling it to search some more, but still nothing. She broadened her search, still circling the small clearing, but going deeper and deeper into the forest while looking back toward the cabin between the thickening stand of trees. When she could no longer see anything but trees, she stopped and bent over, desperately trying to catch her breath.

Tears threatened but she held them in, not sure if they stemmed from anger or fear, or both. Desperation had taken hold, but she forced herself to calm down, knowing she needed to get out of the woods he'd created. All that had been beautifully colorful before now felt stark and dark and threatening.

Fear *and* fury kept her feet moving as the soft ground grew harder and harder until it hurt her feet. The trip back seemed so much longer, making her wonder if she'd gotten confused and had headed the wrong way. But she had a master inner compass so she knew to trust her instincts, even though doubt grew each minute that passed. By the time she finally reached the lagoon she knew she was panicking as terror had fully set in.

The water no longer rippled, the fall was frozen and still. The family of bears was nothing more than masterful carvings once more, though now they were proportionate to her own form. She fell to her knees and screamed her fury, weeping until there were no more tears.

How could he have left her? How could he have done that when she needed him? Wanted him more than life itself?

Spent, chilled, and feeling wounded, Destiny rose and made herself place one foot in front of the other as she walked up the now still stream. She had no sense of time, but she eventually found the scene of the beautiful frightened deer. She approached the frozen buck, unable to believe she had forgotten for a time she was no more real than they. She lifted her hand to reach up and touch the buck's antler as before. And just like that she was standing before the mantel, her finger now looking like a giant's as it touched the tiny carving.

Destiny didn't move other than to pull her hand away. She didn't know what to make of what had just happened, but her heart felt as cold as the hearth below. Weak, numb, she swayed when she turned away from the fireplace so she carefully made her way to the sofa where she fell into its padded embrace. She lay there staring at the ceiling fan until the sun broke the darkness. And was still there a few hours later when her sisters came banging on the door.

Forcing herself to get up, Destiny opened the door to her own face twice over, except theirs were full of smiles. She was glad to see them, but her heart felt broken, and all she wanted was to be left alone.

"Good grief, sleepyhead! I told Rayne to leave you alone this morning; you would be exhausted! But does Ms. Let's All Get Up At The Crack of Dawn and Go See Destiny listen to me? I don't think so!"

Rayne rolled her eyes and pushed past Destiny. "This

place is so much nicer than the one Tom Whitehawk's dad rented to me! Look at that mantel. Oh my gosh!" She looked back at Destiny. "Have you *seen* this thing?"

Destiny ran across the room so quickly to stand between Rayne and the mantel that both sisters looked at her like she was crazy. And maybe she was. "It's beautiful. Just don't touch it, okay?"

Rayne and Haven looked at each other with raised brows then looked back at Destiny. "Okay…" they said together before laughing.

Destiny sighed. "Look, there are some things I have to tell you. And you are both going to think I'm nuts. And maybe I am. But I can do something, or some *things* now, I never knew about before."

Instead of looking at her like she was indeed crazy, both sisters' green eyes lit with curiosity.

"What can you do?" Rayne asked, as Haven moved closer.

Destiny wondered if maybe *they* were crazy, as she suddenly felt like an ant under a kid's magnifying glass. She cleared her throat. "Well, I've been in this area before. Twice."

Stunned looks from both sisters made her smile. "Yeah, only… I wasn't here." Instead of the doubt she expected, Destiny was surprised by their smiles.

"Tell us," Haven insisted, her eyes shining with excitement. Rayne nodded, leaning toward Destiny like she might pounce at any moment.

She looked from one to the other. "I can do what Aunt Soleli does. Sort of."

Both sisters squealed and high-fived each other before turning back to Destiny. "I told you!" Haven shouted before starting a crazy little dance around the room.

Rayne laughed and danced too. "I think we told each other!" She flashed a smile at Destiny. "I knew it! I knew it! Hahaha! I knew it!"

Destiny stood there and watched them, unable to react. They weren't even surprised at her revelation, and she was still trying to get used to it. She held up her hands to get them to stop moving. When they both did, but still looked at her with Cheshire cat smiles, she shook her head. "How did you know?"

Haven and Rayne looked at each other and Haven signaled for Rayne to speak.

"Ok. First, what do you have to drink around here? I am dying of thirst now."

"Me too," Haven added, looking at Destiny expectantly.

"Well, actually I have tap water. That's all."

Rayne frowned. "You are drinking tap water? Since when?"

Destiny smiled. "Wait until you taste it. It is the best thing I've ever put into my mouth."

"Not me," Haven said, drawing a look and a shake of the head from Rayne.

"Keep it in your pants, Haven, this is about Destiny."

Haven made a face at Rayne and sent Destiny a wink she had no idea how to interpret. She headed to the cabinet and pulled down two glasses before going to the tap and filling them.

"No ice?" Haven pouted.

"Don't be ungrateful," Rayne told her.

Destiny ignored them both as she handed them the glasses. Rayne held up the glass and looked at it for a moment as if seeing if there was something she should be concerned about, and Haven shook her head.

"Did you put sea monkeys in here?"

Destiny laughed. "Just drink the water!"

Her sisters slid each other a look, but both put the glasses to their mouths and took sips. Their eyes popped open and they looked at her over the rim of their glasses as they continued drinking. When both glasses were empty, they lowered them and looked a Destiny like she had invented the light bulb. She smiled at them. "Amazing, huh?"

"I don't think water is supposed to make you want it

again after you've just finished an entire glass," Rayne said, her voice filled with wonder.

"You're right. This is amazing. Do you have some special kind of filtration system under the sink?"

Destiny frowned and turned to look. She hadn't thought of that. She turned back smiling. "No. It's straight from the earth. I wasn't going to drink it at first, but I didn't have anything else to drink, and I was so thirsty. I know it sounds crazy but it made me feel so energized."

Rayne nodded. "I see what you mean. I feel…um…."

"Horny!" Haven offered.

Rayne laughed. "You are *always* horny." She turned to Destiny. "But this time I have to agree with her. What is in that water?"

Destiny shrugged. "I don't know."

Haven looked at her speculatively, then at Rayne, before walking to the refrigerator and pulling a small taped piece of paper off the door. She looked at it for a moment then smiled at them both. "I do. Mr. Whitehawk left this note. It says the water is safe. Feel free to drink all you want. It comes from a fresh water spring that runs down the mountain into the lake below." She turned the note over and continued reading. "It says his son, Tom, who owns the cabin, fixed it so he could capture the water in a well that still flows on its natural course once the well fills."

Haven smiled up at them both. "So there you have it."

Destiny frowned. "I didn't see that note there before."

Haven shrugged. "Maybe you were so tired you just didn't notice."

Though she didn't think she would have missed it, Destiny nodded slowly; it was the only plausible explanation.

"That makes sense then…" Rayne said, obviously distracted as she glanced back to the fireplace. "That mantel, he must have carved it or had it done. Gavin says Tom has amazing skills when it comes to home design. I know he knows how to build a shower to die for. He designed and helped Garrison build his."

Destiny thoughts instantly went to the shower house beside her wizard's cabin and she frowned. "What does he look like?"

Rayne smiled. "Well, he's a little taller than us, sandy brown short hair, lean, but not thin. Worrying about his nephew has aged him I think, but that's to be expected."

Destiny shook her head. "What nephew? Did you say short hair?"

Rayne sighed. "The one I told you has been missing for months now. And yes. He has short hair, why?"

No. Something wasn't right. Destiny rubbed the area between her eyebrows. "This Tom Whitehawk has a nephew missing? I thought that was your boyfriend."

"Fiancé," Rayne corrected. "Isn't that who we're talking about?"

Destiny shook her head. "No. Tom Whitehawk."

Haven sighed. "She wants to know about Tom Whitehawk, Rayne."

"Well, I know that now," she said and looked at Destiny. "He's tall. Very gorgeous. Not as old, I don't believe, as you would think since his hair has silver streaks. He...well, he has this face that speaks to his Native American heritage in the very best sense."

Tingles of excitement made Destiny shiver but she didn't want to get her hopes up in case it wasn't her wizard. "Do you know where he lives now?"

Haven laughed. "Since when do you go looking for men just because one of us thinks he's gorgeous?"

"You don't?" Destiny asked.

"I don't need to go after him. I have my man."

Destiny took a deep breath. "I meant you don't think he's gorgeous?"

"I haven't met him."

Destiny turned back to Rayne. "You have. What do you know about him?"

"He's kind of indisposed at the moment," Rayne hedged.

"What does that mean?"

Rayne glanced at Haven then at Destiny. "Well, the FBI took him to the local jail. They found a gun and some marijuana in his cabin."

Destiny swallowed. "He's innocent!" Rayne looked as stunned by her declaration as she was for making it.

"How do you know? Haven said you lost your gift. And you haven't even met him."

Destiny shook her head. "I don't know what is going on with my intuition, but I *have* met him. He called to me and I came here. Well, *I* didn't come, but did, as the mist."

"To anyone else that wouldn't have made sense. But I get it. Your essence came to the mountain of Mystic Waters but your body stayed in Los Angeles. And while you were here you visited with him…in jail?"

Destiny nodded as Rayne spoke until the last, and then she shook her head. "No. He was at his cabin, in a teepee that he had made into a sweat lodge.

"He is… magnificent, to put it mildly, and he knew I was there. He called to me and he called me by name. He called me, 'My Destiny.'"

Rayne and Haven both looked at her like frozen stunned statues. Rayne blinked. "Are you saying he has mystical powers?"

Destiny nodded.

"I need to sit down."

"Me too," Haven agreed as she followed Rayne to the sofa. "I've never heard of anyone else doing the things our family can do."

"Me either." Destiny took the rocking chair facing them. "But it makes sense. Who said the Cavanaughs are the only ones on the planet able to perform magic?" The three sat there silently for a few minutes, and Destiny could only imagine they were as filled with wonder at the possibility as she was.

"Okay, so, you say he called you. What do you mean?" Rayne asked.

Destiny took a deep breath as she considered how to tell her story. "I guess I should start with what was going on before he called me, first. I was feeling pretty crappy. You guys were gone, and I had to go on leave from work because I couldn't read anyone anymore.

"Sure, I had the education and training, but it's crap. People aren't cookie cutter, and neither are their phobias, fears, and reasons for depression. If I had used what I'd been taught and trained to do then I would have steered some of those people wrong.

"So anyway, I couldn't in good conscience keep telling people they needed to look deep inside themselves for a cure to what ailed them because some things can't be fixed by talking about it. I had to close up shop as it were, and then I was home all the time. Alone, bored, and depressed, frankly."

Rayne frowned. "I'm sorry. I wish I'd known."

Destiny shook her head and waved Rayne's comment away. None of that mattered now if she had found her man.

"Don't worry about it. Anyway, like I said, I was all those things. But I decided I couldn't call you guys or the aunts to whine, *Oh woe is me.*" She held up her hand again when both sisters opened their mouths to protest. "*So,* I decided to get more tea enemas for cleaning my system, and start my version of yoga, which is nothing like the actual version, but anyway, I started stretching and moving as much as I could. The song our mother used to sing to us came into my head, and I turned the movements into a dance.

"Eventually, I sat on the floor and was watching the afternoon sun, and then I was soaring in the sky and felt it heating my body."

Rayne held up a hand to stop Destiny. "First of all, you *could* have called. I'm hurt you don't think we would be there for you, and secondly, do you think Momma came to you and put that song in your head?"

As that hadn't occurred to her before, Destiny had to think on it a bit. "I don't know. She never came to me before."

"I think you're wrong. I think she did before I came to Mystic Waters. Remember? You suggested using Momma's crystal and a map to help me decide where to go. And you remembered the words to her rhyme. I think she was talking in your ear then, too."

Chills caused Destiny to rub at the goose bumps on her arms. "But I was so angry at her. Why would she come to me, of all people?"

Rayne smiled, but Haven was the one to speak up. "Because she loves you. Even when people are angry at you, or you are angry at them, it doesn't take away the love."

Destiny looked from one sister to the other. "I hope you know that's true, because I've been an absolute bitch to you both at times. And I'm sorry for it. I do love you both so much."

Three sets of emerald eyes filled with tears, but Destiny refused to get maudlin so she kept talking. "Anyway, as I was saying, I was flying, or at least my spirit was.

"It was amazing. I felt so free, so weightless. And I got to look at the world with a bird's eye view all the way from California to these mountains. It's more beautiful than you can imagine. Even riding in an airplane doesn't compare.

"But then I'm over the mountains, and I suddenly feel like something is holding me in place. So I can't keep flying on past them. Since I didn't feel threatened I started descending, and I ended up over this teepee with steam coming out of its top opening where the support logs were secured together. It sits behind this really old cabin that has a fairly new tin roof. The sweat tent is made of newly stripped logs and animal skins. I sensed that the skins were very old."

Destiny took a breath, wondering if she was talking too much or giving details they wouldn't be interested in. But their attention was so focused on her, and neither said anything, so she knew they were waiting for more. She smiled. It had been a really long time since she had been the storyteller of the three. A very long time indeed.

Knowing now was not the time to embrace childhood memories, she continued. "Anyway, so I'm hovering over this sweat tent, and I'm still feeling this little pull so I float down through the steam. At first my sight was blurry. I think the steam messed with my essence or something. But once my sight cleared I saw him."

Destiny closed her eyes and pictured him. She opened them and shook her head. "He was chanting, or singing, in a language I didn't understand. But he lifted his head and looked around frantically like he was looking for me. Like he *knew* I was there."

"What did he look like?" Haven asked.

Destiny chuckled. "He was sitting, excuse the phrase, Indian style, and he has really long dark hair with streaks of silver. And even sitting like that, I could tell he was tall because his legs were so long and muscular, as were his arms. And he must work out a lot because he had a six pack to die for, very broad shoulders, and, well...he was naked."

Haven's mouth dropped open. "And?"

Destiny couldn't help the grin. "Well...he was well...um, *endowed*."

Haven grinned. "He was well...*endowed*, or he was *well* endowed?"

Rayne rolled her eyes and glared at Haven. "For Pete's sakes! Would you stop?"

Haven laughed. "Hey, I just discovered sex not too long ago. I can't help it if you've been around so much that it isn't the only thing on your brain."

Rayne's mouth dropped open and she looked outraged. Destiny was about to step in, but Rayne beat her to it.

"How dare you? I have *not* been *around*. I wasn't as lily pure as you, obviously, but I had only been with one other man and I thought I would end up with him!"

Destiny kept her mouth closed and made a real effort not to grin. She had forgotten how much fun it could be to be a sister.

"Yeah, well, I remember that boy from high school, too, or don't you count him? And if I remember right, and I have a very good memory about some things, you let him get to third base. Which, if I remember correctly, means he fingered you."

The murder in Rayne's glare had Destiny holding up her hand, although she really wanted to hear what Rayne had to say. She hadn't been told by either of them about Rayne and third base, but it wasn't surprising. She hadn't shared her dirty little secret with either of them either.

On top of her own high school sexual fiasco—which had resulted from her wanting to get close to someone outside of the family, since she hadn't wanted to talk about their mother's death anymore and that seemed to be all the aunts wanted to talk about—Destiny had stopped being interested in anything at home, including her sister's lives. It shamed her to realize how much she had deliberately missed out on.

But that was a past she had long ago buried, and she was more than happy to leave it six feet under. So....

"Back to my story," Destiny said too forcefully. She watched Rayne struggle to turn her glare away from Haven and her attention back to the story. She made her voice soften once she had everyone's attention again.

"I was admiring his beauty, and not just his package, *Haven*, when he said, 'my Destiny.' I think there was more after that, but I didn't hear it because I was suddenly in the fight of my life trying to escape from this mighty suction pulling me backwards. It pulled me up out of the sweat tent, back across the country, spinning me like a top I might add, and then I was thrown back into my body."

"Oh no!" Haven clapped her hands over her mouth, her eyes filled with sadness.

Rayne said nothing, but Destiny knew she was still trying to control the urge to hit Haven. To help her out Destiny kept her story going. "So anyway I'm back in my body, and I'm so dizzy I can hardly stand. But the worst part is I don't know if I had dreamt the whole thing, or if it had actually happened."

Compassion filled Rayne's eyes, taking away the anger. "You must have been devastated."

Destiny nodded. "I was."

"I'm so sorry we weren't there for you."

"Me too," Haven added, keeping her eyes on Destiny, though everyone in the room knew Rayne was looking at *her*.

Destiny shrugged. "That isn't the end. I moped around thinking about him. At night I dreamt about him. I was so sad I finally decided to see if there was some way to get back to him. And the only thing I could come up with was to read the diaries."

Rayne straightened as her eyes lit up. "You read them?"

Destiny smiled. "Not all. Good grief, that would take years! But I wouldn't have been able to read what I had if it wasn't for all your hard work deciphering those Egyptian papyruses. I can't thank you enough. You are amazing."

A sheen of moisture suddenly covered Rayne's eyes as she stared at Destiny. "Thank you. I never thought you felt that way about me."

Destiny knew her own tears were of shame. "I'm so sorry about that. I should have already known how special you are. I just had my head so stuck up my own butt I didn't see it. Please forgive me."

They both stood and met in the middle of the space that separated the couch from the rocking chair. "I'm really sorry."

"It's okay. I've always looked up to you, even though you're only seven minutes older than me. You've always been my big sister."

"If it's any consolation, Destiny, Rayne makes me feel stupid sometimes, too."

Destiny and Rayne looked back at Haven and opened their arms. With a wide smile she joined in the hug and Rayne spoke into her ear, "Not stupid... Ridiculous!"

Haven pulled back to look at her, and she and Destiny

saw Rayne's smile.

"But I love you anyway."

Haven's smile returned. "And I love you, too; even if you are something of a stick in the mud these days."

Rayne shrugged as they separated. "I know I am, especially here lately. But with so much going on in Mystic Waters, 'happy go lucky' Rayne has disappeared."

"Well, get her back. Now that the three of us are together, we will find a way to conquer your fiancé's problems. There has to be some spell or something in those diaries to help us," Haven declared before looking at Destiny. "You brought them, right?"

Destiny nodded, grinning because she felt happier than she had since the day they found out about their mother's death. "I sure did. And I can't wait to work with you two. So tell me everything. What is going on in Mystic Waters, and where do we start?"

Remembering the other reason for her happiness, Destiny held up her hand before either Rayne or Haven could speak. "But first, just where is that jail?"

Chapter Seven

"...one-forty-eight, one-forty-nine, one-fifty."

Tom jumped to his feet and saw Burt Thompson staring at him. The creepy little man was always watching, and it was way past getting on his nerves. "You should try push-ups. It helps pass the time."

Burt made a face, then awful noises in his throat, before spitting a loogy across the distance between their cells. He smiled as Tom stepped back to keep from having the scum's sinus drainage land on him. Knowing he should have known better than to tell the man anything that resembled care or concern, Tom smiled, hoping it came across as snide.

He needed to get Thompson talking so he could get his own incarceration over with. If he was going to have to play a bastard to catch a bastard, then so be it. It didn't matter that it went against everything he believed in. He didn't deserve to be set up for crimes he hadn't committed. "Didn't your mother ever teach you any manners?"

The smile was replaced by an anger that made Burt's face molten red as he grasped his cell's bars and moved his own body back and forth as he tried to shake them. "Fuck you, pretty boy!"

The manic reaction kept Tom from going into the next exercise of his routine. Until now, nothing he had said to the creepy little man had gotten much of a reaction, if any. Thompson's agitation was what Tom had been waiting for. Since finding out he was going to be held after all, he hadn't been nearly as talkative, and certainly hadn't been stupid enough to hand Tom any information the FBI or the Mystic Waters Police Department would find useful.

"What's wrong? Hit a nerve? Guess your momma *didn't* teach you any manners. Did she teach you anything at all?" Tom hated what was coming out of his mouth, but Thompson looked like he was about to explode. Since he needed to make his jail mate lose control, Tom took a deep breath, determined to push on. "Makes a lot of sense. Did she beat you? Is that why you mistreat your wife?"

"Shut the fuck up!" Burt yelled. Within seconds the officer who had brought their lunch was coming through the metal door.

"Something going on in here?"

Tom shrugged and started running in place as the officer turned to Thompson. He winked at his jail-mate behind the officer's back, and got the reaction he was after. Thompson's face was as bright as a fully ripe tomato. The smile fell from his face seconds later as Burt grabbed the collar of the officer's uniform, catching him by surprise.

Though he tried to push himself away, Thompson was quicker, and grabbed the uniformed arm and yanked it into the cell. The officer screamed when his face hit the iron bars, then he screamed louder as Burt twisted the arm in a way that could only have one conclusion.

"Stop that!" Tom yelled, furious and frustrated that he couldn't get through the bars to help. He yelled as loud as he could, pulling on bars he knew wouldn't budge, hoping someone outside of the jail's cells would hear. As the officer's arm snapped then popped through the skin the man let out a scream that would wake the dead, and Tom gagged on the bile flooding his throat. He forced himself to swallow and winced at the rawness of his esophagus, as anger like he'd never experienced tore through him. The earth shook strongly, knocking Tom off his feet, but Burt used the man's arm as a lifeline and hung on while spreading his feet as if riding a boat on rough waves.

Tom crawled to the bars and pulled himself up, knowing Mother Earth was only reacting to his distress. He felt even sicker when he realized the officer had passed out and was hanging against the bars, the chest high stabilizer rail running horizontally across the cell the only thing keeping him up. His limp body was turned in a way that caused his skin to rip even more. The bone stuck-out grotesquely.

Tom heard screams from outside of the door and didn't know if the officers were reacting to the shift in the earth's plates or of someone had finally realized that more chaos was happening inside of the jail-cell area, than out. He almost cried out in relief when the steel door began to open, but it was being pulled back closed just as quickly.

He looked back at Burt and his heart hit the floor. The criminal's free hand was pulling the officer's gun from his holster. Once he had it firmly in his grasp he looked up at Tom and smiled the most evil smile Tom had ever seen.

The officer's unconscious body landed on the floor with a thud as Burt stood up straight and raised the gun, pointing it across the way, directly at Tom.

"Officer down! Officer down!"

Tom couldn't look away as the woman's voice penetrated what had to be a crack left open in the door, before it was closed completely again.

Tom knew he was a dead man if someone didn't intervene quickly. He slowly stepped back, hoping to find the small slice of cover that his cell provided since the cells were staggered and Thompson's wasn't directly across from his, but one over and to the side.

"Not so smug now, pretty boy, are ya?

"Better have you a fast prayer, if you heathens even pray, because once that door opens again I'm going to be a little too busy to play with you. But I'll tell you something you can take to your grave. So you will know for all of eternity that all that just happened is on you.

"My mother was a bitch. She didn't teach me anything except the only person on the planet who cared about me, was me, and eventually the woman who married me. Like I told you, you rotten piece of shit, I didn't abuse her. At least not any more than she wanted.

"But let me tell you about good old Mom, seeing as it's making you kinda green, and I like that color on you. Dear old *Mom* let my father do unspeakable things to me because she was tired of him doing them to her. I was a kid. A skinny little helpless kid, who didn't do anything to anybody. But she didn't take me with her. She saved her own sorry ass and ran away and didn't once stop to think what it would do to me. She left me with that sick bastard of a father who wanted me to be his wife. I got to cook and clean and bend over so he could fuck my brains out.

"But that wasn't enough for him. He had to share me. *What?* You *dare* to look even sicker? Suck it up, pretty girl, because this is what you wanted. You wanted to know every little dirty detail! Where here it is!

"I was raped day after day until sometimes I couldn't stand. I missed school so often that they threatened to put dear old Dad in jail and me in foster care. *But no…* He made me so afraid to tell anyone the truth that I took up for him. And do you know what he did?"

Tom couldn't speak; he couldn't even move to shake his head. He didn't want to hear any more. He didn't want to know that this was what resulted from child abuse because the world was filled with abusers as well as victims, who then became abusers.

He didn't want to know the world was filled with people who had gone mad.

"What? Cat got yer tongue? Well, fine. I'll do all the talking. I'll tell you exactly what *Daddy* did to me. He beat me unconscious because he said it was my fault. It didn't matter that I was so broken inside I should have died. He said I still should have gotten my sorry ass up and gone to school, and if Child Services ever came to the door again I was dead."

The loud speaker over the metal door squeaked. "Burt! This is John Grammar. Domestic assault isn't anything like murder. Put that gun down before you do something you will regret. I'll see you get the death penalty if you pull that trigger."

Tom backed up slowly as Thompson's gaze went to the door. He turned to Tom and raised the gun higher. "You better stand still, pretty boy, while I think about this."

Tom nodded, and stilled, his heart beating in tandem with his harsh breaths.

Burt kept his eyes on Tom though he tilted his head so he could speak to the speaker. "I want to see my wife. I want her in here so she can tell you the truth. If you have her here, willing to confess that she lied about me, within the next thirty minutes I might reconsider shutting this Injun's mouth permanently."

"Somebody get his wife here now!"

Burt smiled. "Good job there, Captain. But you forgot to turn off the speaker. You are sounding a little stressed."

"You are in control here, Burt. I'm getting your wife. But it may take a little longer than thirty minutes. She moved and we have to locate the address and then find her."

Burt's features registered his surprise and then he shook his head. "You're lying. She wouldn't move out of our house."

"I'm not lying, Burt. She couldn't stand, um, what? Oh. She couldn't stand being in the house after my officers tore it apart. She said you wouldn't want her there. She hasn't left town, she just moved across to the other side. We'll pull the information and go get her."

Burt stood there looking at Tom and Tom held his breath, hoping the man was as stupid as he looked. The gun lowered slightly, and Tom allowed a breath to escape but the pistol was back up in the next instant.

"Don't get your hopes up, pretty boy. If that woman has left me, I don't have anything left. And neither will you. You are a dead man for sure."

Tom slid a glance to the speaker and saw the camera over it. Instantly the captain's voice was back.

"I'm not lying to you, Burt. But the longer you hold that gun on another prisoner, the worse it's getting for you. Put the gun down so it doesn't go off accidently and then you're in real trouble. Martha will be here as soon as we can get her. The officers are leaving now. They'll be in the squad car and en route in minutes."

Burt lowered the gun slightly, but it was clear he wasn't dumb enough to lay it down. He looked at the officer on the floor before his cell and then back to the camera. "What about him? What will I get for that?"

There was a long pause, and Tom felt sweat running down his hairline. He swallowed, as he too awaited the answer.

"It will cost you some time. Assaulting a police officer carries a penalty, but we all understand you were under extreme duress. I'll see how much I can help you out. But you have to put that gun down."

"I can't do that, John." Burt smiled. "You don't mind if I call you John, do you?"

"Of course not. John is fine."

"Kind of sucks when you aren't the one in control, doesn't it?"

There was another long pause then, "Yes. I can see where it would have been hard on you never having control."

Burt's face reddened again. "Don't patronize me! I know you don't give a diddly-shit about how it felt to be shunned by you and the others."

"I'm truly sorry you felt that way. I'm not perfect, Burt. I'm human and I make mistakes too."

Burt's features relaxed and the gun dropped a little more. "I'll let the officer come out if someone pitches me some keys. I couldn't reach his."

Complete silence lasted so long Tom was afraid that they were considering his request. If Burt Thompson was free to roam the jail, Tom knew didn't have a chance at survival.

"I'm sorry, Burt. I can't allow my officers to do that. But it would go a long way in helping your case if you showed mercy and let us come get him so he can get medical attention."

Burt shook his head. "Not until Martha gets here. When you send her in, he can go out."

Burt looked over at Tom. "But this one is another

matter. He has insulted me. If I'm going to jail for a while anyway, I might as well get my pound of flesh."

"Burt, if you even act like you are going to shoot that man we are going to have to come in there and shoot *you*. You won't leave us a choice. But if Martha comes in and is willing to change her statement in writing, your lawyer can explain to a jury that you were falsely accused and in your distress you acted irrationally, in a way you never would have normally acted. But if you pull that trigger, you will get nothing but the death penalty if you even make it to court. There is a department of police officers standing here watching to bear witness to what you decide to do.

The officer on the floor began moving, and screamed as soon as the injured arm moved with him.

"Jasper? This is John Grammar. Can you hear me?"

The officer on the floor nodded, though he didn't lift his head again. "I'm holding on, Captain," he said, panting and wincing.

There was a long pause before the captain spoke again.

"Jasper, we have an ambulance standing by. Hang in there."

When there was no response, Tom slid a glance to the floor. The officer's eyes were open, but it was hard to tell if he was even alive. When he finally blinked, Tom exhaled and turned his attention back to Burt.

"Mr. Whitehawk, are you all right?"

Tom looked from the sneer on Thompson's face to the camera and he nodded, too. But he wasn't going to say anything to incite the crazy ex-police officer.

"Good. Okay, Burt. Now everyone says they are doing okay. If things don't go any further, we can resolve this in a way that is better for you. That is what you want, isn't it?"

Burt took a minute this time before answering. When he did, he shrugged. "You know, *John*, I was a police officer too, and I know you can lie through your teeth to get what you want. So how do I know anything you are saying is the truth?"

Burt shook the gun, aiming it at the camera. "How do

I know you won't throw me to the wolves when everything is said and done, even if I fully cooperate?"

"Look, I know you know the ropes and I'm not pulling your leg. I told you, there will be consequences. That is the truth. And I told you if you hurt anyone else, or the officer any more, it won't go well for you. It could even cost you your life.

"And that is the truth.

"I also told you there is a big difference between murder and assault, which you already know as a former police officer. So if you really think about what's happening here, I think you will see that everything I have told you *is* the truth. I wouldn't try to trick a man who already knows all the answers."

Tom watched as satisfaction and maybe even pride straightened Thompson's shoulders. "Okay. You're right. I do know all that. But I want something more."

"And what is that?"

"I want a written apology from you stating you fired me because of prejudice."

After another slight pause John Grammar sighed into the microphone. "I'll consider that, Burt. But that won't get you your job back. Not after what has happened here today."

Burt shrugged. "I know that. But it will cost you yours." He grinned. "Are you willing to give up your job, *Captain* Grammar?"

There was amusement in his voice when he replied. "I consider it every day. I think it's about time for me to retire anyway. Is that what you want? For me to step down?"

"Fuck, no! I want you to be fired like I was. I want you to know what it feels like to have your job ripped away from you! To have your retirement taken so you have to work at some superstore as a greeter until your body is so worn out you have to beg the government for food stamps. That is what *I* want, Captain!"

There was a slight pause and two squeaks before another voice came over the speaker. "This is

Commissioner Halstead, Mr. Thompson. I can assure you, if there is reason to believe Captain Grammar fired you under the wrong circumstances and it is proven his actions resulted in the duress that has brought us to this point, he will lose not only his job but his retirement as well. You have my word on that."

Tom frowned, thinking that the commissioner sounded a lot like FBI Special Agent Thorne.

"How come I don't know you? I never heard of a Commissioner Halstead."

Tom had to keep from shaking his head. The guy wasn't smart by any means, but he wasn't dumb either.

Another squeak. "I'm a regional commissioner. I haven't been to Mystic Waters for some time. And I usually meet with the captain at the Mayor's office. I'm only here at the station today because my private meeting with the Mayor was cut short due to this situation."

"Why should I trust you? I don't know you."

"That is true, Mr. Thompson. But I don't know any of the officers here. It's a situation I will need to rectify in the immediate future."

Burt stared into space, looking indecisive then he looked back at the camera. "Where's Martha? Your time is about up."

****

Martha stood just outside of her closed front door and shook her head. "I'm not going there to talk to Burt. He's lost his mind."

"I understand your concerns, Mrs. Thompson. But if you don't come with me to talk him down, he's going to kill a man, possibly two. All he wants is for you to say you made a mistake and sign a piece of paper, one we will shred and throw away just as soon as we get those other men to safety.

"Look, if we don't go now those men's deaths will be on your head, too."

Martha took a deep breath and thought of all the things she needed to do. But she didn't want them to keep coming to her house. That was the last thing she wanted. "Okay. I'll play like I still want him in my life. But you better be sure I'll be safe."

The officer looked so relieved Martha almost laughed at him. Wasn't it something? Burt had whined about the way he was treated by his coworkers the entire time he was on the force. He would be thrilled to know he had them by the balls now. That almost made her proud of him. "Then we better get going, hadn't we?"

She turned and went inside to get her purse, shutting the door in the officer's face. She wasn't about to let him into her new house. As far as she was concerned, when she finished with this nasty piece of business she was done with the Mystic Waters police force for good, and not a minute too soon.

She ignored the sounds of her pet coming from the back of the house and made her way back out to join the officer as quickly as she could. She pulled out her keys but the officer shook his head. "You can ride with me. It will be quicker."

Martha wanted to protest, but she was afraid after denying him entry into her house he would start getting suspicious, so she nodded and headed to the passenger side of the car. He stopped her.

"I'm sorry. You'll have to ride in the back. It's against policy for a civilian to ride up front."

Martha held her tongue, but she couldn't help the annoyance she was sure was in the look she gave him. He smiled and apologized again as he opened the door. Martha got in and a chill went up her spine. The seat was comfortable enough, but the tightly woven wire between them made it clear she was sitting in the seat usually reserved for those who got caught breaking the law. It was a seat she had avoided many years ago, and had suffered greatly to keep from experiencing at all.

After all she had endured, and yes, she was honest enough to admit she had enjoyed a lot of it, here she was anyway, in the back seat of a squad car. *I guess it serves me right for running to Burt to hide my past*, she thought, irritated, before settling back for the ride.

"Now," Officer Snatch said, as he pulled out of her driveway. "This is the plan. There will be a typed-up confession you need to sign. We will stick it in the door for your husband to read. Once he reads it we are going to require him to release the officer whose arm he broke, then we will try to negotiate the release of the other prisoner. At that point we may need you actually to talk to him."

Martha nodded. He'd already told her that. "So what happens then?"

"Then we add charges to the one you have already filed. The least he'll get is assaulting an officer, and a charge for taking hostages. Beyond that, I'm not sure."

Martha bit her bottom lip then released it. "What kind of jail time will he serve for those charges?"

"If he's convicted, it will depend on what the jury recommends. They may recommend however many years he gets to be served concurrently, or consecutively. The first being at the same time and the second being one after the other."

"So Burt will be locked up for a pretty long time."

"Yes. He could get up to twenty years for assaulting the police officer, at least seven for assaulting you, and if he ends up shooting anyone, and lives through it, then he'll likely spend the rest of his natural life in jail, unless he kills one or both of the men trapped in there with him. Then he may get the death penalty."

Martha tried to keep from smiling. All she had to do was play the game. Then she would be free of Burt, and the police would no longer be a part of her life.

It sucked that Burt hadn't done a better job of taking care of her and his job, but he had served his purpose well enough. Having a husband on the police force had made hiding in plain sight a piece of cake. Now that everyone knew of her as his abused wife, she would be pitied, but never be suspected of the sins she had committed. She would finally be free to be herself again.

And she would make sure she stayed that way.

They pulled into the parking lot across from the police station, and Martha didn't have to fake being nervous. She held her purse close to her side and her head down as she walked beside the officer, trying to ignore the crowd that was gathering. Apparently word was getting out about Burt's little caper. She just hoped she could get what had to be done over with quickly so she could get away before any press arrived.

The squad room looked empty until she got to the area just outside of the door leading to the jail cells. She felt her cheeks heat as the officers who had busted into the house when Burt was raping her looked at her and then away. She held her head up and looked at each one of them until the captain of the force stepped in front of her.

"Thank you for coming. I know this is incredibly difficult for you, ma'am, but your husband has lost perspective, and he's very dangerous right now. I need you to wait here while we try to work this out satisfactorily. We may need you."

Martha nodded. "The officer told me."

The captain pressed his lips together and nodded. "Okay." He looked at his men who were all in bulletproof vests and packing handguns and mean-looking assault rifles. "Let's do this. Are you ready?"

Martha frowned as she was shuttled back away from the action. She wanted to know everything that was going on and see just what Burt was doing on that little monitor they had on the desk sitting just to the left of the metal door. But they were making her wait in a cubicle, so that there was a four-foot wall separating her from everyone else.

Not one to miss an opportunity, she stood as soon as the officer, who had steered her to the mini-office and had her sign the short three-sentence document, left to rejoin the others. Since they all had their backs to her, she waited for the show to begin.

She didn't have long to wait.

Although she couldn't see the monitor they were all looking at, she could hear the exchanges loud and clear.

"Burt? John Grammar here again. Martha is here with us and has agreed she made a mistake. She has signed the statement saying she retracted her earlier statement so you are no longer being held for domestic assault."

"Have her bring it to me."

Martha started to duck back down, but several officers turned to look at her before she could. So she remained where she was and looked back at them. But the captain never turned around.

"We can't do that until you put the gun down. You know we can't endanger another civilian. But I can get the document to you and let Martha talk to you like I am."

There was a moment while Martha figured Burt was thinking about his best course of action. Eventually he came back on.

"Get her on the microphone."

Captain Grammar turned to her and nodded. She made sure she looked afraid as she approached the monitor. The camera inside the cell had to have had a panoramic lens since she could see several cells including the one with the other prisoner. Even in the ugly jump suit, he was a fine-looking man. And she especially liked his long hair.

She made herself look at Burt, and the comparison between the two men made her shake her head. How could she have settled for a frog when she should have found herself a prince? But no problem… She could have her prince as soon as she disposed of the frog.

"It's okay. We aren't going to let him hurt you."

Martha looked up at the captain and nodded, realizing he thought she had changed her mind. Well, that was just fine. Let them think she was the abused little flower all they wanted to believe she was. It only made her case easier to sell.

"Okay, what do you want me to say?"

"Tell him you are sorry, that you were so distraught

when we arrested him you didn't realize what we were having you sign. Mostly just play it by ear. You know him better than anyone. I'm sure you've had years of talking your way out of his abuse."

Martha nodded, although she almost wanted to laugh. The captain had no idea how good she was at manipulating Burt. But she didn't have time to gloat. She stepped up to the desk with the standing microphone and sat down facing the monitor.

"Hi, honey, are you okay?"

"That sounded really good, but I forgot to tell you, you have to hold the key trigger down, like this."

Martha pulled the trigger back and heard a little squeal. She took a breath then repeated herself. "Hi, honey. Are you okay?"

Burt's attention was immediately on the camera. He shook his head. "Hell *no*, I'm not okay. What the hell are you up to?"

"I'm sorry. I didn't mean for this to happen. When they arrested you, I was so embarrassed to be seen like that by all those people, and I was so upset they were hauling you away, and then they confused me even more when they demanded I sign a piece of paper. So I did, but I thought it was just our address and stuff. I didn't realize they were using me to condemn you!"

Martha looked up at the captain and wondered if she was acting just a little too well. He looked confused as he looked down at her, and she knew she needed to back off a little. "Am I doing okay?" she asked, putting a little wobble in her voice.

He nodded and his face relaxed. "You're doing amazing. I would believe you. Keep it up."

Not sure she should, Martha nodded and turned back to look at her husband. He seemed even shorter and fatter on the monitor than he was when he was standing next to her, but she figured it was because the edges of the screen were distorted.

"Bring that piece of paper to me and I'll let this cop

go."

John Grammar leaned down and motioned for her to pull the trigger. "I told you we can't do that as long as you have the gun."

"Well, that sucks for us both then, because I'm not ready to give it up until my wife comes in here to talk to me privately."

The captain's annoyance was clear as he leaned forward again, but Martha stopped him by placing her hand on the one he braced himself with on the desk. "It's okay. He won't shoot me. I'm all he has. And I know him like you said. He won't give up that gun until you give him what he wants."

Captain Grammar looked at her and Martha could see he didn't want to take the chance. "I'm sure about this," she continued. "He wants me so he can see I am still the woman who bowed down to him all these years. I can play that woman again. Just to end all this."

He stood then and stared at the monitor. "Are you sure? I don't feel good about this."

Martha smiled. "I appreciate your concern, Captain. But I can do this. I'm stronger than I look. I've survived this long with that man. I can get that gun from him."

He shook his head. "I just can't. If he starts shooting and hits you or the other two, I won't be able to live with myself."

"But if you don't, I'm sure he'll shoot them. And I wouldn't be able to live with that. I've suffered enough, Captain. Please let me end this with some dignity."

He heaved a big sigh and nodded before looking at another officer. "Get her a vest." He leaned forward and lifted the microphone. "Burt, Martha wants to see you, too. But I'm only allowing this on a couple of conditions. One, you let us get that officer out now. And two, when she steps in the door you place that gun on the outside of the cell and slide it toward the door. You have my word, we will allow the two of you all the time you need.

"But I can't let her come to you if you won't work with

me. You know I can't endanger another person."

Martha allowed the officer to put the vest on her as she turned to see Burt's reaction. He stood there without any facial expression, and she felt he wouldn't budge. He finally nodded, and she knew she wasn't the only one in the room sighing in relief.

"Okay. But this is the thing. I want that Injun out of here, and I want the microphone turned off. I ain't gonna hurt my wife. I love her."

"You got it.

"Jasper, you still with me?"

The officer on the floor nodded.

"Are you able to get up? Are you able to get to the other cell and unlock it?"

He shrugged and started sliding toward the longhaired man's cell. Martha watched as he inched his way less than a foot before he settled back down with his head on the floor. "I'm sorry. I can't. Every time I move I get dizzy and I'm seeing spots."

After a slight hesitation John Grammar nodded. "Can you pitch your keys to Mr. Whitehawk?"

The officer used his good arm and struggled to get the key clip released with trembling fingers. He eventually got them loose and weakly pitched them into the cell. Martha continued to watch as the other inmate quickly unlocked his cell while keeping an eye on Burt. She frowned, wondering what he'd done to piss Burt off so badly.

"Mr. Whitehawk, can you help Jasper?"

He nodded as the door swung open. "Sure." He walked the few steps over to the injured officer, still watching Burt. He spoke quietly to the man for a minute and once the officer nodded, Tom slid massive arms under his leg and around his back and lifted him like he weighed nothing.

Martha felt the stirrings of lust, and she had to keep herself under control. The last thing any of these men would expect was a woman they believed to be abused to show interest in any man. Her heartbeat increased as *Mr.*

Muscles carried Officer Jasper to the door and waited for it to open.

There was a collective gasp and Martha's attention was back on Burt. She grabbed the microphone from Captain Grammar's hand and pushed the trigger. "Burt Thompson, don't you dare get yourself killed! Put that gun down now!"

He seemed so startled by her command his arm dropped to his side instantly. Martha had to keep from laughing. She hadn't used her dominatrix voice for too many years to count, but it was good to know it was still there. It would come in handy in the next year or so when she had her life back on track.

Burt looked at the camera as officers quickly opened the door and pulled the two men from the holding cell. "You still love me?"

Martha was surprised by the emotion's his trembling voice brought out in her. She really had grown to love him over the years. But like everything else in her life, it had died a slow, painful death. "Of course I do. I'll be right in."

She stood and watched as several officers escorted the tall hunk of a man to one of the cubicles. He was so tall she could see the head and shoulders of the officer he carried until he bent down to put the injured man in a chair. When he stood back up, an older officer stepped up to him.

"I'm sorry, Mr. Whitehawk, but I have to cuff you."

Martha watched, frowning, as the officer maneuvered around the man who had angered Burt to the point of stupidity. It was obvious from the look on his face that he wasn't pleased, but was resigned to be cuffed. Then he looked her way.

"Thank you, ma'am."

"Right this way," the captain said, placing a gentle hand on her shoulder to steer her to the door. She forced herself to look away from the finest-looking man she had ever seen as she prepared herself to look at the face of the toad she had married.

The captain stopped her before opening the door. "You don't have to do this. He's only a danger to himself right now. We can go in and handle him. In fact I think we should."

Martha shook her head. If nothing else she needed to close this chapter of her life for good, and if Burt was ever set free, she needed him to believe she'd done her best by him. "You promised I would. And I promised I would. He won't hurt me."

The captain nodded. "Yes, I did. But that was only to get the others out safely." He looked over and so did Martha as paramedics came running in. They popped open the gurney and locked its legs down before helping the officer onto it. They stood there for several minutes while hooking him up to the portable machines hanging from bags at their shoulders, and secured his broken arm with a large plastic board with Velcro straps. He moaned and even shouted through the process before the paramedics were rushing him out the door.

Martha turned her attention back to the man who had made Burt's life miserable. At least from *Burt's* perspective. She knew her husband well enough to know the man set himself up to be disliked by his attitude and actions. "I need to go in there. I need to say goodbye."

Captain Grammar nodded. "Okay. I will keep my word and turn off the microphone, but if he says anything threatening, I need you to flag me."

Martha agreed and went past the officers who had their guns raised when the door was opened. She waited until the captain ordered Burt to slide the gun to the door, and he complied, before she walked in and made her way the short distance to the cell. Burt actually looked like he'd lost some weight now that he was no longer made shorter and wider by the camera lens.

She stopped just out of his reach because she knew what he was capable of. And she hadn't been lying to the captain. She really was here to tell him goodbye.

"Hi, Burt."

He smiled at her; the love in his eyes nearly made her change her mind. But that look of love was too little, too late. She had a new life plan now.

"Come here and give me a kiss. I've missed you so much."

Martha shook her head. "I came to say goodbye."

At first surprise, then anger flashed in his eyes. "What the hell!

"I'm sorry, Burt. But you can't expect me to wait around forever just to have you abuse me again when you finally get out of jail."

He shook his head as his nostrils flared. "You lying little cunt! I knew this was a trick, but because I loved you, I let myself believe I could trust that you wouldn't betray me, too! But you were just waiting, weren't you! You were just waiting for a way to get rid of me and keep all the savings I had worked so hard for all these years. You bitch!"

Martha made herself not react. *Savings? What savings! Whoa! I need to play this differently!*

"Burt, that isn't true!" She thought of the lover she had really lost all those years ago and let her eyes tear up as they always did when she allowed herself to think of him. "I loved you so much, it always broke my heart you would never say the words to me! All I ever wanted was your love, and all I got was slapped around!"

"You like it!" he shouted with absolute conviction. "You did things just to make me mad. Like that little performance on the table! You wanted a reaction from me and you got exactly what you knew was coming.

"I had to talk myself into being mad and rough with you at first, when you first answered my ad for a wife all those years ago. But it got easier over time because I knew I was pleasing you!

"And then I may have gotten too heavy-handed. I don't know. You are the only person that allowed me to be in charge. In my entire life, you were the only one!

"Yeah, I went a little too far sometimes, but I didn't mean to. I only wanted to make you want me."

Martha didn't know what to say. Burt was crying hard

and she knew he was telling the truth as he saw it. She took a deep breath and walked forward, willing to risk his wrath. "I'm sorry. I didn't know. I swear I didn't know. I love you, too."

She was crying in earnest now, actually moved by his confession, though she was still willing to lie. "You are the only man I have ever really loved."

He took her hands, and though he was holding them a little too hard, she knew it wasn't meant to hurt her. "I'll be here. I won't leave. I promise. I'll see this thing through with you, and I'll visit you every time they let me. I won't leave you, Burt. I love you so much."

He nodded as he continued to sob then laid his forehead on the bars. "Thank you. Thank you. I can't lose you, too. You are everything to me."

Martha leaned forward and kissed his forehead then his lips when he looked up. He held her lips with his thick ones, and she was so desperate to make him believe her she deepened the kiss, and knew when she finally had him eating out of her hands. She stepped back and looked up to the camera, allowing them to think what they would. Hopefully they would know that even an abused woman had trouble letting go sometimes.

She looked back at Burt. "They told me I couldn't stay too long. But I want you to know I'm going to get you a lawyer and get you out of here on bond if I can. I want you to come home, Burt. As soon as possible."

He smiled at her as his tears kept flowing. "I won't ever hurt you again unless you tell me to. I promise."

She smiled, pouring her heart into the look she gave him. "I know you won't. If, no *when,* you come home, maybe you'll let me wear a different outfit? And I can be the one in charge? We could start anew. With a new game."

He nodded quickly. "Sure. That would be fun. Anything you want, Martha. I promise you, anything you want."

She leaned in for another long kiss before stepping back. "I'll need money for a lawyer, honey. Is it okay if I use the checkbook?"

Burt nodded. "Sure. But don't spend too much. Once I get out on bond I'll dig up my savings, and you and me are going to start a new life somewhere else."

Wondering just how much he was talking, about Martha nodded. "I'll get you out of here as fast as I can. But I better go now. I need to find you a really good lawyer."

"I need you to move back into our house. You can't sell it. It will ruin everything."

Martha processed that as she smiled at him and let her eyes tear up again. "Until we meet again, my love. And I promise it will be soon."

The kiss was short because Martha broke it off then put her palm on his fat cheek affectionately. "You behave and take care of yourself. I'll see you soon."

Before she reached the door, he spoke. "I love you, Martha. Please don't let this be a trick."

She looked back at him and smiled. "It isn't, honey. I'm not done with you yet."

Burt smiled though he looked at her with confusion wrinkling his brow, so she winked to reassure him. She went through the door ready to tell the captain she was just heartbroken and need time to think things through. Which was the truth. Burt was a fool if he thought they'd let him out on bond. But staying in town and playing the loving wife while she searched for the money might just be worth it in the end. And she was sure he had it buried at the house.

Yes, she would move back in. But only until she found the ticket to her freedom.

Chapter Eight

Destiny couldn't believe they had to go back to Rayne's cabin before she was allowed to head to the jail. Both Rayne and Haven wanted her to meet their men, and she knew it was time she did. So she made a bargain. She would meet her future bothers-in-law, and Rayne would use her close relationship with the captain of the police department to get her in to see Tom Whitehawk.

She still felt they should all talk about the dangers of having men in their lives at all, especially since *theirs* had no knowledge of the Cavanaugh gifts or magic, but with her own heart already seeking a man, she knew it would be two-faced of her to say anything.

So she enjoyed the short ride and smiled to herself knowing the three of them were about to blow some minds. It was just too funny that Rayne and Haven had decided they wouldn't let the guys find out that they were triplets instead of twins until she arrived in Mystic Waters.

"It's so good to be here with you both!"

Haven turned around and smiled, and Rayne looked into the rear view mirror and did the same before speaking. "It's so good to have you here. I can't wait until the guys see you. We haven't been able to do this since…" Rayne's voice trailed off and Haven laughed.

"What she isn't saying, is we haven't been able to do this since we started high school and you know who saw the three of us walking down the hall."

"Shut up, Haven! I don't want to ever hear that boy mentioned again. Or I'll look up a spell in one of those diaries and turn you into something slimy."

"Guess I've ruined high school for her," Haven continued, as if Rayne hadn't spoken.

Destiny laughed at them and was rewarded with

Haven's smile. Rayne sent her a look of annoyance, so she thought she should change the subject. "So where are your men? Don't they work?"

Rayne looked back at Destiny again then returned her gaze to the road. "Most likely they will be in Garrison's shop. While Logan is waiting on his security clearance, and the recommendation from the hospital where he used to work, to be delivered to Mystic Memorial Hospital, he's helping Garrison work on an order that just came in."

"So he builds all this gorgeous furniture that looks like it is a hundred or more years old?"

Rayne nodded as she turned into the short driveway and parked beside two trucks. One was old and worn. The other looked brand new. Destiny figured the new truck had surgeon written all over it.

"Stay in the car until I'm sure they're in there," Rayne said, suddenly sounding like she was getting into the spirit of things.

As soon as she vacated the car, Haven sat back and Destiny did too. "You really shouldn't tease her about that. It really bothers her."

Haven turned in the seat and grinned. "I know. But it's so much fun. So tell me. Who have you done?"

Destiny laughed and shook her head. "No way would I give you that kind of ammunition after seeing how accurately you shoot at our baby sister."

"Aha! So that means you have done at least one somebody. Give. I swear I'll never repeat a word of it."

"Rayne is right! You are obsessed with sex."

Haven shrugged. "Yeah, I am. But mostly just because I'm curious."

Destiny tilted her head. "About what?"

Haven grinned. "I want to know if everybody has these mind-blowing orgasms, or if it's just me."

Destiny shook her head. "Damn. Now I'm just jealous. But I can't help you. I've never had one."

"Oh." Haven looked disappointed. "So you don't have any experience either."

Destiny bit her bottom lip, unable to believe she was opening up about what she had kept to herself for so long. "Not exactly. It just wasn't completely consummated."

Haven's brows rose in interest. "What does that mean?"

Thoroughly embarrassed, Destiny shook her head. "Never mind. It isn't something I'm proud of."

"There is no way you are going to leave me hanging! Hurry, unless you want this conversation to still be going on when Rayne gets back."

Destiny looked toward the doors of the workshop and grimaced. "Okay. You know that guy you were teasing Rayne about?"

Haven's mouth fell open before her nose wrinkled up. "Ewwww!"

Destiny nodded. "Yeah...tell me about it. He got so far that his penis was barely inside of me before he told me that he had been right, and that I was just as tight as Rayne. I was so outraged he had used us both that I punched him to get him off of me, and that was the end of that."

"Really? That's it?" Haven looked at her skeptically.

"Okay, well, not completely all of it. I also pulled out a few of his hairs with the intention of making a voodoo doll, but Aunt Soleli came looking for her special candle. I had melted it and made it into a human form. When she saw what I was doing, she made me stop. She said Cavanaughs never use dark magic. That it's too dangerous, as it would eventually come back to hurt the one using it, and that it could open up doors to the underworld. All kinds of horrible things could happen.

"But I was so angry and so grossed-out that I bought two four-packs of douche and used every one of them. Aunt Lune Brille found the empty bottles the next morning when she was gathering the trash to take it out, and I had to listen for an hour of how we should treat our bodies and how much damage I could do by altering the pH balance in my vagina."

Haven burst out laughing. "I miss her. She could

lecture on the strangest things. She made me sit and read an entire book about ringworm when I was sixteen because I brought a balding stray cat home. But tell me more!"

Destiny nodded, though she had never found the lectures particularly amusing. "It gets worse. As if I wasn't completely humiliated enough, she insisted I go get a pap smear and get tested for venereal diseases. So I had to endure a woman checking me out, and another lecture from her on the dangers of genital warts."

Haven's face crinkled. "Double ewwww!"

"So that's it." Destiny shook her head, unable to believe she'd finally revealed her deepest darkest secret. As horrible as it still made her feel, it was kind of a relief to have gotten it out.

Haven shook her head in wonder. "How did we not know all that was going on?"

"Because I made her promise, once the tests came back negative, she would never tell anyone. And as far as I know she never did."

"I promise, too. I will never mention it. That is too gross."

Destiny sighed. "Make sure you don't, or you will find being turned into something slimy isn't the worst thing you can be turned into."

Rayne opened Destiny's door and smiled at them both. "Come on, you guys! I've been trying to get your attention! What the heck are you doing in here?"

Haven sighed. "Oh, Destiny was telling me how much she enjoyed the diaries and that I need to look at them, too. It seems we may be able cast spells from them even if that isn't our particular gift. I think I might want to learn a couple of spells myself."

She exited the car then walked toward the workshop before turning back to grin at both sisters. "You know, just in case I run into someone in the future who becomes a threat to me."

Rayne looked at Destiny in confusion. "What is she talking about?"

Destiny shrugged, feigning innocence. "I think it's because you threatened to turn her into something slimy."

"Well, for goodness sakes! I was just kidding."

Destiny grinned as Rayne ran to catch up with Haven, and she made her strides longer to catch up, too. They stopped just outside and to the right of the large double doors that had been left open. Rayne turned to Haven and grinned. "Okay. I'll go back in first because I told Logan I was coming out to get you. So you follow me in." She turned to Destiny. "And then give us about ten seconds to make sure they are looking at us and then you come in and stand at our side. Okay?"

Haven nodded and Destiny did too. She could feel her sister's excitement only because it matched her own. Rayne turned and went in and after about five seconds Haven followed. Destiny took a deep breath and counted to ten before she followed and stood at their side.

The two men were at a lathe shouting to hear each other over the machine. Rayne looked down the line then shook her head and shrugged before looking back, as she waited for them to get noticed. Destiny looked from her sisters to the men and after a good three minutes the taller, darker-headed one, who she figured was the surgeon, noticed them. His mouth fell open as he stared. Then he was frantically jabbing at the other one, who stopped carving whatever it was he had spinning, and he looked too, his face as stunned as the first.

The three girls smiled until the sandy-haired one dropped the tool he was holding. It hit the spinning object then bounced back to stab him just below the shoulder blade.

Then all hell broke loose.

Rayne screamed and ran toward them. Haven was right on her heels. The tall dark male was holding up the other one who had gone deathly pale and limp, while he tried to reach over and turn off the machine. Destiny stayed where she was, as frozen internally as her form was externally, horrified their little prank had backfired.

"Destiny, help!"

Destiny took a startled breath and walked toward the chaos. She looked at Rayne who was now helping to support the sagging man. "What can I do?"

"Logan, just hold him. Destiny, just turn the machine off! There's a switch just under there." Rayne pointed and Destiny was instantly searching in the area she had indicated. She pushed the first switch she saw and was relieved the lathe whined down until the room was silent. She looked up to see the tall one had lifted the slightly shorter one and was heading out the door.

Rayne was with him every step, holding onto the long chisel, and Haven was once again on their heels. Destiny took a second to look around and suddenly feeling like a fifth wheel, followed them to the cabin.

She hung back once they were inside. The tall one who had to be Logan was laying the one that had to be Garrison on the couch. Destiny bit her bottom lip when she caught a brief glimpse of Rayne's face as she looked back and up at Haven. Her cheeks were covered in tears, and guilt had claimed her eyes.

Destiny understood. She too felt so weighed down with guilt she wanted to slink away and let the men forget they had ever seen her. But she moved forward instead and caught the attention of Logan.

He quickly looked from her to Haven and then to Rayne before his attention was once again on examining the wound. "You girls have some explaining to do."

Haven laid a hand on his shoulder. "We are so sorry. We thought it would be fun to surprise you. For you guys to learn we were triplets instead of twins when you saw the three of us together."

"It's my fault," Rayne said, her voice hoarse with emotion. "I didn't think. Garrison didn't have the lathe on when I went back out to get them. And I didn't think anything about it when I came back in. All I was thinking was that it was annoying you two weren't paying attention.

"Is he going to be okay?"

Logan looked up at her, his face grim. "I don't know. There may be internal bleeding. I think it's in an artery."

Rayne's eyes widened as she looked toward Destiny. "Call 911!"

Logan held up his hand. "I'm afraid it's too late. He probably won't make it to the hospital."

Rayne wailed loudly and began crying hysterically. Haven shook her head and backed away, as if she couldn't believe what was happening and was helpless to do anything about it. Destiny stayed where she was and looked at the faces of both men.

She focused on the area just above and between Logan's eyebrows first. His brow chakra, or Third Eye, had a strong green aura, which was expected as all true healers held that color, but Destiny also noticed, with her peripheral vision, flashes of a murky orange color lower on his body, which wasn't too bad, but the grey that surrounded it was a dark color and she shook her head.

But before she said anything, she had to be sure. She just wished Rayne would stop the hysterics because it made it harder to concentrate. Destiny turned her attention to Garrison. He too had a hint of gray in an otherwise clean aura, and she knew she had them.

"Rayne, shut up! Haven, get over there and pull that thing out if your good doctor isn't going to do it."

Everyone in the room turned to look at Destiny in shock. Including their *unconscious* patient. Rayne turned back and gasped when she saw Garrison looking at Destiny with curiosity. She jumped up and smacked him. "You pig! How could you do that?" She ran from the room crying as hard as she had when she thought he was dying.

"Crap.

"Get this thing out of me, Logan. I have some feathers to unruffle."

Haven walked up and smacked Logan's cheek just as hard before she huffed and puffed her way out of the room.

Destiny smiled and waved. "Hi guys, I'm what's

behind door number three." She frowned with amusement. "Actually that would be door number one as I'm the oldest. I'm Destiny Cavanaugh by the way." She looked at the face of their dying patient. "So I'm guessing you are Garrison since Rayne's handprint is on your cheek." Then she smiled at the dark-haired one. "And that would make you Logan, though the handprint is the same size, it looks like she might have left you a little more to deal with."

Logan lifted his hand to his cheek then took it back off quickly. "What the hell? I think she burned me."

Destiny grinned. "Woman. Scorned. You know the drill I'm sure. Well, I guess I'll let you pull the chisel out while I go check on the sisters. You never know what kind of retribution those two will come up with.

"Come to think of it. You may want to take a nice long walk."

Garrison and Logan looked at each other before Logan reached out and pulled the chisel out of Garrison's skin. "Ouch! Damn, you could have warned me."

Logan shook his head as he pulled a pad of gauze from the little black bag sitting on the floor. When he saw Destiny's look of surprise, he smiled, and she knew right then what Haven saw in him.

"I was planning on helping out in the shop today. It isn't what I normally do so I came prepared."

She nodded. "Good planning."

He placed the gauze in Garrison's hand. "Better plug that thing up quickly. I'm thinking a long ride might be a better idea."

"Better planning," Destiny agreed.

Garrison nodded as he held the gauze to the small wound that was seeping blood. "Wonder if I need a tetanus shot?"

Logan looked over at him. "How long since you had one?"

Garrison shrugged. "I don't remember."

"Then you do. Come on. Let's run to the emergency room. It will give me a chance to check and see if they got my paperwork today, and we might have them put a stitch or two in that. Maybe Rayne won't be as mad."

Garrison agreed. "I'll take a needle and thread if it will make her feel better." He looked over at Destiny. "What gave me away? I was sure I didn't move."

"I have a sixth sense about these things."

They both stood and Destiny remained still as they approached her. Logan kissed her left cheek and Garrison her right and she couldn't help but smile at them both. "Welcome to the family, boys. You are in for quite a ride."

Once they left, Destiny took a little time to wander around the cabin. Garrison had done a stellar job of making it perfect, but she was sure Rayne was the one who added the touches to give it warmth. She slowly made her way back down the little hall and looked first into one room and then the next, which was a very nice bathroom.

Rayne sat on the closed toilet seat and Haven on a little teak wood bench that could be used inside or outside of a shower. They looked up when she walked in.

"I can't believe they did that. I'm so mad."

Destiny looked at Rayne and grinned. "Why? Because their little prank was better than your little prank?"

She looked up sharply. "It isn't the same. I wasn't faking my death!"

"No," Destiny agreed. "But your little trick could really have resulted in injuring him if that thing had hit him in the eye or somewhere else useful."

Rayne nodded. "I know. That's what we were just talking about. I guess I need to go out there and apologize."

"Ha! Are you kidding? Where is the Rayne I grew up with?"

Rayne's brows drew together and then relaxed when her eyes opened wider. "You are right!"

Haven laughed. "Oh Lord, please don't include me. I was already afraid I was going to have to deny myself my womanly rights tonight. On principle."

Destiny shook her head. "You've got bigger problems, dear sister. Garrison's handprint will turn into a bruise at the worst. Yours will be a little harder to explain. You left a burn outline on Logan's cheek."

Haven's eyes bulged as she gasped and covered her mouth with her hands. "Oh, no! I was so mad I forgot to put up the safeguard before I touched him!"

It was Destiny's turn to look confused. "Come again?"

Rayne stood and Haven did too. "We have a lot to catch you up on, but first we have to check on the guys."

"They're gone."

Panic registered in two sets of eyes, and Destiny didn't have the heart to make them suffer any more. "Just to the hospital so Garrison could get a tetanus shot, and maybe stitches, and Logan could check to see if his paperwork had come in. No big deal. They seemed quite pleased with themselves when they left."

"They did, did they?" Rayne and Haven asked together.

Destiny hid her smile behind a very serious face. "Oh yes. *Very* pleased.

"So you guys can catch me up on why Haven is burning people when she touches them, and how she has learned to control it, and Rayne, what about you? Anything new?"

When they both opened their mouths to speak Destiny held up her hand. "On second thought, tell me on the way to the police station. I held up my end of the bargain and met your guys, now it's your turn, Rayne, to hold up yours and get me in to see Tom Whitehawk."

Chapter Nine

Tom's butt ached since he'd been sitting shackled to the same chair, next to the same desk, for the past three hours. Since Burt Thompson's *coup d'état*, Special Agent Bret Thorne had been at the courthouse waiting for a chance to talk to Judge Maddox, and last Tom had heard more than an hour before, he was still waiting for the judge to finish his session for the day.

"Would you like something to drink?"

Tom looked up at Officer Gishwell and nodded. "Water, please." She gave him a sweet smile then left him for only a moment. She returned, untwisting the cap off a bottle of refined water, then handed him the bottle.

"Thank you."

"You're welcome," she said, as she took the chair facing the desk.

Tom took a long swallow and had to keep from grimacing. The processed water inside the plastic bottle tasted awful since he was used to the pure spring water his Mountain Mother provided. He missed not only the taste, but the energy it provided as well. But there was no use crying over the taste of the water when he had high hopes he'd soon be going home.

Tom turned toward the ruckus at the front of the police station. The buzz of talk set his heart beating in anticipation. It nearly stopped when he saw what all the fuss was about. Instead of the tall FBI Agent, three identical beauties strolled one after the other up to the window.

"Hi. I'm sure you remember me. I'm Rayne Cavanaugh, Garrison White's fiancée. Is Captain Grammar in?"

Tom watched as the young officer nearly toppled his

chair as he backed up to stand. And he could understand why. One Cavanaugh was almost too much beauty to behold, but three of them grabbed a man where he lived.

The startling realization that he was hard made Tom sit up straighter in his chair. He never got hard just looking at a woman. He'd never been built to react to a woman's face or figure. The recent revelation that his spirit woman had brought out the man in him had alleviated a fear he'd harbored since youth, but a walking talking woman had just never done it for him.

He looked back over to them, and his heart thundered like a million horses running across the plains. The first one, the one he'd met, was still talking sweetly to the officer. The second one was paying rapt attention to the conversation. But the third one was staring at him with such joy in her eyes that he felt himself starting to stand, and was startled when he realized the shackle was still attached.

"Whoa there, cowboy."

Tom glanced over to Officer Gishwell then settled back in his seat, but he turned once again to look at the woman who had captured his attention only to realize she was staring at him like she wanted to enter him.

He had no problem with that.

Tom, it's me, your Destiny, I found you.

Tom began shaking as he realized her lips weren't moving and she was talking to him telepathically. He had never met anyone with the capability since his great-grandfather passed away when he was only ten.

Tom, it's me….

Tom didn't know if he remembered how to respond. It was thirty years ago, but he couldn't stand the look of hurt on her face. *My Destiny. I have waited for you all my life.*

Her brilliant smile nearly knocked him out of the chair.

"You know, you aren't allowed to flirt with women while you're in here. Not even if they flirt with you first."

Tom turned to tell the woman police officer to shut up and leave him alone, but then he remembered his manners.

"I'm not. She's mine. We are together."

A look of annoyance crossed Officer Gishwell's features, but she shrugged and pulled a file from the pile of her in-basket. "Then flirt away, cowboy."

The irony of her nickname wasn't lost on Tom, but he could care less whether she meant it as an insult or if it was what she called every man chained to her desk. He turned back to speak with his dream woman again, but she and her sisters were being led away to a room. He felt her pain and panic as she looked back at him.

Tom took several hard and fast breaths before he realized he was at the threshold of full-fledged panic. He tried to get his breathing under control, but it had become a living entity over which he had no control. The next thing he knew he was staring up into the face of Officer Gishwell, as well as several other male officers. She smiled when she realized he was looking at her.

"You're okay. You just passed out. Paramedics are on the way."

"I don't need them," Tom tried to say, but she just kept smiling at him.

"Please, let me through, I'm a nurse."

"And I'm his…fiancée."

Tom noticed the nurse, *if she was in fact one,* sent his fiancée, *who he was certainly ready to claim,* an odd look before they smiled at each other.

"Hi, Tom, are you okay? You know who I am, right?"

The *go along with this* look in her eyes was unnecessary, as he had every intention of doing whatever she said, just as long as her sister got a chance to talk to him too. He nodded. "Of course. Hi, future sis!"

She grinned at him then looked up, her face filled with concern. "Can someone get me a pillow for his head? And I need you to call my fiancé." She pulled a cell phone from her jeans pocket and found the number then handed it to Officer Gishwell. "This is his number. He's a doctor. We need him to get here now!"

"But we've already called Emergency Services. They'll

be here any minute."

"Cancel it. This is a family matter." She turned to look up, and behind her. "Destiny, come keep an eye on your man while I get Logan here. Tom may have a concussion."

She turned back to the officer and snatched the phone from her hand. "Thanks, anyway. But I'll take care of this." She punched the *call* bar on her phone as she stepped away from the crowd.

Tom lay still, enjoying the show until his eyes met *hers*. His heart gave a mammoth yank when his Destiny settled her knees on the hard floor against his ribs and then she settled her butt on her heels.

"Hi, you," she said softly, placing a cool hand on his hot jaw.

"Hi, you," he returned, lost in the wonder of her eyes.

"I missed you so much. I cried for days."

Tom smiled, knowing the officers were taking in their reunion, but he didn't care that the sincerity of her words and actions validated her claim. All he cared about was the sincerity, as his heart had ached for her, too.

"I didn't know when you would get back. I missed you so much. But Mother told me of your visit, but that you left because you thought I was gone."

Destiny nodded. "It about killed me. But I had to go back and close up the house. I'm here now. And I'm here for good. All this…" She looked up and the officers who had been leaning in stood up straight. She smiled at them serenely before looking back at him. "All of this was a mistake… Anyone who knows your soul like I do knows better than to believe you would do harm."

"Be that as it may," Officer Gishwell interjected, "Your fiancé is a prisoner and as such I must ask you to move back."

Destiny looked from Tom's wondrous face to the officer's. Hers was worn out with the annoyance she felt at the world in general. "Officer, *please*. I've been away for a very long time, and I come back to the man I love only to find he's been jailed with charges that cannot be true. Can you just give us a few minutes more?"

Officer Gishwell nodded as if in a trance, and Tom looked from her as she backed away, to Destiny. He shook his head in wonder. "You are a siren, too?"

Destiny smiled. "With you by my side, I am all things." Her eyes held conviction and the emerald green irises swirled as she kept him locked within her gaze. *You are my strength, my light. You send my spirit soaring when you call my name. I am yours.*

And I am yours.

"I will always be yours," Tom reiterated, only this time out loud.

"Well, that's great kids, but I've got to get you up. Agent Thorne is on his way back, and he's got a butt-load of agents with him in full riot gear."

The panic in Destiny's eyes when she looked back at him had him struggling to sit up.

"Not so fast, officer. I'm Logan Hansen, Mr. Whitehawk's physician. Can you please stand back and let me examine my patient?"

When the officer stepped back, Logan dropped to his knees beside Destiny. He pulled a small flashlight from his black bag and shined it into Tom's eyes while he whispered out of the side of his mouth. "What the hell is going on in here? Haven said to get over here and stall. What am I stalling?"

Destiny kept her head down and spoke as softly as she could. "The FBI is coming and they want Tom to get up off the floor, but Haven wanted him to stay down until you got here. If they take him away, I'll...*hurt them.*"

Logan threw Destiny a frown, but he kept his voice low. "You two know each other?"

Tom listened to the exchange and could tell by the way she was struggling that her sister's fiancé had no idea she had mystical powers. He smiled at his little Amazon warrior, so proud she had chosen to come to him.

He glanced up to see the other two sisters standing over him, and he realized she wasn't the only one with powers. They radiated it, though he knew he was the only one able to see it.

Tom smiled at them, wondering if they could see his power and, like their sister, could read his thoughts. But he didn't have a chance to find out as their smiles turned to stark concern as the sounds of many footsteps coincided with the rumbling vibrations coming from the floor up into Tom's back.

He swallowed, hoping against hope he wasn't going back into that jail cell. It would have been bad enough before, but now that his Destiny had come, he had to have her by his side.

"Hello, Doctor Hansen. Is Mr. Whitehawk all right?"

Logan stood and looked at the agent, then nodded. "He appears to be fine. But I think it would be best if he was under observation for the next forty-eight hours."

The agent didn't quite stifle his grin. "Forty-eight, huh? Sounds reasonable to me. He looked at the two Cavanaugh women then frowned and looked down at Destiny. Then he looked back again before turning to Garrison White, who was standing behind his fiancée and her sister. "Three?"

Garrison nodded and smiled. "Yes, sir."

The agent shook his head and turned back to look down at Tom. "And I'm guessing that one is yours."

Tom smiled. "Yes, sir."

"Well, then. Let's get you up and get us a conference room. I think you have all taken up enough of the good officers' time. I'm sure they have work to do, and we're keeping them from it." He looked at them then and they pretty much scattered like rats being chased by a cat.

All of them except Officer Gishwell. "I'm still expecting paramedics, sir."

Haven stepped forward. "No. I sent them away. Doctor Hansen has everything under control."

The policewoman looked at her long and hard before abruptly turning away.

"Watch out for that one. There's something about her

that keeps bothering me, but I can't figure out what," Rayne said, her face pale.

Tom listened to the exchange as Logan bent down to him.

"You ready?"

Tom nodded and did most of the work when Logan began to help him up, but he didn't let it show. He wasn't sure what part he was supposed to play in their next act, so he played it close to the cuff, enjoying himself more than he had since he was a kid.

Destiny was under his other arm and he liked the feel of her there. He pulled her close and they followed the agent into a large conference room where John Grammar already sat with a folder open before him. The captain looked slightly annoyed, but amused as well.

Agent Throne closed and locked the door before walking around the table to sit by the captain. He opened the leather folder with the bureau's emblem on it, put his hands together on the sheets of paper, and looked across the table at the six of them.

"First, I have no idea what was going on out there, but it looked like a circus. I think I've been completely aboveboard with you folks, and I need to be assured what we talk about in this room doesn't leave this room, but equally important, I need to know that you are being completely above board with me and the local police."

"Tom is innocent of the crimes he's being framed for." All eyes turned to Destiny and she lifted her chin, daring anyone to argue with her.

Tom grinned and took her hand. It felt like he had known her forever, but he knew that was because he'd been looking for her forever without realizing it. He lifted her hand and kissed the back of it.

Agent Thorne looked at them and smiled. "Okay. Let's get down to business. Judge Maddox is on board. He's had enough of what's been going on in his town, too. Tom, you'll be taken in to court first thing in the morning, and he's going to grant bond. The bureau is going to cover it and you will be released, but as far as anyone outside of this room is concerned, you are still a suspect, and you will have to wear an ankle monitor."

Tom tried not to let his disappointment show. "So I have to stay here tonight."

Agent Thorne nodded. "Unfortunately, yes. He was conducting a trial and couldn't get away to talk to me until too late to do anything today. But this may work in our favor. Burt Thompson is about to lawyer up. That probably gives us just one more night to try to get information out of him.

"I know he won't get to talk to anyone but you between now and then, and I am asking you to get him talking any way you can."

Tom looked at the agent then at the captain. "That's what got him going earlier today. I was talking to him and he spit at me. I asked him hadn't his mother taught him any manners, and he went off. He said she had left him to a father who had sexually molested him, and who shared him. Then he went crazy, and the police officer who ended up hurt came in. You pretty much know the rest."

Agent Thorne nodded. "I figured he'd been abused. That fits the profile. But I'm beginning to think he isn't the one responsible for the kidnapping or the murders of the young men. I do think, however, he's the one responsible for the death of Grey White and his wife."

Everyone looked at Garrison. He was sitting so still it was obvious he was trying not to react. He exhaled finally, his gaze on the FBI agent. "Why? What do you know?"

Agent Thorne pulled a printout from his folder and slid it across the table. Garrison picked it up and looked at it and then at the agent. "What is this?"

"It's a ballistics report on the gun found at Tom's cabin. The markings on the bullets as they spin through and exit the chamber of a firearm are always the same for the same gun, but are also individual to that gun. The one found in Tom's cabin is an identical match to the ones recovered during the autopsy of your brother and his wife."

The room was silent as Garrison looked back down at the paper in his hands. When they began to shake, he placed it on the table and looked up, his eyes shimmering with unshed tears. He cleared his throat, but his voice was still shaky when he spoke. "Can you prove it was his gun? That he used it?"

The agent shook his head. "Unfortunately, no. But the person who originally bought it, bought it locally." He looked at Tom. "The reason I haven't been able to get back to you before now is because we needed to do a little research."

Tom nodded. "And you found something?"

Agent Thorne nodded and turned back to Garrison. "We got a hit when we ran the bullet's markings in our database. It was used in an unsolved crime nearly twenty-five years ago. The victim was a Samantha Thompson. After checking with hospitals all over the state and the surrounding states, we were able to confirm that the woman gave birth to a son named Burtrum."

"He would have been a kid."

Agent Thorne nodded again. "Yes. We believed the gun belonged to his father. We ran the name we got off of Burt Thompson's birth certificate and took a partial print off the gun. We really didn't expect to find Burt Thompson's fingerprints since he would have known to wear gloves, but using our fingerprint database we got a hit. It was such an old file it took nearly an entire shift for us to find a match."

"But it wasn't Burt's?" Garrison asked.

Agent Thorne shook his head. "No. The father's name on the birth certificate matched the name the partial fingerprint belonged to. A little more digging revealed Thompson senior was a thug and had a long line of charges for petty theft and domestic abuse."

When no one else spoke up Tom lifted his hand to get the agent's attention. "Burt Thompson doesn't know his mother was murdered. He talked about her like she was alive and well when she abandoned him. He hates her for leaving him, for allowing his father to abuse him."

"There's your in," the agent said with satisfaction. "I know you don't want to be here another night." He glanced at Destiny then turned his attention back to Tom. "And I can't say I blame you. But if you tell him you're going to be released in the morning because we can't hold you in relationship to the gun and drugs anymore, he'll ask questions.

"When he does, tell him drug tests proved your system is clean, and since there was nothing else found in or around your property, the captain, who knows you very well and didn't believe you capable of murder to begin with, feels someone is trying to set you up. But don't let him know we suspect that someone is him.

"Make him think you're completely ignorant as far as his involvement goes. If he thinks we are on to him he won't divulge anything."

"And if he says anything about the gun?"

Agent Thorne smiled. "Not if, *when.*

"He won't be able to help himself. He'll be furious he went to all that trouble and now it isn't doing him any good. And that's when you need to really let him have it. He's going to be stuck in there and you are going to get to walk. I expect his mouth to start moving, especially since his earlier behavior proves his dislike of Captain Grammar. That you have a connection with the boss he detested will really make him mad.

"We want you to get him as riled up as you can before you use your ace in the hole."

"His mother's murder."

"Yes, but don't mention his father at all, because again, he'll see the trail leading back to him. Just let him know the gun was used in a locally unsolved crime where a woman was murdered nearly twenty-four years ago.

"Let him put two and two together if you can. But if he doesn't make the connection on his own, you can mention it was some woman that shares his last name, but stress how common a name it is in some way. The shock alone may get him talking."

Tom nodded. It sounded like a good plan. "Are you going to be listening from the speaker system used earlier?"

Agent Thorne looked over to the captain. John Grammar shook his head. "No. We'd like to put a wire on you. We can listen and record everything that is being said. We don't want to take a chance of the speaker squeaking like it does sometimes when it's turned on, even when no one is touching the microphone."

Tom looked at them both and then at Destiny when she squeezed his hand. He smiled at her then looked back and nodded. "Okay. But why go through the farce in front of the judge? And why the ankle monitor?"

Agent Thorne frowned. "That's a little more complicated, and again, I'm asking for your help. If Thompson isn't the one who took Gavin White or murdered those other young men, then someone else is. And we are hoping that they may try to use you, too, since, I'm sorry to say, the town is still going to suspect you've done something since *we* are still watching you so closely.

"It may be a long shot, but right now taking a shot in the dark is all we've got."

"You're sure Burt Thompson isn't responsible for Gavin or the others?"

Agent Thorne shook his head. "No, not completely sure, but about as sure as I can be given the man's behaviors. I've had four different FBI profilers, the best there is, profile him, and they all agree with my assessment. We don't believe he knows anything about the others.

"As you know, we have evidence Gavin was still alive as of very recently. He would have been killed months ago, I have no doubt *immediately*, if Thompson was the one who took him. From the evidence left at the scene of your brother and sister-in-law's murders, it's clear your nephew was there having dinner with them when all hell broke loose. Our suspect wouldn't risk letting the kid identify him as the man who took his parents away from him."

"If you don't think Burt Thompson took him, do you

have an idea of what kind of a person did?"

A frustrated sigh lifted the agent's chest before blowing out of his mouth. "Although I didn't think so at first, Tom, now I suspect it may be a woman."

Garrison's eyes sharpened and Tom felt his distress. He sent waves of pure energy to comfort his friend and again felt the squeeze of Destiny's hand. He looked at her in wonder. *You felt that?*

She smiled. *Yes. I feel everything you feel. I hear all your thoughts. This is new for me. So I know it isn't me, it's our connection.*

Tom had to force his gaze away from her when Garrison spoke, and found it one of the most difficult things he'd ever done.

"Why would a woman take a teenage boy?"

Though the distress was still in his voice, Tom could tell Garrison's anxiety had eased. He felt the squeeze of Destiny's soft hand again and he squeezed back without looking at her. He was afraid he wouldn't be able to look away again if he did.

Agent Thorne shrugged. "That's what we need to figure out. If we can figure out why, then we'll know who.

"There are several possibilities.

"It could be a mother who lost a son and the loss devastated her so badly it colored her sense of reality. If she is the one who took the others, and they somehow threatened the reality her mind had created, she could have killed them in a fit of anger or fear. It would fit with the wounds of the victims we've found.

"They were brutally killed, but it was up close and personal. That alone should have alerted me to the possibility of it being a woman."

"Who else?"

Agent Thorne looked at Garrison, his eyes filled with compassion. "There are several possibilities, Mr. White, many of which you *really* don't want to hear about."

The room was silent as they all waited for Garrison to speak. He eventually did, and Tom knew that his words stemmed from a need to punish himself for not taking better care with his nephew.

"It isn't your fault," Destiny stated quietly, causing all eyes to turn her way. She blinked and then froze, realizing she had spoken aloud.

Garrison frowned at her. "How did you know what I was thinking?"

Tom held her hand tightly, giving her an anchor as the strongest distress in the room was now hers. She sighed and he felt her relax.

"It's what I do. *You* know that."

As she turned to the two Law Enforcement officers, Tom realized Destiny was *commanding* Garrison to know it. He was amazed at her abilities and wondered, as it had been so long since he'd been in the presence of another telepath, just how many different mythical gifts she wielded. He also knew he'd had to hold back his curiosity until later, but it was clear to him that Garrison and his future sister-in-law barely knew each other.

"I'm a psychologist," she explained to two men facing them. When they both nodded, she turned back to Garrison.

"You have the classic symptoms of a parent riddled with unwarranted guilt. The desperation in your eyes, as you so politely demand information, gives you away. The thread of nearly undetectable anger in your voice is self-directed. You want to know what is the worst thing that could have happened to your nephew because you feel responsible for not keeping him closer."

Garrison simply stared at her as Agent Thorne spoke up. "Are you interested in working for the FBI? You are very intuitive."

Destiny turned to him and smiled, but said nothing.

Tom noticed her sisters were trying to hide their own smiles, and he couldn't wait for the night to be over with so he would be free to get to know Destiny and her family. But it wouldn't be over with, until it started.

"Looks like I'm over my fall, and I'm sure my doctor

will retract his statement that I need to be observed overnight, so I guess you better take me back to the cell, Captain Grammar. Let's get this thing done."

The officer smiled. "I guess you had better start calling me John, since we are such good friends."

Chapter Ten

Tom closed his jumpsuit and was glad he didn't have hair on his body. The microphone and wire he wore were taped to his sternum and around his waist to his back. He glanced at the monitor they'd been watching and saw Thompson get up off his bed to stand at the bars. He almost laughed as the senior officer joined him, and they watched Burt do five jumping jacks that made his large belly fly up and then down, before he stopped and grabbed the bars to support his huffing and puffing weight.

John Grammar glanced at Tom and grinned. "I think he's trying to be you."

Tom laughed out loud at that before entering the heavy steel door the captain unlocked and opened. He opened the cell door as well, and stepped back to allow Tom to enter. John gave Tom one last look, then he closed the cell door, and locked him in.

"Well, have a good night, Tom. See you first thing in the morning." He glanced at Burt and nodded. "Thompson."

"Goodnight, John. I'll be ready!"

As soon as the door closed, Tom went to his bed to lie down. He was going to give his jail mate time to start a conversation, and if he eventually didn't, Tom would.

As he expected, he didn't have long to wait.

"Where the hell have you been?"

Tom didn't even try to hide his grin. "Out there getting my freedom." As there was no immediate response, he had to resist the urge to look and see Thompson's reaction. Not that he needed to, the other man's anger was coating the room in dark shades of gray.

"What the hell does that mean?"

Tom did glance down and over at him then, before

lying back so Thompson couldn't see his face. "I'm out of here in the morning."

"Like hell you are! They caught you with the goods!"

"Sure am. They can't hold me. John knew immediately the drugs and gun weren't mine." He left the FBI out of it, figuring the less Burt knew the better.

"John who?"

"John Grammar."

"Since when are you and *him* on a first name basis?"

Tom smiled. The man was as livid as they had expected him to be. "We've known each other for years." Which wasn't a lie. They had known each other. They just hadn't *known* each other.

"That don't change nuthin'! He can't let you off because you two are friends!"

"You're right. That's why I've been in here the last few days. But it did make him work hard and fast to figure out why I had things I wouldn't have, which got me put in here in the first place."

There was a long pause, and Tom couldn't stand it anymore; he had to sit up to watch Burt's reactions. "Turns out my pee is as clean as a shiny new nickel. Not that I had any doubts."

"That don't prove nuthin', either. You could be selling weed, not smoking it."

Tom wondered if Burt realized he'd just mentioned one of the items found in Tom's cabin. To Tom's knowledge, no one had ever told him what was found there. He'd have to remember to ask John when he saw him in the morning.

"They did a thorough search of my property. No pot plants. No building with heat lamps or irrigation systems either. So they realized I was telling the truth when I said someone planted that stuff in my cabin."

"Bullshit! That ain't all they found!"

Tom held his tongue as he shrugged. "It doesn't matter. They know it can't be mine either."

Burt glared at him. "How can they know?"

Tom pretended innocence. "Know what?"

"Dammit! That the gun wasn't yours! You know what I'm talking about, you smug son of a bitch!"

Bingo! Tom kept his expression neutral as he stood and walked to the bars. "They ran ballistics tests on the bullet. Turns out it was used in a local crime about twenty-five years ago. Woman got killed. Shot all to hell from my understanding."

Tom stopped there and waited, but he could see Burt couldn't connect the dots. When his jail mate started cursing and sputtering words about favoritism and injustice, he put a quizzical frown on his face and scratched his head. "Huh! I didn't think anything of it when John was talking because I was so excited about getting out of here, but didn't you say your last name is Thompson?"

Burt stopped fussing and stared at him blankly. Tom knew exactly when realization dawned as Burt's mouth dropped open but no sound came out, and he shook his head so hard it made his triple chin drag back and forth across the closed snaps of his orange jumpsuit.

Tom watched with helpless compassion as Burt went to his knees. He'd been so filled with the essence of the woman beside him while Agent Thorne explained his plan that Tom hadn't thought about the affect their plan would have on a man whose life had already been filled with disappointment and the terror of being an abused child. He hadn't thought about how it would affect him either.

Guilt ate at him. He knew Burt was evil and probably deserved what he would get when everything was said and done, but it went against Tom's nature to do harm of any kind so his own spirit felt the sting.

Knowing things were only going to get worse for them both, Tom forced himself to continue. In the end he had to remember Burt could have chosen another path, no matter what was done to him in the past, and if there was a chance he had a clue about Gavin White, both of their suffering would be worth the pain.

"Hey, Thompson! What's wrong with you?"

With his arms barely wrapped around his large stomach, Burt looked up at Tom, his gaze lifeless. "She was my mother."

Tom cringed inwardly but didn't let it show. "That's too bad, man. But who would want to kill your mother?"

Burt shook his head as his rocking increased. "That son of a bitch! That filthy son of a bitch!"

Tom gave him a moment, knowing to press too hard would make Burt question his interest. But then again, maybe not. Burt wasn't his normal belligerent self, and that was what the FBI agent had wanted Tom to accomplish. "Who are you talking about?"

Burt shook his head again, and Tom was afraid he was still together enough to keep his mouth shut. But the thought had no sooner passed, and Burt lifted his head and looked Tom dead in the eyes.

"My father!" he screamed.

"That son of a bitch bastard killed her!

"And then he lied to me! He used me! He told me she had left me as well as him and that it was my fault! He told me I had to take over her chores to make up for her leaving. He made me his housekeeper and his cook and then he tore my ass up because he said it was my fault that he didn't have a woman to fuck anymore.

"That son of a bitch tore me up! But that wasn't as bad as him making me forget she had loved me. Every time he pounded into me, he told me how much she had hated me, how happy she was to leave me behind so she didn't have to look at me anymore.

"He said she was ashamed to have a scrawny little shit for a son. That I was worthless and unworthy of her love and attention."

Tears rolled down Burt's face as he continued to rock, his head down so Tom couldn't see his eyes.

"Eventually I forgot about everything except the pain. As much as he hurt me, I believed him, and hated her for hurting me more.

"I believed him! What a stupid little shit I was! I

believed him…" Now wailing, Burt's words were getting harder and harder to understand, and his distress caused harsh breath to mingle with the words as he continued to rant.

Tom tried to ignore the pain as each and every word felt like a fist to his midsection. Unable to stomach much more he was forced to lean forward and hold onto the bars for support. As sick as he was getting, he wasn't sure he could continue to torture the man with more questions. In fact, he knew he couldn't. There had to be another way.

When he looked up, Tom realized he wouldn't have to. Saying anything right now probably wouldn't have made any difference. Burt's head was back and though he was looking in Tom's direction, it was easy to see his glazed-over eyes meant he was in shock, and Tom could only imagine he was lost in his past, and completely unaware Tom was still in the room.

Time passed as Tom fought to cleanse his spirit. He continued to watch the broken man, all the while chanting silently for forgiveness. He felt dirty. Diseased. It was something he'd never before known and hated knowing now. In his whole life he'd never sought to cause another pain, even though there were some who had sought to pain him.

Burt stopped rocking and closed his eyes, yet tears continued their course down his cheeks. When he spoke, his voice was barely above a whisper. "She used to read to me," Burt said, his voice breaking. He pressed his lips together, swallowed visibly then continued. "She'd get on the floor and play with me when I was little and helped me with homework when I started school.

"She sang to me sometimes, but not when he was around. If he noticed I had her attention, he'd hit her and she'd have split lips, and black eyes, and bruises on her face and arms. I don't know how many times she took me out of the house after that asshole hit her. She'd stand between us. She always took the hits that were meant for me.

"She protected me.

"She always protected me, no matter what he did to her."

Silence filled the room for long seconds as Tom's heart broke from knowing how sad and painful Burt's life must have been. It was such a contrast to the way he'd been raised. He'd only known love and compassion as both parents raised him with purity of purpose.

A slow smile crossed Burt's lips, and Tom felt his insides churn. His dark grey aura was darkening even more and Tom knew it would likely be completely black were it not for the bright lights overhead and the off-white cell walls.

The stench of purest evil was refilling the man's soul now that he'd gotten past the shock.

"He got his! Hahahaha! Yes, he did, that son-of-a-bitch!

"I found that gun in his sock drawer and beneath it was a pair of my mother's gloves. I remembered them even though I think she only wore them once. They were so white, so feminine. He had kept them for some reason even though she had been gone for over a year at that point. And I though how poetic it would be if the gloves she had worn were holding the gun that took his life.

"Maybe somewhere in the back of my mind I knew. I don't know. But now I'm glad I did what I did. It was more poetically justified than I thought at the time. I pulled out Momma's gloves without touching the gun and put them on. I was thin then. I was so fucking thin because I always had to drink soup. Solid foods hurt too much to pass after the old man got done with me.

"But the gloves were a perfect fit so it didn't matter. I picked up the gun and then, just like it was supposed to happen, he showed up at his bedroom door. I didn't even wait for his reaction. I raised the gun and put a bullet right in his pie hole. And while he staggered backwards I put one in his dick." Burt laughed. "He couldn't even scream because I took his tongue out with the first shot.

"I was just a kid and it was the first time I ever shot a

gun, but I hit the bull's eye both times."

Burt started rocking again, as he laughed. Tom slid a quick look at the camera lens wondering why they hadn't come in yet. He looked back at Burt when the room was suddenly silent. Burt had quit laughing and was staring straight at him. Tom swallowed, feeling like he was looking into the barrel of a gun.

"I'm sorry you had to live through all of that."

Burt shook his head as if waking himself up before he struggled to his feet. "Don't you go telling anybody what I said, or I'll just call you a liar."

Tom nodded, though it surprised him Burt forgot about the intercom system. He hesitated to remind him by looking into the camera again, but he still wondered why no one came. They had their confession, and he needed to lie down before he threw up. Hearing the details of Burt Thompson's pitiful life was doing him in.

"So now you know, Injun. It was mine. I kept it because no one would ever be able to trace it back to me." He grinned then. "I wasn't born in Mystic Waters, you see. I was born in Tennessee just over the mountain. Fucking dick of a father moved us here after he said my mother left us because he knew I wouldn't have anyone who knew my mother to run to. And he made sure I didn't have friends.

"I'm glad I killed him. So fucking glad!"

The click of the metal door preceded John Grammar and three other officer's entrance. He stopped in front of Burt, but stayed back enough that Burt couldn't repeat his earlier performance. Burt looked from him to Tom and pure hatred turned his eyes as black as his aura. "You shit! I'll kill you for this!"

Tom said nothing as he turned to walk the few steps to his cot. He sat down and put his head in his hands as he listened while John Grammar spoke.

"Burt Thompson, you are under arrest for the murders of your father, Burt Thompson Senior, Police Officer Grey White, and his wife, Joy White. You have the right to remain silent...."

****

Destiny paced the floor of Garrison's cabin aware that all eyes were on her.

She hadn't had a chance to talk to her sister's privately since leaving Tom, as *their* men had first wanted to know about the chaos they had walked into and were forced to go along with at the police station. Though she could tell they weren't entirely satisfied with the answers Rayne and Haven gave, they finally let that go, only to hover over her sisters, determined to make up for the trick they had played before leaving for the hospital.

All they were doing was annoying her.

Destiny needed some private time with her sisters to explain what was happening to her. She hadn't had a moment's peace since being forced to leave Tom earlier. If it hadn't been for him sending her waves of comfort, she wouldn't have been able to walk away when she did. But just as soon as Logan and Haven had her in his truck, and they were all heading back up the mountain, Destiny knew she had made a terrible mistake.

The connection Destiny felt to Tom was so strong that at first the unexpected nausea made her fear she wouldn't be able to leave his presences without stomach distress. The further away from him they got the more she realized it wasn't anything to do with her, but rather that Tom was growing ill because of what he had agreed to do. Her stomach pains were tainted with sorrow and regret and worst of all for a soul like his, guilt.

The more ill Destiny felt the more afraid she became for Tom so she searched her memory for the conversation that had pretty much gone over her head at the time. Even with the pain at her midriff, she couldn't help but smile at how captivated she'd been as she'd inhaled the wonder of him, the spirit of him, and the pure clean magic of him.

As she paced the floor at Garrison and Rayne's cabin, the memories started tumbling over each other, and the pains grew too sharp to ignore. She knew she had no choice. She had to get back to him and get him out of that jail.

Only her sisters were no help at all.

Destiny knew everyone was confused by her agitation, especially Garrison and Logan, but she couldn't enlighten Haven and Rayne without exposing them all. So she kept the sick feelings growing inside of her to herself until Rayne spoke up.

"Would you *please* sit down?"

She forced herself to stop moving in circles, but there was no way she could sit and socialize. "I have to go back to town." Her abrupt statement registered on all their faces, but Garrison was staring at her so hard she had to make a conscious effort not to squirm.

"I know this question has been asked a few times by Logan and me *already*, but *how* is it you know Tom Whitehawk?"

Destiny looked from one sister to the other, but their uneasy looks told her they had no idea how to answer either. She looked back at Garrison. "I met him on the Internet."

She instantly knew she'd said the wrong thing. Rayne's features changed drastically, making her look like she just bit into an entire bag of lemons, and Garrison's eyebrows went north then south. She frantically searched for some way to correct her mistake before anyone asked a question she didn't want to answer.

"Well, not *on* the Internet, *exactly*."

Destiny tried to ignore Haven's look of concern and wished she were better at lying. Since there was no help for it, she jumped in with both feet. "But I saw his picture there, and I researched the advertisement for a tribal gathering in this area. He's so beautiful."

The irritation building on both Logan and Garrison's faces at her nonsensical statement made it clear she wasn't scoring any points with them so she gave up.

"Oh... *What the hell!* Okay, guys, I'm going to tell you what really happened."

Destiny ignored the large green eyes and barely

discernible head shaking of both sisters' auburn-covered heads as she geared herself up for the telling.

"I was home in Los Angeles. I was meditating, if you will. Then I was flying in the air, not me, you understand, but my essence. My spirit is capable of transporting to places outside of my body.

"My spirit flew across the country allowing me to see the earth as a bird does, which was amazing. It is quite lovely in spite of mankind's attempts to destroy it. After the long flight I ended up over these mountains. My senses expanded and I could not only see but also smell the richness of the pine-covered mountains. Something, which I now know was Tom, was gently pulling me down and I found myself in Tom's presence.

"He was magnificently naked and so beautifully made, and I was completely entranced. But more important than the call of his body and the response of mine, his *soul* called to my soul. Though I didn't realize it at the time, I know now my decision to come here wasn't entirely my own. Tom needs me as much as I need him.

"So here I am and there he was, and when we met face-to-face for the first time at the jail, everything fell into place. I became his fiancée and he became mine.

"There are things I've left out, but in a nutshell, that's about it."

She was smiling as she had relived every breathtaking moment while giving them the abbreviated version. When she came down from the breezy high of the memories, she noticed the room was as silent as death and that four pairs of very large eyes looked back at her—her sisters' because they were astounded she had told the truth, and their men's because they thought she was full of it. "Any questions?"

The silence was broken abruptly as the laughter started with Logan, but Garrison was a close second. With relief-filled eyes Rayne and Haven joined in, but relief soon changed to gazes filled with retribution. Destiny didn't care. There was really nothing else she could have said that would have made sense to the men, so her only option had been the truth.

As the men shook their heads and rolled their eyes, all she could think was very soon she and her sisters needed to have a long talk about how they expected to live with those men and keep such a vital part of themselves hidden. Destiny was just glad she wouldn't have that problem. In fact, she couldn't wait to find out just what *her* man could do.

"Now, like I said. I need to get back to town."

****

Destiny walked into the police station determined to get to Tom as quickly as possible. Something big was going down, and a loud buzz accompanied officers dashing to-and-fro, filling the station with chaos. She stopped, trying to get her bearings.

A female police officer ran up to her, and Destiny suddenly felt more ill than she had before, so her concern for Tom increased tenfold. But the familiar woman in the dark blue uniform was waving her hands to get Destiny to stop moving any further into the room.

"I'm sorry, but you can't be here right now. You will have to come back later unless this is a life-and-death emergency."

As far as Destiny was concerned, it was. "I have to see Tom Whitehawk. He needs me."

Annoyance crossed the woman's features. "Again, I'm sorry. That isn't possible right now. You have to leave."

Destiny didn't budge. If whatever was happening involved Tom, she wasn't going anywhere."

"Where is he? What's happening?"

Annoyance and many other emotions as well were radiating from the woman, the grey and black auras mixing with so many murky colors it confused Destiny. She couldn't figure out how to read her. But her stomach was sending shock waves to her intestines, and she was sure she would be sick if she didn't get away from her.

"I need to see Captain Grammar, now! This is important."

The officer's face took on a look of determination laced with what Destiny could only gage as evil. The mixed aura and the officer's attitude only made Destiny feel worse. "Please. It's really important."

"Look. I told you that you can't be here right now. The captain has his hands full. If you can come back in about an hour, I'll see what I can do. But right now—"

Several officers burst into the station stopping Officer Gishwell's words. They ran past her and the officer and headed toward the area where Destiny knew Tom was being kept. She pushed past the officer to follow them but was suddenly caught by the wrist. The shock of having a handcuff locked around her wrist stopped her, which gave the officer a chance to capture her other one to lock it too.

"What are you doing?"

"You are under arrest. I told you to leave. Your decision to disobey me will now get you what you want. You are now obstructing justice and can spend a little more time here. Come with me."

Destiny was practically dragged to the area where she had first seen Tom. The woman attached her cuffs to the chair he'd been sitting in. She couldn't find her voice as her outrage was overpowered by the nausea bubbling up her throat. Her fear for Tom increased the sicker she got, but when the officer walked away from her to go see what was happening she was able to take steadying breaths and the nausea abated somewhat.

Destiny tried to jerk the cuffs off her hands, but all she got for her trouble was scraped and sore wrists. She looked around as best she could. No one was in the front office area as they had all headed to the back.

She frantically considered her options as she looked around, but there was nothing she could find to help her escape the shackles. Realizing she had no other option, Destiny tried to calm herself down enough to concentrate in the hope she could send her spirit outside of her body. Her agitation was still so heightened she couldn't clear her mind.

Her mother's voice filled the room with the soothing song that used to put her and her sisters to sleep every night when they were little children. The shock of hearing Celestia's calming voice eventually eased Destiny's distress as she embraced the gift to listen.

Goodnight my loves, my precious loves, to sleep to sleep you go;
Dream my loves my precious loves and in your hearts you know;
You are my loves my precious loves, this I could not fake;
And when you wake my loves, my loves, magick we will make.

Tears flowed from Destiny's eyes as her mother's love cloaked her. She took a shaky breath and exhaled when the song ended but had no time to mourn the loss of it. Her spirit floated free.

Thank you, Mommy. I miss you so much!

Warmth continued to hold her essence, and she knew her mother was still with her. She floated to the area where all the officers were gathered outside of the steel door she knew led back to the jail. Three of the officers were wrestling a heavyset man to the ground, but his strength was amazing as was the fury of his black aura. The others occasionally tried to help, but the small area was so crowded there was little they could do.

Though she wondered if it occurred to them that it would be easier to try to get the man under control if they gave themselves some room, Destiny wasn't interested enough in what was going on to watch. All she cared about was getting to Tom to make sure he was okay. Since she didn't want her essence to pass through so much negative energy she floated back, away from the tussle.

She flowed to side of the chaotic mess before preparing herself to go through the concrete block walls. Although she hadn't had any trouble going through the ceiling and roof of her home, she knew these walls were much thicker and likely more dense. She took a mental breath, pushed against and then through the thick solid substance, and was relieved even concrete couldn't stop her from getting to her man. It disoriented her a little though, so she had to give herself a moment to shake off the strange feelings and to clear her head.

Once she felt more herself, she began to look around. It didn't take long. Though there were several cells, they were all open-faced with only the steel bars fronting them. It was clear there was no one inside.

Her Tom was gone.

Chapter Eleven

Tom sat in the judge's chamber with Agent Thorne while they waited for Judge Maddox to arrive. After he'd been removed from the cell so the police could deal with Burt Thompson—who was acting as if he'd gone completely mad—Agent Thorne took him to his SUV. Tom sat in the back and waited as the agent made a couple of phone calls.

The first was to his boss, the next one to Judge Maddox's private home phone.

Thorne drove the very short distance to the back of the courthouse. They waited until the night guard let them in and led them to the room they now occupied. Agent Thorne had excused himself almost immediately and had been gone for the best part of their wait, but he'd returned ten minutes ago. Tom was glad. Sitting alone for that long had only forced him to relive the entire horrible scene in the jail all over again.

Bret Thorne glanced at the large dial on his black wristwatch. "It shouldn't be too long now. The judge was having dinner with the mayor, so he said it would be a while. But that was nearly two hours ago."

Tom nodded. He could use a meal himself. After the confession he'd tricked Thompson into making, and the upset to his stomach it had caused, his stomach was churning. "Do you think he'll let me go tonight?"

Thorne nodded. "I do. He planned to in the morning anyway. This is just moving things up. My boss is a phone call away if he needs her to back our plan up. He was going to speak to her in the morning before court started."

Tom blew out a breath. He was so worn out all he wanted to do was go back to his cabin, take a shower in the bathhouse, and then crawl into his own bed. As much as he wanted to see Destiny, he didn't want her to be around him until the taint of guilt had been washed from his soul, and the stench of jail washed from his body.

"How are you holding up? Captain Grammar emailed me the video of your talk with Burt Thompson. I watched it a couple of times. The first time I was watching him, studying him. The second time I noticed how it was affecting you.

"I know you are a spiritual man, and I'm sorry you had to be put in the position you were. But it paid off. I hope that's some consolation."

Tom nodded but continued to face the judge's desk rather than looking over at the agent. His shame was still too strong. "I know it was necessary. It's just not who I am. I don't do harm to others. To any living thing if I can help it.

"I don't take life. I don't intentionally deceive. I still ask for forgiveness when I eat meat, and only do so because not doing so caused a deficiency in my system when I was younger, and my mother forced me to. As an adult I've tried to change my diet, but I find I am weakened after an extended period of time abstaining. It is a medical issue that conflicts me."

"I see. Again, I'm sorry."

Tom turned to him then. "I don't hold you responsible. I chose to do it."

Judge Maddox entered the room, and Tom and Agent Thorne stood. He waved them back into their seats as he rounded the desk and took his. He unlocked and opened the long narrow drawer in front of him before taking a manila folder out and placing it on his desk. He opened the folder, and Tom couldn't help but see his name printed in ink on the tab. He looked up then as the judge glanced from the folder and at him.

"Hi, Tom, I'm happy we're getting a chance to take care of this tonight. I've reviewed the information Agent Thorne provided when he came to see me earlier. And I had an opportunity to watch the video from the jail's camera, and listen to the audio from the recorder he forwarded to my email. From what he's told me and from what I've seen, you have been treated pretty badly by our law enforcement people both on the federal and city level. I apologize on behalf of us all."

Tom nodded. "Thank you."

Judge Maddox grinned then. "Now, what can I do for you?"

Agent Thorne spoke up and the judge turned to him. "Although we planned to do this in the morning, I wanted to see if we could get Mr. Whitehawk released tonight."

The judge looked from him to Tom. "Are you still willing to go along with the plan Agent Thorne outlined earlier today? I'm not asking because it's a condition of my releasing you tonight, you are free to go. I will need you to appear in the morning so we can make it official. I'm asking because Agent Thorne believes you are our best hope for flushing out the person responsible for the other murders and possibly the kidnapping of Gavin White, as long as everyone thinks you are still a suspect."

Agent Thorne spoke up again before Tom had a chance to answer. "After what we've put him through today, and the previous days Mr. Whitehawk spent in the jail cell, I believe we should reconsider that. He's a spiritual man and this is taking a toll on his health."

The judge turned back to Tom. "I noticed it was causing you distress when our suspect became agitated and then violent. And I'm sorry we have further pained you. I'm willing to let you go with no conditions but your appearance in court in the morning."

Agent Thorne stood. "Thank you, sir."

Tom remained in his seat and shook his head. "No. I want you to put the ankle bracelet on me and continue with the plan. I agreed to all this in the beginning because I want to do anything and everything I can to help bring Gavin White back home. His family is my family though the relation is very distant. But more importantly, the Whites are my friends.

"What it will cost me is nothing compared to what all this has cost them."

Bret Thorne sat back down and looked at him. "Are you sure, Tom? Things can still get pretty nasty for you. If we still pretend you are a suspect, some people will forget to have manners."

For the first time in what seemed a very long time Tom grinned in amusement. "*Some people* have always forgotten their manners when it comes to me and mine.

"But yes. I'm sure."

"Prejudice is a nasty business," Judge Maddox said as he leaned back into the large chair. "But it is also human, unfortunately. It's a shame though *some people* don't realize those of us whose ancestors came here and turned this land into something it originally wasn't meant to be are the trespassers."

Tom grinned. "I like you."

Judge Maddox laughed. "And I thank you. At least we can mark one case off and start focusing on the others." He looked over to the agent. "Looks like you're back on again. Are you still keeping everyone in the dark with the exception of John Grammar?"

"Yes, sir. Even though I believe Bret Thompson worked alone in the murders of Grey and Joy White, I don't think we can take the chance to exclude anyone else in case there is another dirty cop on the force.

"Captain Grammar is pretty upset by the idea, but he agrees. He was careful not to give any indication Tom is being cleared by us or by you. When I took Tom from the jail to bring him over here, Captain Grammar told his officers I was taking custody of Tom for a while for further questioning. They shouldn't question his not going back in there tonight.

"Once you hold court tomorrow, and they see he is being released but with the ankle device, I'll have the captain let it slip he's being released for helping us nail Burt Thompson, and that without the weapon and drug charges, which are now Thompson's, he doesn't understand why

Tom's still being considered a suspect at all, but it must be FBI business he isn't privy to."

The judge nodded. "He's a good man, never one to let his own pride get in the way. But I hope this mess gets cleared up soon, or we will have to end the charade. As much as I appreciate Tom's help, I don't want Tom hurt, or Mystic Waters' currently law-abiding citizens to commit criminal acts by taking matters into their own hands and ending up in my courtroom."

Bret Thorne nodded. "Give us forty-eight hours. After profiling this Unsub I feel pretty confident the kidnapper is upset a scapegoat is no longer assured. The hint that Tom is still being suspected will give the killer, who I believe is also our kidnapper, a reason to try to set him up before his name is completely cleared."

"I'm assuming you are putting safeguards in place to keep Tom safe?"

"We will. But it's something we need to talk about," he added, turning to Tom. "Your cabin is so remote that, one, I doubt the Unsub knows where it is, although Burt Thompson found it easily enough, and two, it will be difficult for me and my agents to guard it. Do you have an alternate location we could set you, and ourselves, up better?"

Tom nodded. "I have another cabin I haven't lived in for the last several years. It's kept up and is easily accessible but also can't be seen from the road and has forest all around it. It would probably work a lot better. And I can go there tonight if you want. I'd like to go back to the place I live now first, though. I need to."

Thorne nodded. "Understandable. No problem. Give me the address, and I'll get my men out there to set things up. I'd like to put listening devices in the cabin. If the Unsub shows up while you're gone, we'll have ears listening in, if while you're there, we'll know to move fast. I'm going to have John Grammar give a press conference after your hearing in the morning, too. I want him to let it be known that you've been released but are still considered a person of interest in the other cases.

"I'll check, but if you have a regular address at the cabin we're using, it won't be hard for anyone who really wants to, to find it. They may even set themselves up to watch when you leave the courthouse. Be careful, but don't be obvious by looking around for them. We'll have plenty of people doing that."

Tom nodded.

"Well, let me write this down so you will have it on you, just in case, though I don't expect you to need it tonight."

Tom watched as the judge took a plain piece of copier paper and began writing. "What is that?"

"It just says you have been released from jail on your own recognizance but agree to appear in court at nine tomorrow morning." He signed his name and stamped it with a seal and held it out for Tom.

Tom took it and relief swamped him. "Thank you."

The judge stood, as did Tom and the agent. "No. Thank you, Tom. Again, I'm sorry about everything that has happened, but we really appreciate your help. If Gavin White can be found alive...."

"That's all the thanks I'll need," Tom finished quietly. He shook hands with the judge and then followed Bret Thorne from the chambers.

The night was so much quieter in town that Tom couldn't wait to get back to his home so the frogs and crickets could celebrate his release with him. But more than anything he wanted to get through what he knew would be a long night alone, as well as court in the morning, because he needed to contact Garrison White and find out where Destiny was staying. And then move her into what would from now on be their home, not just his.

****

"I think she's dead! *What did you do to her?*"

Destiny's spirit entered her body just in time to hear the horrified voice asking the question. As she was always a little disoriented when she first merged, she wasn't able to question who was talking about whom to find out who they were talking about.

"I didn't do anything to her. I just locked her to the chair!"

Oh. Me! Knowing it would be completely inappropriate to laugh as she opened her eyes, Destiny conquered her amusement and peeked. She jerked back as the face of the woman officer was only inches away from her own. She stretched back even more, wanting to put distance between them, as she suddenly felt ill again.

"There you are! Are you okay?"

"Move over!"

As Officer Gishwell moved back, Captain Grammar squatted down in front of her. Destiny sighed and relaxed as her stomach settled some.

"Miss Cavanaugh, are you ill?"

Destiny nodded then shook her head then nodded again. "I don't feel very well."

His look of concern put her at ease until the other officer moved closer, and her stomach lurched. She looked over at her with a glare, and the woman backed away, eyeing Destiny warily.

"Do you want me to call emergency services so we can have you checked out?"

Destiny shook her head. "No, but can you get this thing off me?"

John Grammar looked at her cuffs then turned to the woman officer. "Give me your key."

Irritation lit the woman's eyes as she pulled the keys from her belt. "She was causing problems, Captain, when all the commotion was going on. I finally had to cuff her to get her out of the way."

He looked back at Destiny. "I'm guessing you're Tom Whitehawk's Miss Cavanaugh?" he asked as he released her wrists.

Destiny grinned, liking the sound of that. "Yes. Where is he?"

The captain looked back at the woman who was

hovering just a few feet away. "Go get Miss Cavanaugh a bottled water from the machine."

The officer nodded and walked away and suddenly Destiny felt a whole lot better.

"Bret Thorne took him away earlier. I don't expect him back here tonight. Is that why you came?"

Destiny nodded, trying to hide her disappointment. She had no idea where to look for him now. "Yes. If that woman had just told me, I would have left. She gives me the creeps."

The captain smiled. "She gives everyone the creeps, but you didn't hear it from me. The good news is that she's put in her notice. She's moving out of Mystic Waters in a couple of weeks."

They both stopped talking as she returned with the water. "Here you go. If that's all you need from me, Captain, I'll head home and get us some dinner before I get back to packing."

The captain nodded before turning back to Destiny then a questioning expression crossed his features, and he turned back to Kathy Gishwell. "I didn't know you lived with anyone."

Destiny watched as the woman's aura exploded in dark matter before her face relaxed into a smile. "Why yes, my...husband."

The captain stood and faced her, his brows furrowed. "You've never mentioned a husband. And I don't remember seeing you were married in your employee file. I just looked it over so I could have it ready if you needed a recommendation letter sent."

She smiled then and everything inside of Destiny cringed.

"Oh, well, we aren't officially married anymore and haven't been for years. It's been one of those on again off again relationships, which is very much on again as long as he behaves, but no matter what, I always think of him as my husband.

"Well, good night!" She smiled broadly at her boss

then sent a less than friendly look Destiny's way before turning to walk away.

"Wait! I'll need to add this to the history in your file. What's his name?"

At John Grammar's question she hesitated then smoothly spun around. "Jimmy. Jimmy Gishwell." She spun in the direction of the doors and nearly skipped her way out of the police station.

Destiny watched her departure as her mind churned. She looked over to the captain once the woman was out the door. "Am I free to go?"

John nodded. "Of course. Do you need a ride?"

Destiny shook her head. "No, thank you. I have my car."

He smiled at her, but Destiny could tell his mind was somewhere else, and she wondered if it had taken the same path hers had. It killed her that she would have to wait to find Tom, but right now she needed to talk to her sisters.

Desperately.

Chapter Twelve

Gavin couldn't believe he'd finally found the camera. He felt stupid for not having thought of it long ago since the view from the air-conditioning vent likely covered most of the room. It gave him the creeps to know she had the camera directly across from his bed at the top of the wall near the ceiling.

Because of the things she'd said or hinted at since day one, he'd known to be afraid she could see everything he did no matter where he was in the room. He'd been as careful as he could be not to do anything to get himself into trouble.

Now that he was *certain* she had a bird's eye view of him in his bed, creepy crawly things had his stomach doing back flips. The only possible silver lining was that his dad taught him all about taking pictures, and he knew there was a good chance she couldn't see the extreme corners of the bedroom. But he'd have to get a better look at the camera to determine that and then assess how it could benefit him.

The only refuge he'd had was the bathroom; although he *had* always worried she had a camera in there too. So the wonderful showers he took, or when he had to relieve himself, were never completely peaceful experiences either.

Well, he had had enough of being looked at and, he feared now, *lusted after* as well.

It always made him mad to know she could watch him any time she wanted. It was even worse knowing, now, for sure, that she saw him on the mornings when he awoke hard.

He'd been dreaming a lot lately, often more than once a night. The dreams always started out as a mixture of happy dreams about his parents but had grown into hot dreams that stirred him like he expected to be stirred had he actually gotten to live the experiences he was dreaming about.

Mostly they took him back to the time before this nightmare began, when he was just a normal teenage boy.

In them all he was still living in the home he'd been taken to following his birth in the local hospital, and his mom and dad would still be alive. His dad would cut up and joke with him like he always had, and his mom would hug him and tell him he was getting too tall and that she didn't want her baby to grow up too fast.

Variations of the same dream he'd have as often was of him with his friends. Sometimes they would be playing ball and joking around, and sometimes his dreams mixed with actual memories of Joe, Jacob and himself, and lots of his friends and more distant cousins swimming in Mystic Lake. Yet every time he'd dream of having fun with his friends, he'd still feel the need to look for his parents. Once he'd spot them, the relief, knowing his kidnapping and their murders had only been a nightmare, would wash over him in waves.

Every night the dreams started the same way. But each night, once he felt the security of his parents' presence, he would venture away from them eventually, and his mind would seek Kaylee. Then every thought, every scene that played out in his head, was about her.

Those were the dreams no one else had a right to know about, especially not the woman whose attention was starting to really scare him.

In the dreams he'd never gotten bolder than kisses and copping a feel, but he'd still wake up with his pajama bottoms tented and his male parts aching, and more and more lately he'd given in and relieved himself of the pressure, either in the bed beneath the sheets, or after making his way into the shower.

It sickened Gavin to think Ma'am had watched over him while he was taking care of his needs. Even though she wouldn't have *seen*, she would have known what he was doing from movements beneath the sheets and when he'd doubled over and cried out his pleasure.

It was stupid of him to forget even for a moment he was being watched, and now that Ma'am was starting to act like she might be interested in him in *that way*, he knew he had to get out as fast as possible.

If she *ever* tried to touch him like that, Gavin knew one of them would end up dead.

The only bright spot in all this mess was that he'd already determined he had to get out as quickly as possible, even before finding the camera was trained directly on his bed. He felt he was a little ahead of where he otherwise would have been.

He'd spent the past week learning to judge when Ma'am was at home and when she was gone. With the television turned down as low as he could get it, but was still loud enough he could pretend he was listening to it, Gavin concentrated hard to keep his attention focused on the sounds from outside of his room. And his efforts had paid off.

Now he knew when Ma'am was walking somewhere close inside the house even when she wasn't heading to his room, as her bare feet made a slightly dull sound on the hardwood flooring, and somewhere close to his door, it even squeaked.

Gavin was certain the sound of a heavy water flow changing to a spray indicated she was showering in the room immediately to the left of his door, and his best guess was that her tub abutted the wall backing his shower. And though he had no idea if it was a personal bathroom within a bedroom like his was, or if it was a common bathroom just opening out into the hall, at least he knew when she was in there and not roaming the house freely.

The more he'd listened, the more he'd learned, and he tried to not only identify the sounds but to also gauge their distance and direction in relationship to his room.

The spray followed by agitation followed by a spin cycle that ended with a beep told him the laundry room was a bit of a distance away, but probably on the right side of the hallway with at least one room separating it from his own.

The smells of cooking food—which had gotten better and was being delivered at a more consistent time for the past week—added to the occasional tinkling sound of dishes hitting each other and the clanging of utensils or pans, told Gavin the kitchen was a little further way from the laundry area. He was pretty sure it was on the left side of his room, likely beyond the room or maybe even a couple of rooms away from where Ma'am showered.

But the most exciting discovery had only happened a couple of days before.

As thrilled as he was to have discovered a good portion of the house's layout, or at least what his mind told him was the house's layout, he'd worried over not knowing when Ma'am came in or went out of the house because he never heard the opening or closing of a door, except before and after hearing the sound of her shower. Since he'd been blindfolded and very ill upon his arrival, Gavin hadn't had a clue where the door or *doors* leading to the outside of the house were. As hard as he'd tried, he couldn't remember if she'd led him straight through the house, or if she'd made turns before delivering him to the bedroom that first day. He'd searched his memories many times, since there was little reason to attempt to escape only to get trapped in another area of the house.

Gavin remembered his mother once saying there was nothing better than a happy accident. At the time he'd asked if she was talking about him since he'd known he wasn't planned. But she had laughed and said that no, he was a happy surprise, not a happy accident. She went on to explain that when something that shouldn't have happened did, and then it turned out to be a good thing, that was a happy accident. And that was exactly what dropping his breakfast napkin a couple of mornings before had been.

The thin paper hadn't had enough weight to just drop straight down to the floor. Instead it fluttered and glided until it was close to his bedroom door. After he'd climbed off his bed to retrieve it, he noticed it still fluttered just a little.

Curious, but not making the connection, Gavin bent over to grasp it, but before he could the paper lifted slightly and flew back toward his bed. Fleetingly he'd wondered if Ma'am was playing a trick on him so he'd stayed where he was and just looked at it. It was then he realized that there was a rush of warm air coming from beneath his door, flowing over his bare feet.

A whooshing suction sound stopped the airflow. He'd looked quickly and watched as the napkin finally settled. His heartbeat had increased and his body shook in excitement, but he'd forced himself to calm down and think.

The conclusion he'd drawn nearly made him cry, as he'd been certain he had finally discovered the door that would lead to his freedom. As the flow of air had been quite heavy he was sure the door was directly in front of his own, which meant his bedroom was at the very end of the hall. That also explained the reason other sounds seemed to lean to the left or the right of his room!

He'd been so giddy he'd gotten lost in the wonder of the discovery. It was some time before he'd realized what he'd discovered meant Ma'am had left the house. He'd almost laughed at himself and reached for his doorknob until he realized he couldn't react. Not then, and not until he figured out how to get past all the locks she kept adding to his door.

If he hadn't caught himself, and Ma'am happened to watch that part of the video when she'd returned, then she would have known he'd learned something new, and she'd be in his face. So Gavin had acted dumb for the camera she'd said she had on him and pretended like he couldn't figure out what to make of the napkin's movements. Then he had prayed she'd be dumb enough to buy it.

Which was how he'd behaved ever since.

With his poor-stupid-me act fully in play, now, Gavin didn't attempt to get to the camera. He didn't even look at it again. Instead he went through his workout routine, took a shower, then spent the rest of the day pretending to watch the television while he mulled over plans of action that would lead to his freedom. He discarded as many possibilities as he felt had promise; the biggest obstacle to all of them, outside of being caught while attempting to escape, was the locks on his bedroom door. As hard as he tried, he just couldn't figure out a way to get the door open without breaking through it, and there was nothing in his room that would aid in that.

Frustrated, Gavin turned off the television, climbed off the bed, and stretched to get some of the kinks out of his body. He headed to the linen closet in the bathroom to retrieve the sheets Ma'am bought, washed, and brought to him the day before, glad that he'd finally get to change from the ones he'd slept between since arriving.

He tugged off and folded the light blanket he used as a bedspread before reaching for the top corner of the fitted sheet to pull it away from the mattress. Gavin didn't know what it was that caught his eye, but he found himself studying the shape of what he'd believed was nothing more than a recessed section of wall like the one Jason's mom once told him was a niche. She had used the one in their living room to display family photos, except at Christmastime when she'd set up a little Nativity scene in there and run tiny white lights and a fake garland around the arched exterior of the hollowed-out wallboard. He'd thought it pretty cool at the time, but Jason said it was just another place to have to dust when it was his turn to dust the living room.

Gavin sighed, wondering what his friend was doing...what all of his friends were doing, and wondered if they ever still thought of him.

Remembering the camera was aimed straight at him and realizing he'd probably been lost in thought and standing there for too long, he pulled the sheets from the bed and dropped them on the floor. He fretted over what Ma'am would think if she watched the video and saw him standing there that long, but there was something about the way the niche was made that bothered him.

Inspiration struck. Gavin ran his finger over the low metal headboard of the bed as he angled his body so that the camera would catch him lifting his finger to inspect it. Thinking he'd found the perfect reason to spend some time looking the wall over, Gavin went to his bathroom and returned with a washcloth. He put his back to the camera and ran the cloth slowly over the square frame and then up and down the round metal bars that ran vertically within the square, followed by a flat piece of steel that ran through and around the bars as if needed for stabilization. Since his pillows and the raised angle of the bed were always blocking the view of the headboard he'd never paid any attention to the design.

While his hands were busy performing for Ma'am's camera, his mind processed how much the headboard resembled the bars of the jail cells his dad had shown him once, when he'd visited him at work. Since he'd asked to see them, and the Mystic Waters Police Department wasn't housing any prisoners at the time, his dad took him back to take a look.

Gavin tried to ignore the goose bumps that suddenly raised the hair on his arms and the chills that ran up his spine. He rarely forgot for even a minute that he was nothing more than a pampered prisoner, but having it thrown in his face made him want to hit something.

He pushed his anger down and kept dusting as he turned his attention back to the wall. Not only did the recessed area look to be about the size of a small window, the paint within it was a slightly different shade of the same color as the rest of the room. He knew if he wasn't standing so close, he'd never have noticed the minute difference.

Gavin's hand itched to touch the wall and to inspect the area more closely, but he had no idea what view the camera's angle actually provided Ma'am. He continued to dust over the same areas he'd already dusted as he tried to build up the nerve to take a chance. But wishing he had the nerve to pick at the corner of it to see if what he suspected was true, and actually doing it, could be the difference between life and death.

Mine.

He swallowed, biting his bottom lip until it hurt as he fought the urge to throw caution to the winds. The possibility he was very close to an avenue of escape made his knees knock together when his body started trembling. He studied every inch of it, noticing that unlike the smooth transition from flat wall to recessed wall at Jason's house, the transition here wasn't as smoothly accomplished. If he wasn't mistaken, there was an itty-bitty piece of drywall tape peeking out at the bottom right corner that hadn't been completely mudded over. He only knew that because he'd taken a handyman course at school as an elective, and one of the lessons had been on replacing drywall.

Excitement made his heart pound and he knew he was going to lose it if he didn't calm down. That thought had barely registered when there was a hard thump on the wall. Gavin jumped and stepped back to stand frozen as he waited in fear for Ma'am to come in and tell him she knew what he was up to. When he didn't hear the locks clicking, and she didn't appear after several seconds, he allowed himself to relax a little.

That was a mistake.

His knees nearly gave and his body shook so hard he knew his fear had turned into a delayed reaction of panic. Tears brewed and his throat closed, making him lightheaded. He tried to gather the strength to make it to the foot to his bed, but his body wouldn't cooperate and he landed on the floor at its side. Pain tore through his shoulder where it hit the lowered rail, and he screamed inwardly, not daring to make a sound.

Huffing through the pain, he tried to think, and to get his body under control, but neither seemed a possibility at the moment. He gave up and lowered himself slowly until his back was flat against the floor. He forced his mind to regulate his breathing until his body relaxed. Though it took what seemed like an endless amount of time, he eventually had enough strength to roll onto his side, then his stomach. Using all his remaining strength, Gavin pulled himself up and rolled onto the bed.

The house seemed very quiet. So quiet in fact Gavin was worried.

More and more lately there was always something making noise outside of his room, and he'd been so intent to discover Ma'am's routine and her placement in the house at any given time that he came to look forward to the sounds that happened at around the same time each day.

Even though the sounds of her footsteps were never a reliable indication of anything, five days out of seven, about midway through the weekly morning news, he now knew the soft suction sound was her closing what he had come to think of as the front door. It was never done loudly, and had he not experienced the napkin-floating incident, he would have never even made the connection. From that point until several hours later when *Wheel of Fortune* came on, everything outside of his room would remain very quiet. Except on her days off. Then sounds would carry to him on and off throughout the day. Tomorrow wasn't a day off for her since only three of the five days had passed.

Being equal parts excited and fearful had Gavin so jittery he got off the bed and hit the floor to do a hundred pushups. When he finished those, he pushed his bed into the middle of the room and jogged around it without counting his laps until he thought he heard a sound.

He stopped abruptly and rolled the bed back into place. With sweat rolling down his face and coating his neck beneath his extremely long hair, Gavin headed to the bathroom for a quick shower. He'd been so busy plotting his escape, he'd forgotten to take one earlier, and the last thing he wanted was for Ma'am to ask why he'd completely changed his routine, especially after he'd spent so much time facing his wall while he'd dusted and re-dusted his headboard. He was pretty sure she still made a habit of scanning his day after being out, though she hadn't commented about anything he'd been up to lately.

But until today he hadn't really done anything to garner her attention either.

If he could make it happen, and he was certainly going to try, tomorrow was going to be his Fourth of July. And Gavin could hardly wait to celebrate his independence day.

****

Kathy Gishwell pulled into the driveway furious with herself, wondering why she'd felt the need to rub her victory into the captain's face. It was a stupid thing to do, and her reaction to his simple question could have been deflected as a slip of the tongue and nothing else. It was that woman's fault. Her superior attitude was bad enough, but Kathy's irritation had reached its limit over the reaction her captain and every other man had when in contact with those sisters. Men fell all over themselves to please the triplets, and she'd finally just had it.

After being so careful all these years and never giving any indication she was anything but on the up-and-up, Kathy's gut churned, as she was really concerned. John Grammar had looked at her funny after she'd spouted that bit about having a husband who wasn't a husband, and that Cavanaugh woman had looked at her with suspicion too.

Kathy entered the house as quietly as she could and went straight to the room where she kept the surveillance equipment. The kid was coming out of the bathroom pulling a shirt over his head. His long hair looked wet as it hung down past his shoulders. She studied him for a minute then turned the monitor off and headed for a shower of her own. She would check out his day later, after she got them something to eat. With all that had happened during the day, she'd ended up working well past her shift and she was hungry. And she was sure he was too.

For the first time in hours, Kathy smiled to herself. He was growing at a rapid rate, and those chest muscles and tight abs she saw before he pulled down the pajama top made her heart beat a little faster. Maybe she wouldn't have to wait quite as long to teach him how to please her as she'd first thought. From the looks of him, he wasn't really a kid anymore.

But first she had to figure out what to do.

With nearly a week and a half still left to work at the station to cover the two weeks' notice she'd handed in just a couple of days before, Kathy now had to consider the option of telling the captain she'd have to leave earlier. But she wasn't prepared to move the kid yet, and she was really depending on a good recommendation to get her into the next job.

Being a law enforcement officer was the sweetest gig she'd ever had. It sure beat the hell out of stripper and cocktail waitress, and since she'd accidently killed Jimmy, it had also provided her with an opportunity to see if she was being pursued before anyone else got a chance.

The captain never realized her taking control of the fax machine feed-outs before everything was sent in email form was because she had needed that control all those years ago. He probably had figured she was just a rookie trying to impress the boss, and she'd let him believe it. It was no skin off her teeth if he was as gullible as the rest of them. The only one who had ever wanted to look at the *Wanted* posters as much as she had was the man now in custody for the murders of the parents of her new *Jimmy*.

After years went by, and by the time *Wanted* posters came through the Internet and went directly to the captain, she hadn't worried about it quite as much. Seven years was a long time, and she hadn't seen even a hint of herself being pursued. At one point she'd wondered if it had been a waste of time and money buying the illegal documents to use her long-deceased mother's name. She'd done so because she had access to her mother's personal information, as well as the bank account that she still used.

But she lived by the creed *Better Safe than Sorry*, and at this point she never thought of herself as anyone but Kathy Gishwell.

It had just been lucky when she applied for the job that

the captain who had hired her left the job immediately afterwards, and Captain Grammar made assumptions her records checked out, as best she could figure, because he'd never questioned her education or employment documents.

Kathy just hoped her stupidity didn't cause the captain to look back at her records too hard now or, more importantly, to dig beyond that. If he did and confronted her, she'd have a mess to clean up that wouldn't end too well for either of them.

She'd always had a sixth sense about when it was time to move on, and she just didn't have time to bury another body on top of packing up and somehow getting her boy to go peacefully. If it hadn't been for that *redhead*, she wouldn't be in this mess.

Damn that Cavanaugh woman for finding those bodies to begin with!

Kathy retrieved dry pasta and laid it on the counter before opening a jar of spaghetti sauce that she dumped into crock cookware. She stuck it in the microwave and set the temperature and timer then filled a pan with water and placed it on the stovetop. As she waited for the water to boil she went back to check on Jimmy again, but he was doing what he always did, which was lay on his back and watch TV, and she wondered how the little bit of exercise he did kept him in such good shape.

On her way back to the kitchen, Kathy stopped and turned to go back and look again. Since she'd had the kid for so long now, she didn't really spend that much time watching him anymore. She'd glance at the monitor each day and watch just long enough. Then she could comment on something that would keep him aware she could see his every move, though she'd had so much to do lately she hadn't really even done that for some time. But maybe that was a mistake. What if he was doing things he shouldn't be doing and she hadn't watched long enough to catch him?

The last thing she needed with a suspicious captain was to have the kid causing her problems.

Kathy heard the timer buzz and knew the sauce was

ready. She bit her bottom lip and then headed back to the kitchen. She would get their meal finished, eat, and then she would spend as long as she needed watching to see what was what. If he was behaving himself, as she believed, then all she had to focus on was getting them out of there as quickly as possible. If he wasn't, she would have to leave Mystic Waters without him.

What a shame it would be to have to leave him behind after all my hard work. What a shame it would be to have to cut him into little tiny little pieces, when he's grown into such a nice-looking young man.

Kathy approached the stove and frowned. As she registered that the pasta still had several minutes left to boil she heard the buzzing again and realized it was her cell phone. She hurried across the room as her stomach tightened. No one ever contacted her at this time of night, and she feared it might be the captain asking questions she had no intention of answering.

She dug through her little purse quickly and pulled it out. Her stomach eased some; it was only a group text message from the sergeant. She read it quickly, and her stomach eased even more. As she thought about the coming change in her work routine, she smiled, and as her thoughts turned to the reason for it, excitement made all other thoughts fly away.

Apparently there was to be an early morning hearing involving her landlord, and those in charge were concerned a rowdy and possibly dangerous crowd would appear. They were calling everyone in to work crowd control.

Kathy laughed out loud and quickly put the kid's meal together. As she threw crackers and a couple of canned soft drinks onto the tray, she considered her next move. By the time she'd delivered his meal, told him good night, and turned up the television to mask any sounds of her leaving, she had forgotten she'd wanted to check up on what he'd been doing all day.

Chapter Thirteen

Destiny hated to bother Garrison and Rayne, but she had no choice. If what she suspected was true, they needed to act as fast as possible. She had to get Rayne to come with her, and then they had to go get Haven.

The lights were low inside the cabin as she parked beside the old pickup. Wishing she had called just in case they were locked in a passionate embrace that would embarrass everyone, Destiny honked the horn and got out of the car. Relief washed over her as soon as Rayne opened the door. But Garrison was right behind her, and it was clear they were both ready for bed.

Destiny smiled as she approached the porch wishing she could telepathically communicate with her sisters like she did with Tom. Since that wasn't an option, she gave Rayne a look that had once been all the communication the sisters had needed.

Apparently it still worked because Rayne turned to Garrison and gave him a kiss. "Looks like Destiny needs me for a minute. I'll be inside shortly."

Garrison nodded and said, "Hi," before he turned back into the cabin.

As Destiny reached the porch, Rayne's brows lifted. "What's going on?"

"I think I know who has Gavin White."

Rayne moved forward quickly. "What? How?"

Destiny explained the entire experience she'd had from the time she reached the police department, until she left it, and Rayne's eyes got colder and colder as she listened.

"That bitch! I knew something was off every time I was close to her! We have to tell Garrison. We have to call Captain Grammar!"

Destiny caught Rayne's arm as she started to turn back

to the front door. "And tell them what? That I think because this woman makes me feel sick to my stomach every time I'm near her she must be the kidnapper? No, Rayne, we have to get Haven, and we need to go to my place. The diaries are there. We need to look through them even if it takes all night until we can find a way to be sure."

Rayne nodded. "But wait! Can't you pull your out-of-body thing and find out?"

Destiny nearly groaned. "I wish I'd thought of it. I could have followed her when she left. But John Grammar was still talking to me about Tom, and I was so busy trying to get over the nausea that it didn't occur to me."

Rayne looked at Destiny closely. "Are you okay now?"

Destiny nodded. "I'm fine. My stomach still hurts, but that will go away. Can you come with me?"

Rayne nodded. "Of course. Let me go tell Garrison you need me for a while. Hopefully he won't question it because I frankly have no idea what to say."

Destiny nodded and headed back to the car after the first few drops of rain hit her head. She got in and put the top up and waited. Fortunately, Rayne had a small bag in her hand when she stepped out onto the porch. Garrison stepped out too and waved to her, and then gave Rayne a kiss.

Destiny looked away to give them privacy, wondering if the time would come when she could feel the touch of Tom's lips against hers. When Rayne got in the passenger seat, she let thoughts of him slide away and backed out of the driveway. Within a couple of minutes, they were both standing on Haven's porch.

"I asked Garrison to call Logan to tell him we needed Haven for the night, and also because if I know her, they are hot and heavy at it."

Destiny hid her grin. "Good thinking. I was afraid that may have been what you were up to too, but didn't think about it until I was already there."

Rayne shrugged. "We have a great love-life. Unfortunately it's tempered by the chaos going on.

Garrison has been sick with worry for months now, but with all that's gone on in the last several weeks, and today in particular, it's like he's just completely worn out."

"That's understandable."

"Yeah.

"I know he's glad at least one case is solved, but finding out about Burt Thompson's involvement has revived the pain of losing his brother and sister-in-law all over again. He told me he had to stop mourning and start searching when Gavin went missing. I think he left it there through all that's happened since.

"I try, but I don't feel like I help ease his suffering much, although he says I do. If you're right and we can get Gavin back, it will make all the difference in the world. I just pray we can do it quickly."

Destiny nodded then knocked on the door. "Me, too. That woman has turned in her notice at work and is leaving Mystic Waters soon. If she has Gavin we have to hurry before she takes him away…or kills him."

Haven opened the door with a sheet wrapped around her, and it was clear that was all she had on. Her hair was a disheveled, her lips swollen, and she had the indication of a hickey on her collarbone. Rayne looked over at Destiny with annoyance, which almost made her smile, but at the moment little seemed amusing.

Before either sister could speak, Haven stepped out and closed the door behind her. "If you could have just given me about five more minutes.…"

Rayne looked her up and down. "Sorry to interrupt your fun, but you need to get dressed and come with us."

Haven laughed at that. "Like hell!"

Destiny stepped forward. "I'm sure I know who has Gavin White, but I need you two to help me get him back."

The laughter fled from Haven's eyes immediately, and she glanced at Rayne who nodded solemnly. "I'll be quick. What do I tell Logan?"

"Tell him we have a family emergency, and you hope to be back by morning, but you aren't sure."

Haven hesitated then nodded at Destiny. "Okay. I'll be out as quick as I can." She turned to Rayne with a hopeful smile. "This is great news. It's going to be okay."

Rayne sent her a small smile in return before Haven reentered the cabin. They turned to make their way back to the car as the raindrops increased in both size and speed. Both ran when the sky opened up. What had threatened to be an annoyance turned into a downpour.

Soaked, Destiny jumped in the driver's seat, and Rayne pushed the passenger seat up and climbed into the back. Destiny started the car and turned on the wipers and then the defroster when their warm breaths caused the windows to fog. Less than five minutes later Haven stepped onto the porch. Destiny watched through the downpour as she stopped then slowly walked down the steps as she made her way to the car.

"Look at that!" Destiny said in wonder. "It isn't raining on her!"

For the first time since she'd been picked up, Rayne laughed. "Oh yeah, there is still so much we have to catch up on."

Haven opened the door and got in. She smiled over at Destiny then laughed. "You aren't the only one with special abilities."

Destiny looked into the rear view mirror and smiled at Rayne. "You're right. We do have a lot to talk about."

There wasn't much talking as Destiny made the drive back to her cabin. The wind increased, and the rain was nearly horizontal by the time she parked the car. This time Haven was nice enough to share her invisible umbrella. All three sisters got to the porch as dry as they'd been in the car.

After unlocking and opening the door, Destiny flipped the light switch, but nothing happened. She flipped it a couple more times but it made no difference. "Damn! Electricity is off."

Haven pushed past her and entered the dark cabin and rubbed her hands together. "Do you have candles?"

Destiny watched as her sister's hands began to glow, and she knew they needed to have a talk immediately. "Yes. Two large ones behind you on the table and a couple more on the kitchen counter."

Using the light from the flow of her hands Haven walked to each candle and touched the wick with her index finger and thumb. One after another the flames shot up then settled to put out a soothing glow.

Destiny turned to Rayne. "You didn't tell me she could do that!"

Rayne shrugged. "Actually, I didn't know myself. But it's a handy little trick."

They both turned to Haven as she approached them with the candles from the kitchen. "Here, take one." They both did then she lifted one of the others and turned to Destiny. "What do you want us to do?"

"Well, first of all I want you to tell me how you can stop rain from falling on your head, and how you can light these candles with hands that had only once healed."

"Oh, that's easy. I'm trying new stuff all the time. I figured if I can call in a storm and then can control the aspects of it, I should be able to do the same even if the storm isn't of my making. And since my hands are capable of burning flesh now, I figured they could start fires. So I was right on both counts."

"That's amazing." Destiny turned to Rayne. "What about you?"

Rayne shrugged. "I don't know. I'm beginning to wonder if I've completely lost the ability to do anything. I don't even see my Indian guide anymore. And he was the only ghost who has spoken to me since I moved here. I'm a little bummed about it."

Without thinking Destiny sent waves of sympathy to her sister. She was surprised when Rayne's eyes lit up and she quickly looked her way.

"Did you just do something? I suddenly felt your spirit touch me."

Destiny laughed. "Looks like I can radiate my feelings

as well as my body."

Rayne smiled. "Well, thanks. I suddenly feel…I don't know, *all tingly* and warm inside."

Haven looked from one to the other. "Seriously? You were able to help Rayne? That's never happened before."

All three sisters sat in stunned silence before Destiny remembered their purpose. "Okay, that *is* weird. But we'll have to think about that later. Right now we need to figure out what we are going to do to get Gavin White back. I was hoping we could look through all the unread diaries to see if we can find a locator spell.

"Rayne, if what you said you and Haven discovered before is true—and it seems so even more now than ever, that means I'm *Divine* like Aunt Soleli, and able to discover the truth even if it requires me to travel through space and time, (although I haven't tried time yet). Haven is the Regulator, and is able to take control of the elements and the earth, like Aunt Lune Brille. I think there is the very real possibility you are more like Momma than you know. As the Enchantress, you should be able to cast spells.

"*What if* it were possible to conjoin our powers and compound the strength of yours? Do you think you might be able to locate Garrison's nephew?"

"Wouldn't it just be easier to ask for her address from Captain Grammar? Or look her up on the Internet?"

Destiny frowned at Haven. "Sure. Do you want to be the one to tell him why we need to find one of his employee's home addresses?"

The affront on Haven's face made Destiny regret her harsh words. "I'm sorry. But we can't involve anyone else until we are sure I'm right. I know in my heart I am. But we have to make sure. If we make a false accusation against her, and I'm by some chance reading this all wrong… Well, it will just be bad."

"I guess she's right," Rayne said, her eyes distant. "Although it isn't *that* bad of an idea."

"Why are you even thinking about another option? Don't you want to be able to make magic?" Destiny asked.

Rayne looked from one sister to the other. "I really do. I just don't know if I'm willing to risk losing Garrison to have it."

Destiny sighed. "From all I've read in the diaries I've gotten through, it has been a tragic, sometimes *fatal*, mistake to assume love will conquer the fears that come when someone else can't comprehend the Cavanaugh gifts. So I think it would be a good idea for you both to practice your abilities in secrecy but not give them up.

"I made a terrible mistake thinking I could ever be normal. Because once I had no power, I realized I was nothing. We have to hone what gifts we are given, but until our dying days, it would be best to be careful. And whoever is the one to have children must teach them just like we were taught."

Destiny took a long slow breath as she watched her sisters' struggle with what would be a lifelong lie to the men they loved. It went against the grain for them all, but she hoped they understood that their very happiness, and the safety of all, would hang in the balance.

"What about Tom?" Haven asked.

Destiny shrugged. "He already knows. Not everything, of course. But he knows I have powers, and I bet he knows you do, too. He's no threat, not only because of his own powers, but because his spirit is pure and to harm another causes greater harm to himself than to anyone else.

"He will be the keeper of our secret and, I have no doubt, our protector should we need him to be."

"We need to swear on it," Rayne said, as her eyes filled with tears.

"I agree. Haven?"

Haven nodded slowly. "I agree too. I just hope I don't accidently do anything to expose us. At least I've gotten a lot better at controlling my gift now."

Destiny placed her candle on the coffee table before going into the kitchen for a paring knife. She returned and waited as Rayne and Haven lowered their candles, placing them against hers. She took a deep breath then gently ran the small blade across the veins at her wrist before holding it above the flame of her candle.

She bit back a moan as she passed the knife to Haven. Looking a little ill, she did the same before passing it on. Rayne followed suit before placing the knife on the table. Destiny watched as a blood drop plopped onto the flame of her candle and put it out then her sister's did the same over theirs.

With only the low light of the remaining candle illuminating the kitchen they stood, and Destiny placed her palm on Haven's thin wound then wrapped her fingers around her sister's wrist. Haven repeated the action with Rayne, and then Rayne with Destiny until each wound was covered and the three were connected.

Destiny looked at Rayne. "Seal our pledge."

Looking a little doubtful, Rayne closed her eyes. "On this night, in this place, and by our blood, I pledge upon threat of death to never divulge the gifts of our family to any other who does not share our blood or gifts, save Tom Whitehawk."

When Rayne opened her eyes, Destiny turned to Haven. "Your turn."

Haven repeated the pledge and then opened her eyes to look at Destiny. Smiling she closed her eyes. "On this night, in this place, and by our blood, I pledge upon threat of death to never divulge the gifts of our family to any other who does not share our blood or gifts, save Tom Whitehawk. And so it is, and so it shall be."

The lights came back on immediately and all three girls jumped. They looked at each other before they burst out laughing. "Well, we *were* being a little melodramatic!" Destiny said. "Serves us right.

"Now that we have electricity back, let's try something. Since I was able to transport my concern to Rayne a few minutes ago…Haven, see if you can heal our wounds."

Destiny held out her arm and so did Rayne. With a *here-goes* look, Haven placed her palms on her sister's wounds and folded her fingers around their wrists before closing her eyes. Destiny smiled at Rayne's look of surprise as the fire burning inside of their sister radiated from the connections, and warmed Destiny to her toes.

****

It was a good thing Destiny had planned for it to be an all-nighter, as it had taken the three of them an entire night, and a good two hours after the sun came up, of reading several different diaries apiece, before Rayne squealed in victory.

"I found it! I found it!"

"Thank God!" Haven said before dropping the book she was assigned.

Rayne frowned at her. "Hey, take better care with that!"

Haven closed the leather bound book as it landed open to the page she'd been reading before shoving it toward Destiny. With a sign she slumped back onto the couch. "*You* take care of it. For Pete's sake, most of this stuff is boring as hell. I was reading Citri Cavanaugh's diary. That woman detailed how often she had to take a crap and what color it was every day during the several months the family joined a wagon train heading west.

"I mean, seriously. The woman was obsessed with her poop!"

Rayne looked at Destiny. She shrugged as she gently laid the book aside. "Well, for the most part they *are* pretty boring, but every once in a while you get to really good stuff. The amount of sex in the one I'm reading right now would curl your toes."

Haven sat up quickly. "Give me that one."

Destiny laughed. "You can have it when I'm done. I'm getting some really good pointers here for when I finally get a chance to tackle Tom."

Rayne glared at both Haven and Destiny. "Would you guys stop? This is really important. I have to go back to my place and get a picture of Gavin, find some of his hair if I can, and grab a few other things. Then I'll be right back. This spell, if it works, looks really simple."

She smiled with excitement. "I think we might actually find him today," she said before grabbing her purse and racing toward the door.

In the ten minutes it took to get to her own cabin, Rayne worried about what she'd say to Garrison about the stuff she needed to gather, so it was a relief to find Garrison's cargo trailer gone. That meant he was gone, too, and no explanations were needed.

She wondered if he was finally getting a chance to deliver Tom's furniture even though she had no idea if Tom had been released—oh darn! She had forgotten he was supposed to be at court and she bet Destiny had too, or if Garrison simply knew where to take all those tables and chairs.

Or…maybe he was taking them for delivery after he attended the hearing… *Crap!*

Destiny was going to kill her and Haven.

Regardless, it freed her from having to make up something to cover what she and her sisters were doing. And as far as she knew, Tom was in the clear, so their mission took precedence anyway. And Garrison being gone, no matter where he was gone, was perfect!

Until she was certain they could locate Gavin, Rayne didn't want to get Garrison's hopes up. She didn't know how much more he could take. He was really starting to look way too old for his age, but even though she had tried to tell him without actually saying it outright, he either hadn't caught on or he just hadn't cared.

Rayne liked it that he wasn't vain in the least, but Garrison was still too young to look so worn out. If she could help bring his nephew back to him to alleviate some of his loss it would be the most important thing she'd ever done, not only for the kid, but for the man she loved.

Rayne entered the cabin and went straight to Gavin's room. Since Garrison's breakdown she had gone in while he was at the shop and completely cleaned the room. Having everything as it had been before he went on his mad searching spree was more to help him have peace than because it had so desperately needed it.

At the time she'd cleaned, she hadn't thought of the possibility of needing to have some of Gavin's hair for any reason, mostly because the possibility of her being able to cast and conjure hadn't been a thought. But now that she saw what her sisters were capable of, she knew she had to at least try to see if she was able to carry on the tradition of one of the three sisters being a…well…*witch.*

Rayne laughed at the thought as she searched around Gavin's desk, in his drawers, and finally on his bed. And there, in bookcase headboard was a simple black comb. And, *Wha-la,* the hair she so desperately needed.

Finding a picture of Gavin was simple. She had replaced hundreds of him at various ages with all his family photos in the dresser when she'd cleaned. Next she went into the little cubby on the desk where she'd seen the small bowl with the fingernail clippers and the fingernail clippings Gavin had left there before disappearing. While cleaning she had almost thrown them out but thought better of it, and now more than ever she was glad she did.

At the time her thought process had been only about Garrison, thinking if he had kept them for all the months he'd kept the dust out of the room, then she couldn't throw them out either. Now she knew Garrison's need to hang on to Gavin in any way would enhance the spell she was going to try to perform.

There are *no mistakes.*

Hearing Celestia Cavanaugh's voice stopped Rayne in her tracks. She had to take a moment to gather her wits so she walked the few steps to Gavin's bed and sat down.

"Momma?"

Mists of sparkling bright pinks and deep lavenders formed and swirled in circles a few feet in front of her and Rayne held her breath in awe. When her mother's beautiful face and lithe form solidified but was still transparent, Rayne's breath whooshed out in a sob. She stood and ran to her mother, only remembering to stop before going right through her.

Tears washed over her cheeks in an endless stream as she stared at the face that she hadn't seen for way too long. "You are so beautiful."

You, my love, are as beautiful as the fresh bloom of a rose, as are my other babies. It has been my joy to watch you three grow into such wonderful women, yet I worried over you all stifling your gifts to near nonexistence.

Celestia's hand extended to touch Rayne's cheek and wipe away her tears. Rayne felt the warmth of her touch and placed her hand on her mother's. Though she touched her own cheek she could feel her mother's spirit intertwine with her own.

"I have missed you so much!"

I am always with one of you girls, although you made it difficult when you separated. I am so joyous you are all back together again. You must never part by so large a distance. It weakens each of you, until your powers reach their full potential, as they are beginning to do now.

"Yes. We found that out the hard way. But I never lost my ability to speak with spirits from the other realm. It was only Haven and Destiny that lost their gifts. I even met an Indian that knew our ancestors."

Celestia smiled, her face filled with peace. *Ah, yes, your great-grandfather many times over. It was not by your will that Qaqeemasq came to you, but by his. He was a very powerful mystic when he lived, and is still, it would seem. Had you been able to call other spirits to you once you left your sisters?*

Rayne shook her head. "No. I thought that was also by my will, though, and have only questioned it recently.

"Are you saying that Qaqeemasq is family? Did he have children with Fawntain Cavanaugh?"

Celestia's smile deepened. *It is good that you studied the history I only learned of once I was on the other side. I should have taken the time to learn, but like Haven, I was too busy enjoying the fruits of the flesh.*

"There is no easy way to ask this, Momma, but did you ever regret knowing our father?"

Something you will learn with time, my child, is that what is meant to be is meant to be. If I had lived and had more time to raise you girls, I would have spoiled you rotten and probably made you selfish. My dearest sisters are forever my champions. They taught you three the most important things about being a Cavanaugh, and that is service to others and kindness to all. Even while denying your gifts all three of you girls chose to help others, even when it was at such great cost to yourselves.

"You helped others too. It isn't fair that we lost you so long ago. We needed you so much. Destiny most of all!" Rayne's tears reignited as hurt and anger replaced the joy of seeing her mother again.

My love, do not weep. I made a decision that ended badly for us all for a time. But you would not be here and neither would your sisters if I hadn't fallen in love with your father. He was so good to me every moment we were together. But once he found out I was capable of magic, he became frightened. His act was not intentional; he never meant to harm me and he has paid a great price for his actions. Perhaps one day you will seek to know him better.

Rayne was certain her heart had stopped. "You mean he is alive?"

Light laughter filled the room, bathing Rayne in happy memories. Her mother was a woman of joy, and she had laughed often.

Indeed, my love. He is here in Mystic Waters. Had you or your sisters read your more recent history, you would find that all roads lead us back here eventually. There is no greater power source for us than that which flows into the lake from a spring at the crest of the mountain. You only grew up across the country because I left him as soon as I found out I was with child. That's what Cavanaugh women do when they mate with mortal men, except in the rarest of cases.

Our highest calling is to protect our children, not only because it is instinctual, but also because there was only one of the three who ever gave birth, and the line could end so easily. I did my duty by leaving him. But I mourned the loss of him for years after your births, as he was a very good man, and the love of my life.

The night of my physical death, I was torn from him once again. Only the result was much worse than a loss of life.

I don't know what you remember of that time. I'm sure my

sisters sought to ease some of your pain, but I left you with my sisters and came back to Mystic Waters to gather crystals from deep within the mountain where it opened to the lake. There I saw him again as he was playing in the lake with his son.

Though my love for him had never waned, I still fought the urge to approach him and to try to rekindle his love for me. But I gave in to my desires and sought him out and found that he had never stopped loving me either.

He had only recently buried the woman he'd married on the rebound, and he was raising the child she'd had with her deceased first husband as his own. The trip, which should have only lasted a couple of days, turned into four, and our love built and burned like an inferno that was magical in its burning.

As woman-to-woman I can tell you now that he'd come home from work for lunch to be with me as we were together every moment we could steal. Since his child was at school we were together and locked in passion's embrace, but someone knocked on his bedroom door right as our love reached its peak. I was mindless with lust and riding an orgasm, and I thoughtlessly slammed all the doors in the house and locked them.

It was such a little thing, but it woke him from the passionate trance he'd fallen into, and he realized we were floating high above the bed. His reaction had been instinctual, and had resulted in my being thrown away from him to slam my head into his bedside table.

My sisters knew immediately that I was gone—as each of you will when one of the others passes—and they hid their grief while Lune Brille stayed with you girls, and Soleli rushed here in spirit and put him into a sleep. She had to put his child into a sleep as well since he was the one who had knocked on the door.

"Why was the boy home from school early?"

The child had only had a half-day at school that day. My love was so filled with thoughts of me he forgot the change in his child's schedule. So you see, I was entirely at fault for what happened. And yet he paid as big a price.

Rayne followed her mother's story wondering why the aunts had never told her or her sisters what had really happened. "Did he end up in jail?"

Celestia shook her head. *No. My sisters immediately made*

arrangements to hire a private airplane. Lune Brille stayed with you girls as Soleli flew across the country to get me. She basically hypnotized the pilot and other men into helping her remove me and get my body to the airport and onto the airplane, and even more people to clean up the scene. No one ever knew. Not even my love or the child he had made his son.

That is the price he paid… All his memories of me were washed away, even those from the time before your conception. But he didn't just lose me. He lost you girls, too. I had already decided I couldn't live without him ever again. I told him about his three baby girls, and he couldn't wait to meet you.

Rayne's heart broke for them both as one question collided with another in her mind. She knew her sisters had to be wondering what was taking so long, and she knew they would be upset that they weren't here with her once she told them, but there was one question that took precedence over all the others. "So who is he? Even if I can't tell him who I am, I need to meet him."

Celestia smiled so serenely Rayne couldn't help but smile back at her.

You already know him, and you already know he is a good man. John Grammar is his name.

Chapter Fourteen

Tom awoke slowly and stared at the ceiling of his little cabin. He hadn't meant to spend the entire night. He'd planned to be at the other one to welcome the agents who were going to set up the surveillance equipment so he could let them know where it was *not* acceptable to put the cameras. But it felt so great being in his own bed again that the lack of rest from being in the always lighted jail and with all the issues regarding Burt Thompson, his mind and body had just crashed the night before.

Now he was running late, though, and he needed to get ready and head to town for his hearing. Making short work of the trip to his shower-house, Tom scrubbed from head to toes as quickly as he could. Although he'd taken a quick shower the night before, just getting to shower in private and when he wanted to, rather than when he was told to, made taking the time worthwhile. He just couldn't wait for the hearing to be over so he could contact Garrison to ask him where his fiancée's sister was staying, if she wasn't staying with him and Rayne.

Destiny... he still couldn't wrap his mind around her name. He'd called for her that first time, without realizing, until she came, it was a mystical woman he'd been seeking. But not just any mystical woman, *his* Destiny.

Tom knew he could have never imagined what would happen when he'd decided to build the sweat tent to meditate, nor that The Great Spirit would send him a sign of what was coming, and the salvation that would follow, if indeed salvation was his to grasp.

He'd known trouble was coming. Everything inside of him that was normally filled with peace had been agitated and on high alert for months. At first he attributed it to his being one with the mountain. He had always felt her pain.

As body after body was discovered, it explained why Mother Mountain had wept and trembled.

But the extent of discontent had grown so steadily over the past several weeks that he'd come to wonder if what was coming was targeted at him specifically, rather than just an imbalance in his universe.

Now he knew that it was both things. But he hadn't known that at first.

Frank Whitehawk was, and always had been, considered a wise and good man, and no one understood that better than the son he'd raised. Tom had sought his father's council many times throughout his life when he couldn't pinpoint a problem or situation on his own, or if he'd just needed to work out a problem out loud. And this time had been no exception.

Frank had listened to Tom's explanation of all he'd felt and the strange dreams he'd had. As always his council was sound, and together they'd built the tent using lumber Mother Mountain had given up freely, and the well-tended animal skins Frank's father had passed down to Frank. And that Frank had now passed down to Tom.

He treasured those mementoes of his family's history, and he hoped to one day, now that he'd found the woman who knew his soul, to pass them down to their own son, or daughter; whichever was fine.

Once the sweat lodge was assembled and large, round, satiny smooth stones from the banks of the lake were gathered, Frank did what he'd always done and that was to step back and allow Tom to follow his own path.

Tom's need to call to those who had come before, to seek understanding through fasting and meditation and even submission as he sought The Great Spirit's power, resulted in that which he'd unknowingly sought.

He'd prayed and chanted for days until his body grew weak and his heart began to doubt that his questions would be acknowledged or answered. And just as he'd been about to give up The Great Spirit released the destiny he sought, though at the time he'd had no idea his destiny was a woman of flesh and bone, and that she would be that which he had called by name.

Destiny Cavanaugh was the most beautiful of creatures, and though one of an identical set of three, her beauty for him outshone the others because his heart was meant to see only hers. He was still uncertain how she was to play a part in finishing the quest he was on, but even if she was meant to be nothing more than the mate he'd always ached to know, then that would be more than enough.

Tom dried himself off and stepped from the shower wondering how late he might be. He hadn't meant to get lost in thought about the woman he couldn't wait to see again. But the last thing he needed was to miss the hearing that would set him on the new path he must take. And once everything was said and done then he would make Destiny his own.

Determined to hurry to his cabin and get dressed, he wrapped the towel around his waist and headed out the door at a jog. The hot pain at the back of his skull, and the flash of white before his eyes, was all he knew before everything went black.

****

Destiny was trying really hard not to get irritated. "What is taking Rayne so long?"

Haven glanced over from the diary she was reading and shrugged. "I don't know, but you're right, this ancestor was really something. It's a good thing she was discreet."

"You don't have to tell me. I read it. I can't imagine all those positions she tried out on those men are physically possible.

"Right now I just want to get to town to see about mine!"

Haven turned her attention back to the diary. "I guess it's a good thing this one wasn't in our direct line. Can you imagine what kind of life we'd be living now if our great-great-great grandmother was a madam?"

"Would you put that away? I think I hear a car."

Destiny kept waiting as the sound of an approaching vehicle finally rounded the line of forested land on either side of the long driveway. But the car wasn't Rayne's and it wasn't just a car, but a line of black SUVs.

"Crap! The FBI is here! We have to hide the diaries!"

Haven jumped up and started gathering as many as she could, and Destiny did the same. Together they replaced them in the suitcases as gently as possible, but with the need for speed, Destiny was worried about the lack of respect they were giving the family tomes.

They finished zipping the suitcases closed only seconds before the knock at the door. Sending Haven a *what-the-hell-is-this-about* look, she went to the door, pasted a smile on her face, and opened it.

"Hello. Can I help you?"

The agent was obviously as surprised to see her as she was to see him and it took him a minute to speak as he was looking at paperwork atop a clipboard. He finally looked up and *kind of* smiled.

"Hi. Is this Tom Whitehawk's cabin?"

It took Destiny a moment to respond as she watched four SUVs filled with as many agents stepping out to stand by their vehicles. She had forgotten the cabin she'd rented belonged to the man she planned to spend the rest of her life with, but she couldn't even let that sink in too deeply as her stomach was starting to churn. She flashed the agent a smile. "It is. But he's not here right now."

"I see. He's supposed to be in court right now. But he isn't there either."

A sick feeling washed over Destiny and her smile melted. "Wasn't he taken to the courthouse from the jail?"

The agent shook his head. "No, ma'am. He was released last night, and Special Agent Bret Thorne took him to his other cabin. He was supposed to have come here later last night, but a couple of agents were sent there when he didn't show up at court on time. Special Agent Thorne thought Mr. Whitehawk looked pretty worn out when he dropped him off. He figured Mr. Whitehawk might have decided to rest and then fell asleep. But I got word on the way over here that he isn't there. So I was expecting him to be here."

Haven appeared at Destiny's side. "What's going on?"

Destiny took a deep breath. "Tom's missing."

The sound of an approaching car had all the agents turning to see who was coming. Destiny tried not to let her disappointment show when she saw her sister's car and, seconds later, the wary look on Rayne's face through the windshield. No one spoke as Rayne left her car to join them on the porch.

"What's going on here?"

"Tom's missing." This time her voice shook, and the look of concern from both her sisters was the last thing she needed as tears began to flow.

"I hate to have to ask you this, ma'am, but do you know of any reason he would deliberately disappear when he has been cleared of the murder charges?"

Destiny shook her head. "No. It was our understanding he would be held overnight and released today at the hearing. If he was released last night, there is no way he would purposefully mess up putting an end to this."

"Are you aware, ma'am, that he is still being considered a suspect for the kidnapping of Gavin White and the murders of the other men found recently in the area?"

That didn't make any sense to Destiny at all. Had they talked about that at the meeting? She couldn't remember. Regardless, she knew Tom. If Tom could get to court this morning, no matter what the outcome would end up being, he would be there.

"Tom is a man of honor. He would have even shown up if he believed he wasn't going to be set free. I think you need to get busy and find out what has happened to him. If the kidnapper thinks he's going to be set free, that person may be responsible for his disappearance. What could make him look guiltier than not showing up for his hearing?"

The agent nodded with a look of respect in his eyes. "That's what we have deduced also, ma'am. I can assure you we will do everything possible to locate him quickly. But just in case, the agents in the last two cars are prepared to set up the surveillance equipment Mr. Whitehawk was expecting. Do you mind if they go ahead?"

Surveillance equipment? "Um, no, I guess not. Not if Tom already approved it."

The agent nodded and walked back toward the SUVs as Rayne turned to her. "Destiny, listen. We have to get this spell going quickly now. Gavin was kept alive for a long time, and I feel he still is, but if this person has Tom, I don't know that they would chance keeping a full grown man alive."

"But we can't do it here. And the book with the spell is in the suitcase. Haven and I put them all back in there when we realized the FBI was coming up the drive."

Rayne bit her bottom lip then released it as she kept her focus on Destiny. "I think I remember it all. If we can get to Tom's old cabin, I think our chances of locating him are even better than using the locator spell to find Gavin.

"I've never met Gavin, and other than concern because he's Garrison's nephew, I have no real connection to him. But you have a strong one with Tom. Your soul crossed a continent to get to him. If we can get some of his personal belongings, especially those that came from his body like hair or fingernails, or even dead skin cells on a washcloth or towel he used, I believe we can locate him quickly. If the same person who has him has Gavin, then we're good. If it isn't the same one, then we'll do Gavin's as soon as we find and rescue Tom. I really feel Tom is in more danger at the moment."

Destiny nodded then hugged her sister. She was going to tell her she agreed, but four agents arrived on the porch and waited for them to move away from the door. "Excuse us, ladies."

Destiny stepped back and so did Rayne, but Haven stayed where she was and smiled at them. "I hope you don't plan on putting cameras in the bathroom or master bedroom."

The agent was young, and to Destiny's amazement, he blushed as he shook his head.

"No, ma'am. Just in the main areas of the house. We understand you and Mr. Whitehawk will require a degree of privacy."

Haven didn't correct his assumption and neither did Destiny. She sent Haven a smile as her sister stepped out of the way and allowed the agents to enter the cabin.

"We need to get the suitcases. I don't feel good about leaving them here. What if those men get nosy and want to look inside them? I know they are law officers, but the monetary value of the original historic documents equals the ruckus that would be raised if anyone ever read them, and let's face it, we already know of two dirty cops."

Haven smiled. "They aren't here."

Rayne and Destiny looked at her with their brows raised and she laughed. "I figured if I can move clouds in the sky surely I could move the suitcases."

Both of her sisters grinned.

"Where are they?" Destiny asked.

"In the woods behind the cabin being guarded within the protection of a dense growth of vines."

"That's ingenious!"

Haven smiled at Rayne. "Thanks. I'm really starting to have a lot of fun with all this. I can't believe I once resented having magical gifts. Was I stupid or what?"

Destiny laughed. "We all were. But let's get out of here and get to Tom's other cabin. I know where it is as the eagle flies, but I'm going to have to do a little guessing from the ground." She turned to Rayne. "And then it's time for you to try *your* wings."

"It is," Rayne agreed. "And once all this is over, I have the most amazing story to tell you."

Chapter Fifteen

Martha Thompson stayed low in the seat of her car and kept her head down as much as possible while she watched the shackled men being led one at a time from the courthouse to the white prison van. She hadn't planned to stick around after the lawyer she was going to hire said a cop killer didn't have a chance in hell of bonding out. Burt was looking at a death penalty case. Knowing that, she'd torn up the backyard and hadn't found where he'd stashed the money. Now she had to have a *Plan B*.

Because of the danger Burt represented, and the outpouring of hatred from the community he was supposed to have protected, the judge ruled Burt couldn't stay in Mystic Waters little jail either. Judge Maddox had remanded Burt to be incarcerated inside Fulton Prison until he was to stand trial for the murders of the police officer and his wife, as well as the more recent injury to the cop inside the jail.

There was no way Martha was going to leave the buried treasure behind. Since she hadn't been allowed to talk to Burt to get more details on exactly where he'd hidden the money, she knew she had to rescue her idiot of a husband before he got locked up inside the prison. Fortunately, she had slightly more than two hundred miles to figure out exactly what she was going to do to free him before her time ran out. If opportunity presented itself that would be great, but if it didn't, she would make her own no matter the cost to the others in the van.

Martha sat up a little when it was Burt's turn to be led from the courthouse, and she felt a moment of sympathy. Though Burt was only nearing forty he looked decades older. The shackles attached to his wrists were attached with a chain to the shackles around his ankles. This made him look like a hunched-back old man with wild whiskers on the sagging skin of his face. He hadn't been jailed long, but it was obvious the stress had taken a toll and he'd lost weight. But then she remembered what a rotten scoundrel of a man he was and could do nothing but smile.

"Won't you be surprised, my love, when your loving wife saves you? You'll be so grateful to me for hiding you until it's safe to go back and recover the money that you'll be kissing *my* butt for a change."

Martha laughed at herself, clamping her mouth shut when Burt turned to look in the direction of her car. Having no idea if he saw her or not, she still put on a mask of hurt and sorrow as she stared back at him, just in case. The guard pushed him forward when he'd hesitated too long, forcing Burt to climb awkwardly into the van.

Martha dropped the act and straightened up while wallowing in the thrill of her quickly hatched plan. Once she had Burt convinced of her devotion and she got her hands on the money, his standing trial wouldn't be necessary.

After all, a death penalty was a death penalty. Her plan was *genius*. Not only would she take the treasure Burt no doubt stole over the years from the impound, she'd save the state loads of money and do their job for them. It was a win-win situation for everyone involved.

Except for Burt, of course.

Chapter Sixteen

Pain!
Pain!
Pain!

His head pounding, Tom blinked his eyes until he could open them completely. The acid in his empty stomach roiled and boiled until it burned its way up his throat and projected from his mouth, to cover the plastic covered floor he was lying on.

"Waking up, I see."

Tom tried to turn to look, but the slightest movement magnified the pain and caused white flashes of blinding light. But even as muddled as his mind was, he knew the voice. He'd heard her speak for days. It was the woman officer from the Mystic Waters Police Department.

"Why?" It was the most Tom could ask since speaking had his stomach threatening to revolt, again. She walked around to stand in front of him, but he could look no higher than the stun gun in her hand.

"Because I need you to disappear."

As her statement made no sense, he attempted to look up at her again, and suffered the pain just to see her face. She had her head cloaked with a hat covered in black netting. Tom tried to process what that meant, then felt a ray of hope that she didn't know he knew who she was.

"Why?"

Kathy Gishwell hesitated a second then laughed. "I don't guess it matters if you know. You won't be around to tell anyone else. I'm the one they were looking for. But they'll never know it because by now they'll really think it's you. And I need them to continue thinking that.

"Since you missed your court hearing this morning they will assume you're on the lamb." She laughed again. "I love that phase, *On the Lamb*. I wonder who came up with that."

Nausea was building again. Tom fought it as he laid his head back down on the hard floor. His throat was already horribly sore, and he was so weak he was afraid he was about to pass out, but he needed answers. "I don't understand. What are you talking about?"

She squatted down and he saw a flash of white teeth beneath the netting.

"I killed all those boys. Well, they were men really, *mostly*. That's why I kept Gavin White once I had him. I should have known I couldn't change a man. But a boy is a different matter. They're trainable." She laughed. "Ah, I see you understand now. Well, I'll let you in on a little secret. He's going to be my lover very soon."

Which means she hasn't violated him yet. Tom was thankful for that at least and hoped Gavin was rescued before the crazy woman messed him up for life. *If she hasn't already messed him up in other ways.* "You're sick."

Pain exploded when she hit his head, but he fought the darkness overtaking him. He opened his eyes and watched as she wiped blood on his chest. It took him a few seconds to realize it was his blood she was trying to get off her hands.

"You're going to kill me."

Again a flash of teeth before she stood, and all he could see was the hem of her blue jeans and the points of her leather shoes.

"I already have.

"Blood is still pouring from the wound at the back of your head so you will pass out very soon. You may as well give in now and just go peacefully."

I don't think so. Tom kept the thought to himself as he struggled to stay awake. He knew if he allowed himself the release of sleep she was right, he'd never wake up. "And then what?"

Her laughter held such evil that Tom's stomach lurched before he felt the burn of acid scorching his throat.

"Just give us both a break and go to sleep. I have things to handle in the other room, but I won't be long. I hope you give in easily because I'd hate to have to cut you into disposable pieces while you're still alive."

Tom let her evil words flow over him, but he didn't waste time dwelling on them. As soon as she shut the door behind her, he struggled to push his protesting body into a sitting position, while trying to ignore the resulting spots dancing before his eyes. Once he settled he could see he was in a large laundry room. A washer and dryer set sat next to a very large, very deep freestanding sink. Beside it was a long counter topping built-in storage cabinets.

Tom half-crawled, half-dragged his way across the hard floor, but it took much longer than he felt he had. Once he reached the cabinets, he had to take a little break but only allowed himself a moment. By will alone, he forced his weak body into a standing position. He climbed his way up and leaned against the counter's edge.

Nausea and head spinning intensified when he focused on the instruments atop the counter. A canvas cloth used to roll up hand tools was filled with instruments meant to torture and dismember, and for a moment Tom could do nothing but stare at them in horror. He turned abruptly and nearly fell before catching himself by anchoring his body against the cabinet and locking his elbows onto the surface at his back.

A rage as he'd never before experienced took over, and Tom felt a little strength return to his body. Knowing it was only adrenaline and wouldn't sustain him for long, Tom pushed himself up and grabbed a deadly looking hooked knife before lumbering his way to the door.

He grasped the doorknob and was surprised it turned so easily in his hand; he'd fully anticipated it being locked. But Kathy Gishwell thought him seconds from death when she'd left the room and expected him to be too critically injured to make it up off the floor. Her assumption was working in his favor.

He gently pulled the door open a crack, but almost

jumped back and was prepared to close it again when he saw a flash of movement. His heart stuttered then resumed its hard beating as he watched her walk further away. Since her back was to him Tom's confidence grew, and he opened the door just enough to track her activities.

Kathy approached the door at the end of the hall where she began releasing a series of locks. When he started getting lightheaded, Tom realized he was holding his breath, and he allowed the air to leave his lungs slowly. If she heard even his sigh, he knew he'd lose any advantage he now held. He was certain Gavin White would be on the other side of that door, and Tom knew he had no choice but to stay alive, at least long enough to give the kid a chance to escape.

****

Everything had changed.

His hope that there was an escape route behind his bed *had* ended with there being a window, but it had been bricked up at some point. But now that he'd torn up the drywall to find that out, it would be clear to her that he'd at least made an attempt. That meant it was now or never time.

Gavin stood on the inside of the bedroom door as he listened to one after another of the locks being released. He'd waited all morning for her to get back from wherever she'd gone the night before. As much as he'd hoped to be able to escape while she showered, Gavin had finally accepted that he'd have to wait until she unlocked his door and surprise her, and most likely injure her, if he was to have a chance at success. It was the last that worried him most however, as he'd never expected he'd have to harm a woman. The thought of doing so went against everything he believed.

What he hadn't anticipated was hearing her not only come back without immediately checking on him, but the other sounds that came with her. Because he'd never heard her talking outside of his bedroom, and the only other voices he'd ever heard in the house were on the television or radio, he'd been surprised by the conversation that carried over the air conditioning vent when the blower cut off.

Ma'am had a man in the house and he was hurt really bad, and she intended to kill him. But that wasn't all he'd heard. His greatest fear for himself had been voiced, and it came directly from the horse's mouth.

Though the meanness of her words had made him ill and more than a little scared, Gavin was grateful he'd been working out and was now stronger and bigger than he'd ever been before. Knowing someone else was in danger also gave him the last push he'd needed to try to take the woman down.

When the final lock released Gavin was ready, standing just a couple of feet behind the door. He tried to control his breathing, as he knew she was always on the alert when she first came in. This time he'd started the shower in the hopes she'd look or head in the direction of his bathroom before realizing he was behind her.

But now that he thought about it, he knew there was a possibility she would shut the door behind her as she sometimes did. He gathered his courage, and as the door opened he counted to three and threw his body against it.

Her shout of surprise was followed by a thud and then another, and Gavin jerked the door open to see her rolling over to pick herself up off the floor. She reached for the stun gun but he didn't give her time to grasp it as he moved quickly and kicked it away from her hand.

"You little shit!"

Gavin reached down to pick her up with the intention of wrestling her into the room and locking her in while he went for help, but she kicked him in the stomach and sent him flailing backwards to slam into the wall. Ignoring the pain, he moved forward again, but she'd grasped the stun gun and then rolled to her feet. Staying in a crouching position of aggression, she glared at him with murder in her eyes.

It was only then that he realized her hat had fallen off,

and that he knew who she was.

Anger burned through him as he faced her down. "You're a cop!"

"You stupid fool! I could have given you the best life! I was going to treat you like a fucking king, and now you've gone and ruined it for us both. You have two seconds to get your ass back in that room, or I am going to fry you with this thing."

Gavin stood up straighter as reality set in. She was going to kill him anyway, but there was no way he was going down without a fight. He looked at her a second longer then started to turn away. "Yes, Ma'am."

Hoping she bought his submission, he pivoted back around and charged at her.

The last thing Gavin saw before the barbs entered his chest and threw him into electrical spasms of pain was the rage of a woman scorned.

Chapter Seventeen

It took Destiny all of twenty-eight minutes to figure out where Tom's cabin was located from the road and another twenty to drive the path that led to it.

Returning to the property felt like coming full circle, but until she was with Tom again, her life would never be complete. She sent her sisters in the direction of the cabin as she headed to the back, and it wasn't until she stood outside of it that she realized how tall the sweat tent was.

Destiny took a moment to go inside, and her heart instantly jacked up its beats. She could feel Tom's presence in each and every inch of the round structure, as well as his need for her. Though passion was a part of the tent's memory, the strongest call was one of fear. Knowing Tom as she did, Destiny recognized the fear he radiated wasn't for him.

They are together.

Torn between knowledge she wanted to share with Rayne and the need to gather the things they needed, Destiny decided to quickly look around. But Tom hadn't left so much as a hair behind. She forced herself to abandon the tent before she ran to his shower house.

The structure still held the moisture of a shower, and just as if she'd been there to witness it, Destiny knew exactly what had happened. Though there was no taint of evil intent within the structure, she had passed through some before entering the door. And she'd recognized it as belonging to the policewoman.

Destiny looked all around as she walked to the large shower stall where she searched some more. Everything was perfectly clean; not one hair lay on the floor or was attached to the grill covering the drain.

Feeling defeated, she returned to the door, and it was

then she saw the blood coating the grass. She knew her frantic need to get to the shower house had caused her to miss it. She'd never looked down, but now that she saw it, she was torn between fear and gratitude.

There was nothing stronger within a body than the blood that kept it nourished, and Tom's would be all they'd need to lead them to him and Gavin.

With tears rolling down her cheeks, Destiny gently picked a handful of blood-soaked grass before running back to the cabin. Rayne met her at the door.

"I've never seen anyone live with so little stuff."

Destiny tried to smile, but her fear for Tom was increasing, as she was getting ill again. "Tom's needs have nothing to do with things. But we don't have time to talk about that right now. Look at this."

Rayne looked at the crumpled bloody grass in her hands before looking back up into Destiny's eyes. "He's been injured."

"Yes. We need to get Haven and get her fast. Tom is in serious trouble and so is Gavin. I think their lives are in imminent danger." The sharp pain that hit her stomach caused Destiny to bend over, solidifying her fears. "Get her now!"

Haven stepped forward. "I'm here and I heard. Are you okay?"

Destiny shook her head as her stomach threatened to expel whatever was inside. They hadn't yet eaten, so she knew it couldn't be much and had the potential to be brutal. "No! We have to start this!"

"I already have," Haven said, walking forward. She helped Destiny to stand up and turned her to face away from the cabin. "Look."

Destiny took several deep breaths as she took in the line of boiling clouds and the bright flashes of lightning moving toward them. She looked at her sister. "How is a storm going to help us?"

Haven's face was filled with contentment. "It's my power source. We need the storm and so do they."

Not fully understanding but trusting that Haven knew what she was doing, Destiny turned to Rayne. "Are you ready?"

Rayne took a deep cleansing breath. "I've already started, too. Look," she said, pointing to the closest line of trees. Destiny and Haven gasped at the same time; they were able to see that which only Rayne had known before.

Destiny shook her head. "I can see spirits! There are hundreds of them!" She turned to Rayne. "How?"

Rayne's face also reflected her calm and Destiny realized why. "Because it is *your* will. You made them appear to us as they appear to you, and you can make them do what you wish."

Rayne nodded. "Yes. We can't call the police once we find Tom and Gavin, but we can send an army. An army *you* will lead."

The pain in her stomach subsided as a peace-filled calm engulfed Destiny. She nodded and dropped to her knees as lightning flashed, thunder rolled, and the increasingly darkening clouds swirled in angry circles. Dirt and leaves lifted from the ground to mimic the developing tornadoes as one after another teasingly threatened to drop from the sky.

Haven fell to her knees at Destiny's side, and she placed her arm around her sister's shoulder, and Destiny, with half the bloody grass clutched in her hand did the same by placing her arm around Haven. The storm advanced rapidly and Rayne dropped before them both. Both sisters pulled her into their huddling hug.

Once they were locked together, and resting their heads against each other so one auburn-covered head could not be distinguished from another, Rayne began to site a spell of protection, following the words her mother whispered in her ear.

"We are the three whose powers shine bright,
"We are the three beseeching light,
"With the strength of Mother Mountain,
"With the *magick* borne of our endless line,

"We ask for guidance and sight Divine,

"Shine now a beacon on those that we seek,

"Protect them and shield us while havoc we wreak."

Lightning flashed and thunder rolled as Destiny's spirit shot into the air above her body. She sent silent waves of gratitude to the sisters, who now held her shell in their protective arms before heading to the stand of trees where her army awaited instruction.

She stopped before them, sending gratitude their way as well. The warmth of their support made Destiny's heart sing, but it nearly stopped altogether when her mother's lovely spirit glided toward her then wrapped her in a glittering blanket of love.

Momma!

Weep not, my love. I am with you always. It is only because of Rayne's love for you that you can see and hear me now as well. Let us follow the emblem of Haven's love for you. Her lightning is our guide as it lights the way to the man you love. But we must hurry. His time on this earth is short if we tarry even a little.

As hard as it was to turn away from the mother she had mourned for so long, Destiny nodded and took off toward the sky, aware her mother and the army followed close behind. She entered the twirling explosive clouds and was amazed by the energy filling her essence, finally understanding Haven's pleasure in tempests and admiring her strength. The storm wasn't of nature, but of Haven's will alone.

Destiny and her minions were carried away from the mountain as the storm beat at the earth below. She marveled at the speed with which they travelled, yet her sense of urgency made her fear it wasn't fast enough.

We are moving well, my love, and they are yet alive. Already the one who seeks to harm is distracted by the wind beating at her home. Storms are not her friend, and Haven's tempest senses it and is growing more violent to distract her from her intent.

Look now. The lightning no longer points to the east but is heading straight down. We are arrived, my love. Behold the power of my beloved three.

Smiling at the way her mother worded things, Destiny look down through the tunnel of circling counterclockwise winds spinning within the clockwise spinning clouds. Lightning cracked and thunder boomed; rain and hail were sent to batter the house below. *Yes,* Destiny thought with growing satisfaction; *Look out, bitch, if you've hurt our family. We* are *the three, And we* are *arrived!*

****

Before the storm hit Tom knew his strength was almost spent, but he knew he couldn't give in or he and Gavin were dead. For the first thirty minutes or so, the hand-to-hand combat with a woman who trained for it on a daily basis had been touch and go. And though he would normally be capable of defeating her, and then taking her down and disposing of her, it went against his beliefs to do harm, especially when it went as far as taking the life of another.

Even knowing it gave her great advantage, Tom couldn't force his mind and body to seal the deal and put an end to her brutality. He'd taken more of a beating than he'd given in an attempt to stall for time.

Because time was all he needed.

Everything became so clear when Kathy Gishwell sent the fire of electricity into Gavin White's young body. Tom suddenly understood the meaning of his visions while meditating in the sweat tent, as well as the dreams of the past months. With renewed clarity of mind, he knew his Destiny would come and slay the fire-breathing monster to spare him from destroying his soul. It was her mission to accomplish; all he had to do was hang on and ignore the lack of nourishment for the past twenty or so hours, and the loss of blood that was an ongoing problem.

And for a while there, he had wondered if his will alone would sustain him until she arrived.

But all that changed when he felt the oncoming storm. It held and heralded the power of magic, and his body suckled at the surges of energy sent his way. Tom's strength intensified with the howl of the wind, and he felt almost himself by the time rain and hail pelted the rooftop with such ferocity he was certain the shingles were giving way.

As the storm fed his strength, it seemed to drain hers. Tom found he was no longer the one at a disadvantage. He toyed with Kathy then, as her flailing arms and kicking feet no longer reached his sore stomach or swollen manhood.

He knew the instant his Destiny arrived, but he was amazed as she was not alone. His warrior princess brought an army of ancestors, which quickly stepped between Tom and his foe. Her essence caressed him and backed him up to lean against the wall. She left him and went to deal with the woman who stood with her fists still held high, but her mouth was now hanging open in terror.

No longer needing to maintain a defensive stance, Tom hurried over to Gavin's prone form. He didn't look back as Kathy Gishwell screamed over and over until she screamed no more. He gently touched Gavin's face. The boy's eyes fluttered open, and the look in his gaze said it all. As Destiny's warmth wrapped around Tom, and tears slid from the outer edges of Gavin's eyes, Tom smiled reassuringly. "You're safe now, Gavin. When you feel up to it, I'll take you home."

****

Had it not been for her sisters' support, Destiny's body would have collapsed with the renewed weight of her spirit entering her body. She allowed them to hold her and whisper words of comfort, though she knew both were waiting for news.

She pulled herself up once she could, and smiled at Rayne first. "It is done. They are safe. But we need to get help there immediately."

"What is done and who is safe?'

All three sisters gasped and turned to look at Garrison and Logan. The men were drenched, their hair plastered to their heads and their clothing to their bodies. Rayne and Haven slowly rose, pulling Destiny up with them.

"Rayne? What did we just witness?"

The caution in Garrison's voice sent dread down

Destiny's spine, but she knew it was nothing like what her sisters would be experiencing. She pulled on the remaining strength as the weakening storm abated even more and then stopped as if shut off with a valve.

"This was my doing. It has nothing to do with them except I needed them to help me."

Rayne turned from her lover to Destiny, shaking her head. "No. Momma came to me and said something that matters here. I'll tell you more about her later, but their presence here means something. She said, 'What is meant to be is meant to be.'"

Rayne left her sisters and approached the man she loved. "I am Rayne Cavanaugh, daughter of Celestia Cavanaugh, and I am filled with mystical powers that have been passed down from my ancestors for over three thousand years."

Garrison stared at her as Haven approach Logan. She smiled at him. "And I am Haven Cavanaugh, daughter of Celestia Cavanaugh, and I too am filled with the powers of my ancestors."

Destiny's pride in her sisters nearly took her breath, so she stepped forward to stand between them. She looked from one man to the other. "I am Destiny Cavanaugh, sister to Rayne and Haven. We are The Three." She turned to Garrison, smiling at the stunned but accepting look on his face. "We found Gavin and he is alive and for the most part seems well, but we need to contact Captain Grammar and tell him to meet us at that policewoman's house. Tom is there as well, and he and Gavin both need medical attention."

A relieved cry tore from Garrison's throat as he stepped forward and pulled Rayne into his arms for a tight hug. Logan smiled at Haven and pulled her to him as well. "I knew something was up since you kept burning me!"

Haven pulled back to look at him in surprise. "You knew? Why didn't you ever say anything?"

Logan grinned over at Destiny and then down at her. "Because everything about you sets me on fire. A little scorched skin here and there is something I can learn to live with." His eyes grew serious. "But really because I didn't know what to make of it, and I was afraid confronting you would cause you to run from me."

Haven laughed. "Not likely."

Destiny smiled at them then turned to watch as Garrison placed kisses all over Rayne's face before holding her away enough to look into her eyes.

"I don't care what you are or what you can do. I love you with everything I am."

The sky crackled loudly overhead. They all looked up as lightning, in the shape of their Egyptian ancestor's profile, covered with the queen's headdress, appeared and then shattered into fireworks to rain down from the sky.

The Three looked at each other and smiled, knowing the family curse was broken.

Epilogue

Destiny snuggled against Tom's back, amazed an entire year had passed since the triple marriage ceremony. She yawned as he turned her way with sleepy eyes, and he yawned in response as he pulled her closer. She settled against him as comfortably as she could and he kissed her with a gentleness that never failed to set her on fire.

"Happy Anniversary, my Destiny."

She always grinned when he called her that. It usually was followed by his lips taking hers in a long kiss that had her toes curling and his manhood seeking. But they both knew it just wasn't going to happen today. He reached down to run his hand over her large belly. "And how are our girls?"

Destiny laughed as Tom was the only one of the husbands who hadn't insisted on an ultrasound to know the sex of their children, since he was also the only husband who knew the entire history of the Cavanaugh family. "They are making me very uncomfortable. My back is breaking, I can't poop, and they were fighting so much during the night I expect at least one of them to come out with a black eye or a busted lip."

Tom laughed as he wiggled his way down her naked form to put his lips on the skin covering their children. "Young ladies! This is your father speaking. Stop tormenting your mother. Do you hear me? Don't make me come in there and get you!"

Destiny laughed so hard it took her several seconds to realize the strange sensation she felt was wetness on her inner thighs. As it was absorbed and spread over the sheets, her bottom was getting wet as well. Her laughter died in her horror to have lost control of her bladder too. "Oh my gosh! I just peed all over the bed!"

One of Tom's brows rose, but nothing ever bothered him enough to get more of a reaction than that. "Good thing we can afford another mattress."

Destiny swatted at him and attempted to rise, but midway up pain squeezed her abdomen so hard it took her breath, making her hold her position until it subsided. She looked at Tom while he looked from her to the sheets. Then his gaze flew back to hers.

"That isn't pee, is it?"

Destiny grinned. "I don't believe it is."

In less than three minutes, Destiny had to revise her opinion about her husband's temperament. Her calm, cool, "the world was meant to be walked in peace" husband was practically bouncing off the walls as he ran from the bed to his dresser and then from the dresser back to the bed.

He plopped his fine ass down on the edge of the mattress and jammed both of his large feet into the same leg of a pair of Levis. Destiny felt another abdominal squeeze, but she just rode it out then scooted back to a drier spot on the bed. She grunted as she pushed and pulled at her pillow until it hit just the right spot at her lower back before she leaned against the headboard to watch the show.

Tom ended up spending more time untangling his feet than either of them expected. Destiny attributed it to losing his balance while pulling at the unoccupied denim leg, and the end result was a roll off the bed to hit his head on the oak flooring.

It wasn't until a good five minutes later that Tom finally had the pants on correctly. He flashed Destiny a smile of success and then noticed his boxers were still lying on the bed beside his shirt. He frowned at them and looked back at her before he dropped his jeans to the floor.

Five minutes and two contractions later, Tom was dressed and dragging Destiny off the bed. "I'll help you dress."

Destiny felt awkward enough on her own, and since Tom's forehead was still seeping blood, she wasn't sure his help was what she needed. "I want to take a quick shower before we go. I can't go with this stuff on me."

Tom's eyes grew with panic. "You don't have time. We have to go to the hospital now."

Destiny looked down at her naked form but all she could see was her swollen breasts and the top of her *gianormous* belly. "Why?"

"Your contractions are too close together. We need to go now."

Destiny stretched and yawned. "No, they aren't. I still barely feel anything." No sooner had the words left her mouth than it felt like something inside of her womb broke off and fell with a hard thud as it landed against the opening of her cervix. Her gaze flew to Tom's. "*Oh! My! Gosh!* What are you doing just standing there? Get my clothes!"

With a nightgown quickly thrown over her hugeness, and the fuzzy slippers Tom bought early in her pregnancy as a joke—which she secretly loved—stuck on her swollen feet, Destiny allowed her husband to lift and carry her to the front door.

Tom grunted as he crossed the threshold leading to the wide front porch. "You have gained a little weight, honey," he teased.

As it now felt like a tiny person was sliding down her cervix riding a bobsled, and the pressure from the widening passageway that was unprepared for such a rapid expansion was taking her breath away, Destiny was not amused. "Just shut up," she panted several breaths, "and get me to the hospital."

Being a smart man, Tom closed his mouth and nodded while hurriedly placing Destiny in the new crew cab truck she'd insisted they buy. Being a spiritual and loving man, his concern was for the moaning wife whom he was afraid had waited too long to leave, but being just a man as well, had him cringing at the thought of blood and gore getting on the new leather seats.

Not that he was dumb enough to voice that concern.

"I can deliver these children here, my love. The drive out is going to be hard on you."

Destiny grasped the backs of her thighs and pulled them to her so she could rest her feet on the dash. "There is no way in hell you are looking down there while these children come out of me!"

Tom shut her door and hurried to the other side of the truck to get in the driver's seat. He started the engine without saying a thing. Since they'd attended the childbirth classes, and Destiny saw the video of what a woman's bottom and vagina looked like as a child emerged, she had refused to let him see that happening to her times three, so she'd scheduled a caesarian section for the following week. Now that the babies were determined to make a grand entrance on their own terms there was no way in hell he was missing the show.

But again, he knew better than to voice it. Mostly this was out of respect for her tolerance for pain while bringing his children into the world, but also because he wanted a chance to practice making more in the future just for the fun of it.

"You knucklehead! I can hear your thoughts!"

Tom grinned at her as he started the truck. "Then stop listening."

Destiny glared at him until another contraction hit, and Tom threw the truck into gear. She moaned and he cringed as they flew over each bump, but they finally made it to the road without a baby flying out and hitting the floorboards.

Sweat was pouring out of both of them by the time they reached the hospital fifteen minutes later, and Tom parked at the emergency entrance. A member of the hospital's staff told him he couldn't leave the truck there, but he barked for them to have the damn thing towed as he lifted Destiny out of the truck and rushed with her through the sliding glass doors.

Destiny was rushed on to the delivery ward while Tom

was left to fill out paperwork. He didn't care if they could read his handwriting as he made short work of it and used the stairs three at a time to climb the four flights.

Logan and Garrison were both waiting for him when he emerged through the doorway and a paper pantsuit was shoved in his hands. He saw that Logan and Garrison both wore the same outfit.

"Are you guys going to be in there too?"

Logan laughed and Garrison looked terrified as both shook their heads. "No. Our girls are being prepped too, so we are all going to be daddies today."

Knowing he wasn't the only one going through the torture of watching his woman give birth, Tom took a breath and calmed down enough to pull the scrubs over his clothes. "All of them at once, huh?"

As the other two nodded it struck Tom as funny he was the only one of the three who knew what was happening was not just unusual, but unheard of, in the world of Cavanaugh women. He grinned at his brothers. "Well, best to you both, guys. I better get in there before Destiny decides she made a mistake taking me on."

Understanding lit both Garrison and Logan's eyes, and Tom suspected their women weren't any more gracious than his when it came to bearing so much pain and looking at the prospect of expelling three babies each. A nurse appeared at each of the three doors leading to the birthing rooms and called them by name. They sent each other a look of encouragement before heading to their assigned rooms and Tom felt on top of the world.

Until he stepped inside and Destiny glared at him over the paper sheet draped across her bent knees. He hurried to her side. "I didn't look. Would you stop worrying about that? You are beautiful to me no matter what. And these are my babies, too. I want to see."

A contraction hit, and this time Tom got to hear and watch its strength as the monitor's high tone and ticker tape printout showed small and large peaks. He turned to the nurse who looked at it before going down to check

Destiny's progress.

The nurse smiled at them both. "You are doing great. It's a good thing you got here when you did because it's time to get the doctor in here."

Destiny nodded as sweat popped out of her pores to coat her forehead. The tone sounded again, and he could tell she wasn't breathing through the contraction like they'd been taught. He took her hand and made her focus on his eyes. "Breathe, Destiny. Like this!" He inhaled deeply through his nose and exhaled in a long cleansing breath. Then did it again and was proud of her as she focused and followed.

The next breath was accompanied with a moan and the tone as another contraction grew, crested, and waned. Tom slid a quick peek at the monitor and knew the doctor needed to hurry. She was peaking off the chart, and the contractions were barely allowing Destiny to take a breath and a break before they'd start again.

"Good morning!"

Tom turned to the doctor to greet him, but Destiny grabbed his hair and pulled him down to her. "Get these things out of me!"

The doctor laughed at her and at Tom's look of horror. "Don't take it personally for yourself or the babies. Nearly all women get cranky right before giving birth. Once this is all over with you will be her hero and they will own both of your hearts."

Destiny turned angry eyes on the doctor then closed them tightly as another contraction hit and made her roll forward with the instinct to push. The doctor sat down on the rolling stool positioned for him by the nurse. "Ah, there we are. The head is emerging and there's lots of dark hair."

The doctor's eyebrows jumped and he made a quick movement, and Tom watched, quickly pulling the mask up over his own nose and mouth. The doctor looked up at Tom as a nurse approached. "You want to cut your son's umbilical cord?"

So stunned he couldn't move, it took several seconds

before Tom could finally nod. He slid a quick look at Destiny but he wasn't sure she'd heard that they had a son instead of a daughter, as she was in the middle of another hard contraction.

"Better make it quick, Dad. I'm seeing head number two."

Tom moved down quickly and took the scissors from the nurse and he cut through the thick cord that had nourished his son. He stepped back as the baby was practically tossed into the blanket the nurse held open before she hugged him to her chest. She ran to the warmly lit receiving table with him as the doctor caught their second son.

"Quickly, Dad! Baby three is already making an appearance!"

Tom cut the second cord and saw the long tiny penis with the very large testicles before that son was handed off to a second nurse. And before he knew it, he was once again severing the gestational lifeline of his third son before he too was whisked away.

Torn between wanting to go look at the three little miracles, or in this case three *big* miracles, and his need to check on his wife, Tom returned to Destiny's side and watched as she finally lay back and took a relaxed breath.

He smiled down at her as he lifted a washcloth and dipped it in a small tray where ice was melting then wrung it out to cool her forehead. "You are amazing."

Destiny smiled up at him. "How are our girls?"

Three nurses lined up to hand over swaddled babies, and Tom took them one at a time and kissed them before placing the first two in their mother's waiting arms. The last he held gently in his own. Tears filled his heart and flowed from his eyes as all the love in the universe spilled out and overwhelmed him. "Meet our sons."

Her own eyes full of tears and her face awash in joy, Destiny's gaze flew to his. "Sons?"

Tom nodded. "Yes, my love. We have three boys. So now we have to think up new names."

Destiny laughed as the doctor stood and grinned at them both. "I've never had multiple births happen so quickly. Those little guys are going to be a handful."

Tom turned to look with love and admiration at his beautiful wife. "I don't doubt it for a minute."

The doctor and then the nurses handled the necessary cleanup. Finally Tom and Destiny were left with their bundles of joy. They looked toward the door at the knock and smiled when Gavin stuck his head in. Tom waved him forward, his affection for the eighteen-year-old as strong as the love he felt for the child he held in his arms. Gavin's recovery was still ongoing. Though he no longer suffered any physical repercussions from his long ordeal, and a year had passed, the emotional baggage was heavily strapped to his back.

They were all so proud of him. Though he'd somehow managed to test his way through school and had ended up graduating with his class, he came out of the ordeal such a different person that his close friendships were never the same, and even his involvement with the family was guarded. Though he tried to hide it, it was clear he was always uncomfortable. Tom figured *that* was why Gavin ended up spending more time with him than with the Whites, rather than his belief that Tom alone had been the one to rescue him.

The past year of freedom had been joyous, but in the early days following his rescue, Gavin told Tom it hurt to see all the Whites celebrating life the way they always had. For him it was just a reminder that those he'd loved most were still gone and would be forevermore.

Gavin came to stand by Tom's side and looked at each baby in turn then he sent a gentle smile to Destiny. "I heard you got the boys."

Destiny opened her hand though she couldn't stretch it toward him since a baby was anchored in the crook of each elbow. "Hi, sweetheart. I wish you would reconsider. These guys should grow up knowing all their cousins."

Tom looked from his wife to Gavin as the boy briefly

reached out to squeeze her hand before stepping back. "You have to do what's right for you, but you know you are always welcome to come back. To any of us."

Gavin nodded slightly and smiled at them both, but it was obvious he'd made up his mind.

"I'm flying out in the morning. I was just waiting for the babies to come. Now that they're here, I have to go."

Tom and Destiny nodded as her eyes filled with tears. "Come back as often as possible."

Gavin nodded and leaned forward to kiss her on the cheek. "I will. And thank you again. You and Aunt Rayne, and Haven... I just really appreciate you all letting me live in the house in LA. I'll take good care of everything."

"There's no need to thank us. You're doing us a big favor by being there. But don't let it be an obligation. The aunts will pop in every now and then, but mostly you'll be alone. So enjoy the university and make lots of new friends. You'll love the beach, but be safe. But mostly, if it isn't a good fit for you, come back. Don't ever feel like you can't come back."

Gavin nodded. "I'm heading out now so you can get some rest. I've already said goodbye to Rayne, Haven, and Logan. I'll see Uncle Garrison at the house tonight, and he's taking me to the airport in the morning.

"I love you guys. You and Haven are as much family to me as any of my own. Rayne is too, but she gets the aunt title so I didn't include her. I'll be in touch often." He looked at Tom. "*Often.*"

Tom nodded and swallowed. "I'll walk you out, little brother." He placed the baby he held by Destiny's side and looked at each one of his boys before smiling at his wife. "I'll be right back."

They left the room and Gavin walked to the waiting area at the end of the hall to look out the large windows that displayed the parking lot below. He sighed when Tom made it to stand by his side.

"John Grammar called while I was on my way over here. A Missouri couple found Burt Thompson's wife yesterday, dead, behind a grocery store. No sign of him though."

A chill ran through Tom but he hid it and nodded. "Guess she got what she deserved." He knew the news had to be hard on the boy he'd come to think of as *little brother*. Gavin tried not to let the others know, but he'd revealed his fear to Tom following Burt's successful escape from prison transport. Tom knew, too, this had as much to do with his leaving Mystic Waters as anything else. "I can't say I'm sorry. That woman shouldn't have killed the guards transporting Thompson. He'd be where he belongs now, if she hadn't helped him escape."

"He wanted to kill me, too. That night. But he got spooked and ran away. You don't know how many times I've wished he had. Nothing that happened afterwards could have happened if I'd died with them… I wouldn't still miss them so much either."

Though Gavin had expressed the same sentiment to him in one way or another over the past year, each time broke Tom's heart. He placed his hand on Gavin's shoulder. "You are so loved by so many, little brother, if they'd lost you too…."

Gavin nodded. "I know. And I feel guilty for always feeling guilty." He smiled slightly at his words. "But that man is still free, out there somewhere, and until I know he's dead, I'll never be free from it."

Tom knew there was no point in telling Gavin that Burt Thompson's death would likely change little in that regard, that he had to grasp his happiness regardless of circumstances. "I hope you seek peace in your new life, little brother, and that you find joy."

Gavin turned to him suddenly, and Tom found himself in a tight hug.

"I couldn't have gotten through any of this without your help. Thank you." Abruptly he pivoted and quickly pushed the door leading to the stairs. Tom's eyes filled as he remained where Gavin left him, before he shook them away and started back toward the room where his beloved and his sons awaited his return. As Tom entered the door he saw Destiny on her knees, her messy auburn hair sticking out in all directions, her sparkling emerald eyes filled with laughter, and her enormous smile as she made silly noises at the three little boys lined up before her. His heart nearly burst with the love he felt, and he could only pray Gavin would one day know such joy.

THE END

Take a sneak-peek into the fourth book in the
Cavanaugh Family Series!

COMING SOON
From Turquoise Morning Press

Jewel of the Nile

A Mystic Waters Book
By

JC Wardon

Jewel of the Nile
Prologue

His shoulders and chest were silk covered muscle, his abs a rippling washboard that teased her palms and fingertips as her hand glided downward beneath the sheets. She gasped as she grasped the serpent's head while she trembled in both fear and desire.

She heard his gasp, his moan, and almost cried out in protest when he moved her hand away and smoothly rolled her onto her back. She could do nothing but whimper in sweet agony as his lips captured hers, and his large hands began a less tentative exploration of their own.

Tears slid from the corners of her eyes as his knee nudged her legs apart and his muscular thighs slid between her much softer ones. She wanted to tell him no. That she didn't want him. That she didn't want this. But she had no right to protest. Her fate was now sealed.

"Open to me."

She shook her head, refusing to look at him, though the hours they'd been doing this was weakening her resolve.

He said no more as he took her mouth again, still taking his time, still handling her with a gentleness she hadn't expected. His lips knew magic, witchcraft, trickery. His kisses were gentle one moment, teasing and tantalizing the next, and hard and demanding as his passion built, only to soften again when she reacted in what he believed was fear.

She tried to hate what he was doing to her. The aching tightness of her nipples, the butterfly-flutter of her belly, and the aching anticipation at her core, was a betrayal. His patience seemed endless, his temperament even, no matter how many times she denied him. The gentleness of his actions while he was forcing her to comply to her father's edict almost persuaded her to cooperate. His ability to make her degradation and punishment seem more like a dance than a demand, an enticement rather than chastisement was confusing. Were it not for her hatred of what he represented, she was afraid she could desire him.

And then her father would win once again.

She pushed at him abruptly as all the hurt and anger came flooding back. There was no way she would lay with him willingly. Not after what he'd done. What he'd taken from her. It mattered not that he'd had no more choice than she. It mattered not at all! Wedding-night or not, she would fight her imprisonment to the death. Her father had every right to force her to marry the guard as a punishment for her actions, but she would never give him the satisfaction of liking it!

"Jewell! Get up! We have to go!"

Jewell awoke abruptly, momentarily befuddled, as her gaze darted from one corner of her room to another. Gone was the colorful netting hanging from the ceiling. Gone was the extremely large round bed covered by pillows made of the finest Egyptian linens. Dressers her father built replaced the tightly woven papyrus shelving. Highly polished hardwood replaced hand-woven rugs that had covered a bricked floor. And gone was her dream-self's lover.

She crawled from her bed slowly as her head still spun with the images, the *feelings*, and the sexual desire that even now had her aching and wet between her legs. More than a little disoriented, she made her way to the bathroom to splash cold water on her face but was momentarily startled at her reflection as she stood before the sink's vanity.

Her heart pounded wildly as she took in the swollen lips, the disheveled hair, and what looked suspiciously like a hickey on her collarbone. Jewell shook her head, wondering how she'd bruised herself, knowing the man in her dreams couldn't have actually left the mark on her when he'd stopped at that one particular spot to suckle at her skin.

"Jewell! Are you up?"

Startled into jumping, Jewell nodded even though she knew her sister couldn't see her. There was no way she could speak as she stared at the reflection of her swollen nipples and the tiny bruises he'd put around them with nibbling nips of his teeth while he'd breached and readied her core with his long, skilled fingers. Her knees buckled as her body reacted to the memory of his passionate onslaught and she had to capture the edge of the vanity's sink to keep from falling completely. With a shaky breath she pulled herself back up.

"Jewell? Come on! You promised to go with me! We've got to do this before Sapphire finds out I broke those dishes!"

Though she couldn't gather her thoughts enough to remember when she'd promised anything, Jewell nodded again and then shook her head in an effort to clear it. She tried to respond, had to clear her throat when her voice barely worked, then took a deep breath before trying again.

"I'm coming, Dia. Five minutes. Ten tops."

"Okay!"

Jewell smiled at her sister's happy response, glad she had Dia to keep her grounded in reality. The small bruising on her collar and breasts were obviously the result of her running into something, sometime, without her being aware she'd hurt herself. What she was *feeling* was lust, pure and simple, and a result of the erotic dream. True, she hadn't seen his face, and had for some reason resented being with him, but the passion and desire on her part, and the erotic onslaught on his, had felt just a little too real to ignore. And the aftermath still did....

She laughed at herself as she turned on the shower. *Boring, dependable, studious Jewell Cavanaugh-White...* Passionate? Adventurous? Desired by a man with a killer body? "As if!"

Jewell took one last shaky breath, determined to put the dream behind her and get on with her day. Of course she couldn't help but wish that kind of passion really existed.

The Cavanaugh Series Books Now Available!

(The Cavanaugh Sisters Trilogy)
#1 Mystic Thunder
#2 Touch of Lightning
#3 Tempest's Embrace

(The Cavanaugh Series continues!)
#4 Jewel of the Nile
#5 Sapphire Blues
#6 Diamond in the Rough
#7 Luna's Landing
#8 Celestial Liaison
#9 Zeus: *Unbound!*
#10 Apollo: *Unleashed!*

The Cavanaugh Series Books still to come!

Heracles: Undone
Soleli's Secret
Gavin's Ghosts

The Blood Moon Chronicles

Blood Moon Rising

Read on…

Available now in ebook at Amazon!

BLOOD MOON RISING
JC Wardon

In the beginning, before the time of man, there was a great battle between those angels who believed in One True God, and those who did not. At the battle's end, those who did not believe were damned by the Creator, destined to a life in the pits of despair with the leader of the revolt, the master of vanity, Satan.

But there were those angels who realized their mistake immediately. Filled with regret and repentance, they begged an audience with the Creator, prostrating themselves as they asked His forgiveness, even if they remained damned for all eternity.

The Creator looked upon those who had followed what was once His most beautiful angel into ruin. A God of mercy, as their repentance was sincere, He forgave all. As a God of justice, He knew a price was still required. But instead of damning the repentant, God gave them a sentence of eternal life in service to Him, cleaning up the wreckage He knew Satan would design.

Those few angels who had repented would be known as The Brethren, sheathed in physical form, commissioned to reproduce, and capable of magic. They were to become an elite army of guardians who would watch over and protect the Creator's newest creation. *Man.*

Now, many generations later, Satan's son has risen to a power so deviant even Satan fears him. Natas, the ultimate spawn of evil, is master-mining the cataclysmic destruction of mankind to prove he is greater than his own father, and of God Himself.

With the battle for all mankind rapidly approaching, The Brethren are desperately seeking the destined mates the Creator designed just for them. These women, once the mating ritual has occurred, enhance The Brethren's powers and become the vessels to reproduce the Creator's future warriors.

But the prophesied blood moons approach, the mates have all but disappeared, and evil is gaining ground on the earth. With so much at stake The Brethren know they must prevail with all haste, as time is rapidly running out for all.

Prologue

Riagan Absalom flew low over the ocean as fast as his large wings would carry him. His heart beat at dangerous levels, not because of his always heightened need for haste in the sleek hawk's body he preferred for solo flight, but because she was calling to him in a panic that terrified him.

For centuries, no, *forever*, he had waited for her, looking for her on every continent, in every time period, until finally, only a decade or so before he had come to the conclusion that he, the hereditary Prince of his people, was meant to spend an eternity alone, without his destined mate.

It was happening too often now. The Brethren never knew who their mate was, or what her gift was, they only knew that a life with that one special female was their required destiny. Together they were both stronger than apart. Their individual gifts, once harnesses and sharpened, not only doubled in strength, their lives were almost always instantly enriched with offspring which would bear one or both of the talents of their parents.

The lack of mates and offspring for centuries had seriously depleted the army. An army needed to protect those to whom the Creator gave the earth. With reports that Natas was raising his own army for a major onslaught against all humankind, and with the majority of his own brothers-in-arms still without their mates, he feared the world in gravest danger.

Riagan didn't know what had happened. His father, the first of the original fallen who had repented, had been promised by the Creator that mates would be created, one each for every one of the brethren. Since he didn't doubt the Creator for a moment, it meant that Natas and his *vamphere* were getting to the mates first.

It made him sick to think of it. The mates were pure. Females who would instinctively know that to lose their purity before mating with their destined master would cost them their place in paradise. Such degradation would be worse than death to these women. And the loss of them would be worse than death to each male.

Age held no meaning to the brethren except it was a burden to spend century after century in limbo while risking their very lives. Waiting and wanting that which they were designed to crave. Alone and lonely. With nothing more than an entire existence filled with nothing to look forward to; with only pursuing evil to pass the time. These burdens, after centuries, would destroy the spirit, slowly, until one after another of his brothers had sought the only escape available to them. They would seek that which they were sworn to destroy, and allow themselves to be slain.

Until recently.

Natas was as wicked as his father, or perhaps even more wicked as he'd been the spawn of two evil souls. Satan had once been God's beloved servant, and though he had done a stellar job of tempting man to sin, even he hadn't gone to the lengths Natas had to destroy that which the Creator made into flesh.

Now, somehow, Natas found a way to destroy the reprieve of death for the disheartened brethren by keeping them barely alive until continual exchanges of blood from those demons known as vamphere would turn his brother's silver blood, black. The brethren would then turn into creatures that needed human blood to exist. To deny the need would mean certain death and an eternity in Hell, with all the other forever damned.

Accepting that he would never give in to such a fate, thus accepting that he would spend eternity alone had been a bitter pill to swallow for Riagan. He, as Prince to his people had a duty to perpetuating his breed. To create a successor should he fall in battle. To help his brothers find their own mates even if he could not find his. And he had done his best to do his duty. To be obedient. To remain humble. To ignore that need that sometimes made him forget that his first and only real purpose was servitude, first to God Almighty, then to mankind.

The irony that the Creator had made him and all his kind with a physical need that was as strong as it was powerful sometimes felt like a mean joke. The need to breed, to share his seed, was absolutely necessary for his, and the brethren's happiness, he knew, and for all their well beings. Sure, he was capable of dalliances with human women if he felt so inclined, but none of those encounters would ever produce offspring, as children could only result with a true mate. And those encounters would not satisfy in any way that mattered. Only his destined mate could satisfy his needs, as he would be the only one ever able to satisfy hers.

But after thousands of years, she'd failed to appear. She'd never sought him. Had never even given him a hint that she existed. And now, after he had all but given up she summoned him. Not with the subtle scent he'd expected, but with so many pheromones filling his senses, as well as the universe, he feared that Vamphere would find her, too. Which meant he had to hurry.

Now that he'd found his way to her, there was no way he'd lose her.

Not to man.

Not to beast.

Not to the devil, himself....

About JC Wardon

JC Wardon loves writing fantasy and spends her days weaving stories for those who love it as well. Though she has great appreciation for romances, a juicy and complicated plot is what she holds most dear. Danger, mystery, and magic are the life's blood for her Mystic Waters Books. She hopes you are captivated and stimulated, and your hearts become engaged.

If you enjoyed **Tempest's Embrace**, please consider telling others, and writing a review.

www.jcwardon.com,

www.facebook.com/jc.wardon

www.facebook.com/JCWardonNovelist

Tweet: @jc_wardon

Thanks for sharing my world. I'd love to hear from you!

JC Wardon

WWW.JCWARDON.COM

MYSTIC WATERS BOOKS